THE TRAIN OF SMALL MERCIES

This Large Print Book carries the
Seal of Approval of N.A.V.H.

THE TRAIN OF SMALL MERCIES

DAVID ROWELL

WHEELER PUBLISHING
A part of Gale, Cengage Learning

GALE
CENGAGE Learning·

Detroit • New York • San Francisco • New Haven, Conn • Waterville, Maine • London

GALE
CENGAGE Learning·

Wheeler Publishing Large Print Hardcover.
The text of this Large Print edition is unabridged.
Other aspects of the book may vary from the original edition.
Set in 16 pt. Plantin.

LIBRARY OF CONGRESS CATALOGING-IN-PUBLICATION DATA

Rowell, David.
    The train of small mercies / by David Rowell.
    p. cm.
    ISBN-13: 978-1-4104-4629-9 (hardcover)
    ISBN-10: 1-4104-4629-8 (hardcover)
    1. Kennedy, Robert F., 1925-1968—Death and burial—Fiction. 2. Funeral rites and ceremonies—United States—Fiction. 3. Nineteen sixty-eight, A.D.—Fiction. 4. Large type books. I. Title.
PS3618.O8738T73 2012
813'.6—dc23   2011045241

Published in 2012 by arrangement with G. P. Putnam & Sons, a member of Penguin Group (USA) Inc.

Printed in the United States of America
1 2 3 4 5 6 7 16 15 14 13 12

For Katherine

"Is everybody all right?"

— Senator Robert F. Kennedy, moments
after being shot, in the Los Angeles
Ambassador Hotel, June 5, 1968

MARYLAND

Every morning Ellie West listened to her son get out of bed. With her husband, Joe, not yet awake, she tuned in so intently to the sounds two rooms down that she could feel some part of her leaving their bed and drifting down the hall. First she heard Jamie push his covers off and turn his body to the edge of his mattress. Then she followed as he reached for his crutches, which were propped against his wall, and she could even make out the *pff* sound of the foam padding coming off the surface. She heard the rubbery thud of his crutches push into the wooden floor; then she heard the same thud three times until there was a pause, so that he could stop, lean over, and turn the doorknob. When he moved down the hall to the bathroom, Ellie listened to the crutches creak under the weight of him. With one crutch he pushed the bathroom door until it swung lightly against the doorjamb, and then he let one crutch rest against the wall while he stood over the toilet to pee. When he was done, she could hear him linger in front of the bathroom sink — sometimes for a few seconds, sometimes for a minute or more — but he was not washing his hands or brushing his teeth or anything else she could think of. And then most mornings he bounded back down the hallway to his room and closed the door. The crutches connected with the floor three more times before he was back on the bed; there would be no other sound from his room for at least an hour or more.

Jamie's two years of being in the army had erased any ability to sleep late, which had taken Ellie by surprise; she had imagined the strict structure and routine of his days would have had the opposite effect.

"Won't it be good for him to just catch up on all the sleep he's missed," she said to Joe two days before they met him at the airport, just outside of Baltimore. "He's still just a boy. He can sleep all he wants to. I want him to do whatever he wants for as long as he wants."

Four months earlier, east of the village Than Khe, the morning mist was just beginning to evaporate. For several days Jamie and

10

Alpha Company had waited for orders while falling into soggy boredom, and now the slate sky was a kaleidoscope of mortar fire. The air hissed all around, and Jamie, with one arm thrown over his helmet, scrambled toward the foxhole he and "Bulb" Landreaux had dug the previous night when he caught sight of Landreaux covered in flames — still on his feet, but wavering like a tower of blocks. As Jamie barreled toward him, a missile landed a few meters away, knocking Jamie so high into the air that he had time to wonder how he would land — and sending shards of shrapnel as big as bottles into his leg. Two days later, he woke up on a cot in a nearby aid station. When he opened his eyes there was an army nurse standing over him with thick curls as soft-looking as anything he had ever seen; she smiled at him in wild surprise, as if he were very mischievous for waking up only after the doctor had left. He understood then that nothing about his life would be the same.

Ellie was frying bacon when she remembered to reach over and turn the radio on. The funeral service for Bobby Kennedy would be on in a few hours, but she wanted to listen to the commentary beforehand. The radio was next to the toaster, and she moved the dial past "Stranger on the Shore," which she would have otherwise liked to have listened to, to the one station that ordinarily broadcast classical music. Then she heard the announcer say, "As we said at the top of the broadcast, Senator Kennedy's body is scheduled to be taken to New York's Penn Station and put on a train around eleven thirty, and from there it will begin its historic journey down through New Jersey, Pennsylvania, Delaware, Maryland, and on to Arlington National Cemetery, where the senator will be buried next to his brother, President John F. Kennedy. And I remind listeners —"

She could smell the bacon burning and moved to lift the pan off the stove. "Are they talking about the funeral?" asked Miriam, who lately had stopped saying good morning in favor of asking a question right off or making some bold proclamation. Miriam had turned seventeen the week before, and she had been following every development since the senator was shot in the early minutes of Wednesday morning in Los Angeles. The train would follow tracks used by the C&O system, the newspaper had reported, and those tracks were just forty yards from the Wests' back door. Ellie knew Miriam planned to watch the service on TV, and didn't know about Joe or Jamie, but all of them planned to watch the train pass by.

Miriam considered a long thread hanging from the arm of her pajama sleeve and said, "And that reporter is still coming today to interview Jamie?"

"They haven't said otherwise," Ellie said, and she could hear the fatigue in her voice. She hadn't slept well that week and wondered if Miriam had noticed the puffiness in her face. While working her shift as a highway tollbooth operator a few days earlier, she had dozed off in a rare lull between cars, until the owner of an aquamarine Chrysler honked his horn. "They still have a newspaper to put out. I'm sure not all of the reporters are going to be covering Bobby Kennedy."

A week ago, the editor of *The Gazette*, Avery Tate, had called the Wests, whom he knew, like most everyone else in town, from PTA meetings and being at the Friday night football games in the fall, from waiting in line at the Piggly Wiggly and seeing most everyone in town at church at least on Easter Sunday and the Christmas Eve service. He asked Joe and Ellie about the paper possibly doing a piece on Jamie — what he had gone through in Vietnam, the challenges he faced now, after losing his leg.

13

He told them they wanted to do a profile of Jamie and make it "a portrait in courage." That phrase rang in Ellie's head off and on all hours of the day. When she first asked Jamie about the idea, he was sitting on the edge of his bed, his long foot sweeping over a stack of *Hot Rod* magazines that had been saved for him. He took a full minute before he shrugged his shoulders.

"They must be short on story ideas these days," he said.

Avery Tate had planned to send his best features writer to do the piece, but when Senator Kennedy was shot, he wanted her covering the funeral train. In fact, three City reporters would be following the Kennedy funeral or be camped out with a group of mourners who were standing by the tracks for a glimpse of the senator's coffin. But having made the arrangements with Ellie, he was concerned that rescheduling might send the wrong message to the young man, who was already struggling. That was what he had heard, anyhow, or rather, what his wife had heard. Instead, he assigned the story to Roy Murphy, who had just completed his junior year at the University of Maryland and was, as a journalism major, interning with the paper.

What Avery Tate had forgotten to ask —

and in the last year, he had been forgetting more than usual — was whether Roy knew Jamie, since they had gone to the same high school. Roy wouldn't be studying ethics in journalism until the fall semester, and in the days before beginning his reporting and interviewing, it never occurred to him that he was the wrong man for the job.

The Wests knew to look for the reporter at one that Saturday. Beyond that, not having ever been interviewed before, they didn't much know what to expect.

DELAWARE

When Edwin Rupp woke up that morning, he turned on the radio beside the bed and searched for a weather report, despite having followed the forecast for Saturday all week long. His wife, Lolly, rolled over, annoyed and not ready to open her eyes.

"Just go outside and look," she said in a raspy voice. "That's your forecast."

Instead, Edwin opened the blinds of the bedroom window. The sun poured in. "Blue skies," he said, and exhaled deeply.

The radio was playing the Doors' "People Are Strange." For a few minutes Lolly tried to sort through her dream about their new pool brimming with fish, then, understanding it no better now that she was awake, she pushed her way through deep morning fog and thought about Saint Patrick's Cathedral, in New York, and how many people must already be lining around the block. She lifted the top sheet and reached over to

16

find a station broadcasting any news about the service.

"Hey, you're turning Jim," Edwin said.

"I want to see if they're saying anything about the funeral. Jim won't mind." She went around the dial but couldn't find anything.

"We're going to have fun today, right?" Edwin asked. "We'll see the train, but I really don't want that to just hang over the whole day, with the party."

Lolly yawned. "It's just Ted and Georgia, so I hadn't really thought of it as a big party. But sure, we'll try to have fun. It's just that it's going to be kind of a heavy day. I mean, there's some very sad shit going on right now." Since growing her hair out, she had developed a habit of tugging on the ends when she was irritated, and now she held her auburn strands with two hands.

"I know," Edwin said. "It's heavy, I know." Edwin glanced out the window again. He tried to offer Lolly a smile, but his mouth turned into a pucker, and then he gave up. "I'm going to go ahead and fill it up," he said. "Chlorine needs to sit for a couple of hours before you can get in." He changed T-shirts and stepped into his old madras shorts, which had become as thin as tracing paper over the years, then glanced over at

Lolly before walking out of the room.

Lolly wrapped herself in the sheets again. The house began its quiet rumble when Edwin turned on the hose, and it was not a noise she could listen to for an hour or however long it would take. The water hit the bottom of the pool with a loud smacking sound, like a hailstorm. From the window she could see Edwin holding the hose, his face set gravely in concentration.

MARYLAND

"You want to come to breakfast?" Ellie whispered outside of Jamie's door. "Or do you want me to bring it in? I'm glad to."

Joe was lying awake in bed, and his face was twisted as he listened. As Joe saw it, the more Ellie pampered Jamie, the more Jamie was going to see himself as an invalid. He tried to never look at what remained of Jamie's leg.

"He's not six years old," Joe told Ellie one night, a week after Jamie had come home. "You've got that old singsong voice you used to use when the kids were little and sick. Jamie's lost a leg, but that doesn't mean he's a little boy again. And you can't treat him like one."

Ellie, who had been quietly crying herself to sleep since Jamie had come home, bristled when Joe spoke to her that way.

"Don't you tell me what my own son does and doesn't need," she said. "A mother

19

knows what she should do. Don't make it your business to start monitoring everything I say to him."

Now, both Ellie and Joe waited for Jamie's reply. A truck — probably Dilbert Ray's tow truck — drove past, causing the house to shake like a subway car.

"All right," Jamie said after a while. "I'm coming."

Joe hoped Ellie would not respond with high-pitched enthusiasm, but she did.

"Breakfast for you, too," she said to Joe, sticking her head in their bedroom. He could see that she had erased her grin, lest he see it. Lately they were constantly studying each other's expressions.

"Coming," Joe said.

Joe heard Jamie push himself off his mattress and onto his crutches. And because he had to stop himself from listening to Jamie negotiate his way from one room to the other, he got up and forced himself to cough.

In the kitchen Miriam had turned the radio up, and her grim expression told everyone not to try to talk over it. Jamie rested his crutches against the wall and took two hops over before working himself into a chair at the end of the table. Miriam reached over and ran a hand over his hair.

"I want to hear, too, but it's too loud," Ellie said, and indicated with her fingers how minimally she was lowering it. "What a day for that family. My God."

Joe wanted coffee but didn't feel like making it, and he hesitated to ask Ellie. She had stopped drinking coffee much lately, and now that she was doing so much for Jamie, she didn't want to spend any more energy on Joe than she had to. These days, he thought about coffee as much as he drank it.

"Jamie, do you still feel like talking to that reporter today?" Ellie asked. "This was the day he was going to come over. I still don't understand what they want to write about, exactly." Since Jamie had returned home, she had come to enjoy pretending to be uninformed.

"It's all right with me," Jamic said. "I don't know what I have to say, though. I lost a leg. Charlie's winning the war. And does anyone want to hire Captain Peg Leg for a job?"

They were used to his making comments like this, but even now it could still make them skip a breath. "Don't say stuff like that," Miriam finally said. She tried to scold him with her version of a glare, but he wouldn't look over. "So how do you know

21

exactly what he's going to ask?" she said. "I mean, what if it's one of those reporters who accuses soldiers of killing women and children?" Before the last words had come out, she felt a great tightness in her chest. This was not an altogether new sensation for her; Miriam frequently said the wrong thing, and her family hadn't grown more tolerant over the years, but instead, seemed to, in ways only she could measure, move further and further away from her. She had been acutely aware of this in recent weeks as she watched her parents stare at Jamie. And when they did return their gazes to her, she was sure they remembered again their disappointment in her.

Before her mother or father could speak, she was going to beat them to it.

"I'm just saying, you don't always know what someone wants to say about the war. I know Jamie didn't do anything like that — God! Of course I know that. Don't even *look* at me like that. I just want to protect Jamie. How do we know what this reporter wants to ask? How do we know, is all."

Ellie kept her mouth open, but it was unclear when a reply might come out of it.

"That's enough of that kind of talk," Joe said. "*The Gazette*'s not that kind of paper, and Jamie shouldn't have to hear that garbage in his own house. From his own family."

There was a hint of enjoyment in Jamie's face then — not for the scolding that his sister received, but for how quickly such upset could befall them all. He knew better than anyone how on edge his family had been since his return, and he was grateful when the hushed reverie and manners could be so easily pierced. He only wished that it happened more often.

Miriam studied Jamie's face, wondering if she needed to apologize. She could see that she didn't.

Ellie was content for once that her husband had more or less expressed the appropriate message in a reasonably appropriate manner. Still, she cocked her head toward Miriam out of habit.

"I've got to get this house in order is what I need to do," she said to all of them and to no one. "I can just see the first sentence of that article now. 'Jamie West lived in cleaner quarters while serving in Vietnam than he does in his own home.' "

"I'm going to go listen in my room," Miriam said, feeling confident once more, "where I can actually *hear* it." She put her hand on Jamie's shoulder and squeezed as she moved past. "Do you want to come?"

she asked him.

Jamie shook his head. He could see that his parents were interested in his answer either way. Generally they seemed to worry that he was spending too much time alone — alone on the front porch, alone in his bedroom, alone in the backyard, where Joe had set up two round targets at the yard's end for Jamie to practice archery. As a soldier, Jamie was an expert marksman, the best in his company with the M-16, the M-60, and M-79, and Joe had encouraged him not to let those skills recede just because he had lost a leg. In junior high school Jamie had placed third in the state's national target archery finals for his age division, and the summer before he was drafted, he briefly considered trying to get into the *Guinness Book of World Records* for most consecutive bull's-eyes from forty meters. Now, seated on an overturned wooden barrel, he spent a couple of hours most days shooting with his longbow; Joe had bought him thirty arrows and a backpack so that he wouldn't have to keep getting up and retrieving them; Ellie was only too eager to sit out there with him, sorting through the wet laundry and hanging it on the lines and pulling the arrows out every few minutes to hand him, and in the evenings Joe liked to do the same, though he didn't busy himself with anything but watching Jamie shoot. Or often Jamie's friend Sutton came over and held a small tin of chewing tobacco out for himself, watching Jamie shoot into the two small yellow circles. Sutton walked with a limp because of a football injury in high school. A tackler had crushed his left femur as Sutton tried to take the ball into the end zone, and it was poorly reset. Jamie was one of the team's wide receivers, and when he watched Sutton's leg bend left when the rest of his body was knocked right, he knew that Sutton would never play football again. Now Sutton worked as a driver for Pepsi. He didn't have to worry about the draft.

"Do you know how long this reporter will take?" Jamie asked. "Sutton was coming over later to watch the train pass by. Since the shooting, Sutton thinks he's Walter Cronkite. Last night all he could talk about was Sirhan Sirhan and Arab nationalists."

"I keep wondering if there is going to be a Jack Ruby in all of this," Joe said. "I keep thinking Mr. Sirhan is going to meet the same fate as Oswald."

"Then more killing and more killing," Ellie said, untying her apron strings. "More violent chaos. I hope they don't shoot that man. Or when is it ever going to end?"

She stopped to look at Joe and Jamie. Jamie's thin face looked like Joe's when they first married, like the picture from their honeymoon in Ocean City they had gotten a stranger to take, with Joe's arm around Ellie on the boardwalk, the ocean breeze lifting a lock of his hair and sending it across his broad forehead, his expression almost stunned. Had he really just met this girl Ellie two months prior?

NEW YORK

The first woman Lionel Chase passed that morning, a heavyset white woman in a sundress marked by giant sunflowers, took pleasure in the appearance of the new train porter's suit and offered him a shy smile. Without thinking, he reached his fingers to the tip of his hat to acknowledge her. Already the uniform, with its six brass buttons and dark jacket with gold trim at the cuffs, was doing what it was supposed to do.

When he picked up the suit at the Penn Central office the week before, the company tailor who fit him studied his shoulders without speaking. "You want them edges so sharp, someone bump into you, they get *nicked*," the man said.

Lione offered the man a chuckle, but the man said, "You think I'm joking, son? You want everything *goddamned* right."

On the sidewalk his patent leather shoes

squeaked terribly, but he was sure that inside the train they would be drowned out. Even at its quietest rumble you couldn't outduel the power and crudeness of the locomotive engine. Lionel worried that by summer's end the roar of the train would be difficult to get out of his head. Before retiring two years ago after a massive heart attack, his father, Maurice Chase, had worked as a Pullman porter for thirty-seven years. When Lionel was a boy he heard his father say that the train was always running around somewhere in his head. "Trying to make up the time," he said.

As Lionel walked toward the Queens Plaza subway, he checked his front jacket pocket to make sure the letter from Adanya was secure. He had read it a half-dozen times in the two days since it had arrived, but he wasn't about to leave the house without it; his mother might happen upon it while delivering clean clothes to his room.

In three pages, sprayed with a perfume called Lotus, Adanya had started out by saying how much she missed him already. On the second page, she wrote that she had gone to see a doctor. She was pregnant. The rest of the letter was skillfully vague. She was just shy of four weeks along, she wrote, and then added, "It's a good time to find out, I guess. Not too late to give us plenty of time to think about what we should do." She wrote that there was a joy she couldn't deny about carrying Lionel's child in her, and she followed that by saying, "We have our whole lives ahead of us, and I know this is sooner than either of us imagined being parents. We haven't even started our sophomore year!" By the third page, Adanya steered back to where the letter had begun. "If you were drawing me in one of your comics right now, draw me with my arms wrapped around you so tight, and a caption bubble (is that the right word?) that says, 'Never let go.' "

It was still early, but his father had insisted on Lionel's getting out the door well in advance. Maybe before reporting in he could step into a diner, order a Coke, and read the letter once more. If he did that, he thought, he could clear his head for the rest of the day and fully concentrate on the job. His father was going to want a report of his first shift in excruciating detail — there was no getting out of that — and when he asked Lionel how he thought he did, Lionel wanted to be able to say, "You're asking the new star of the Penn Central how he *did?*" and be convincing.

Down on the subway platform, the heat

draped riders like a thick blanket until another train could sweep it away again. Lionel started to remove his hat when he felt the gaze of a little girl holding her mother's hand. Lionel smiled at her, and the girl produced a little tremor of a wave. The mother watched her with some amusement and said, "She said you look nice in your uniform."

"Well, thank you," Lionel said to the girl, who was working up the nerve to speak.

"Do you work on the trains?" she asked in an elfin voice.

"That's right," Lionel said.

"Do you work on this train?"

"No, not this one," he said. "One that goes farther, that leaves New York."

The girl then whispered something to her mother, who didn't catch it the first time and needed her to say it once more.

"She says have a good trip."

The lights of the E train grew wide in the tunnel, and Lionel tipped his hat once more as the crowd shuffled a few steps back. When the train doors opened and Lionel stepped in, he stood next to three nuns who gripped the vertical pole as if the train were still moving. Their faces were as pale as onion skins, and one of them was crying softly, her tears flowing around a large mole on her cheek.

"It's all right, dear," one of the nuns said to her. "It's all right."

Even as a small child in Cahir, Ireland, Maeve McDerdon had always had a special gift with babies. She was the oldest of four girls, and at six, only she could soothe the piercing cry of Derry, the second child, even when Derry had an ear infection or diaper rash. Maeve wasn't allowed to hold her sister while standing up, but she liked to cradle her in the softest chair in the house — her father's chair — and lock eyes with her and say, "There, there," in such a way that soon held Derry in a state of mysterious calm. "That's right," said Maeve as her parents looked on in equal parts admiration and bewilderment. "Listen to Maeve," Maeve said, and she couldn't help smiling a little with pride. "Sister has you. There, there."

She had this effect on all her sisters as babies — after Derry was Christine, then Fran — but it was to her father that she felt the most drawn. Larney McDerdon and his brother owned a small pub together, selling fish and chips, champ, and boxty, but Larney was mostly useless with the cooking. Instead, he played the role of regal host, making sure everyone's glasses stayed filled with the bitter ale they served or whiskey, and mostly by telling stories.

"Did I ever tell you about what my brother did to me when I was five years old?" he would say to a table after setting down their plate of soda bread.

Or: "Did I ever tell you about the time my father's bull got loose and made it to Dublin?"

"Did I ever tell you about the time Old Man Dyer went and grabbed a hatchet after me?"

"Did I ever tell you about the time I nearly drowned while sitting in a bucket?"

Some of the stories he told his customers bore some scrap of truth, but he enjoyed the fuller freedoms of making up stories from whole cloth. His wife had long ago grown bored and irritated by his endless stories, and if he and his brother hadn't opened up a pub so that he could tell them to someone else, she claimed she would have gone mad. But Maeve hung on to every word of every tale — even the ones she had heard countless times, even when the stories deviated dramatically from their last telling. Sometimes, that was for the better. At a young age she understood that when her father winked as he spoke, he had broken any obligation to stick to the facts, and she, too, found this possibility joyous.

"Daddy, did you know that Jack Moan came into school with a balloon where his head was supposed to be?" she said to her father one night as he was putting her to bed.

"You don't say," he said, and even in the darkness she could see his face lighting up.

"It was a red balloon," she said, "and since that's my favorite color, I didn't tease him the way other children did."

"They teased him, did they?"

"Yes," she said. "And one boy tried to pop his head with a pencil, but I took the pencil away and said to leave him be. It was a very red balloon, and I thought it looked nice, and for the rest of the day I had to protect him so nothing would happen to it."

"Oh, that makes me so proud," he said. "Raised you right, I have — and your mother."

Maeve nodded that that was indeed true.

Soon Maeve and her father found themselves trading stories at every turn, and he was so impressed with her imagination that one night, while attending to a dying fire in the stone fireplace, he said to his wife that their Maeve might have found her calling. "Maybe she'll go on to write plays, or write stories same as Joyce," he said. "I don't see why not, with the mind she has. Why, just the other day she was telling me about —"

"It's all just foolishness," said his wife. "And please for the love of *God* don't be telling me that her fantastical stories are the thing that she should set her sights on — that *that's* what to do with her life. She's telling lies is what she's doing, and lying is a sin. Or have you forgotten that? It's one thing to have you telling her all the crazy tales of things that happened to you that never happened at all. That may work for your sodden customers at the pub, but do you have to encourage the girl to spend all her time thinking of the same kind of silly rubbish? Really, Larney, what are you thinking?"

In the mornings Maeve was the first to wake up, tending to the littlest girl, and when she had diapered her she crept into her parents' bedroom and looked to see if he was awake yet. If he wasn't, she would tiptoe out again, but not before her mother, eyes wide open, could say, "So I'm of no interest at all to you, is that it?"

As Maeve got older, her body remained as flat as a post, but she was pleased about this, since she had no interest in any of the boys she knew. Instead, she liked working at the pub, cleaning and drying glasses. She had become just as quick to say to a confounded patron, "Did you ever hear about the teacher I had that choked on a poem?" as her father looked on with enjoyment — and some sense of inadequacy, since she was producing new, remarkably detailed stories every day, and he was only recycling his, adding variations and side stories, yes, but he knew she had surpassed him as the better storyteller.

"You should start writing them down — the best ones," he told her one night while closing the pub.

"Why would I go and do that?" she said. He had never mentioned such a thing to her before — out of fear of what her mother would say if Maeve ever brought it up.

"That's what the best storytellers do," he said. "How can you be known as a great storyteller if you don't get any of them down?"

"Do you? Write them down, I mean?"

"No," he said. "But I run a bar, love. My telling stories is just part of the menu, if you see what I mean. I already have my livelihood. But there should be more to it for you. You've two gifts, Maeve: your way with babies and storytelling. And you can do both, of course. No one's saying you can't. But you've got a wonderful imagination that goes well beyond this pub or talking for fun back at the house. I'm just wanting you to know how grand you are, is all."

Two weeks later, as Maeve was drying the last of the shot glasses, a terrible clatter came from the kitchen. All night Larney had gotten the orders confused and said his head felt like it had been worked on by a potato masher. When Maeve and her uncle raced in, they found him doubled over on the rubber mat of the floor. He would only live for another couple of hours.

With both her parents and now her husband dead, and her only sister having moved away to America, Maeve's mother decided the only way to go forward was to start their lives anew and leave Ireland. By that point she had no interest in running her half of the pub, and her sister, Meg, had done fine opening up her own dress shop in a small town in Massachusetts. They packed up and moved just a few months after the burial.

In that first year in America, no one could

remember Maeve saying anything. She was fourteen and seemed to go about her life just waiting for it to be over. She was still attentive and good to her sisters, but at school she could barely look at anyone — not even the few boys who worked up the nerve to whistle at her in the hallways.

Mostly Maeve found ways to avoid being around kids her own age, who bored her with their ridiculous fascination with "the Twist" and *The Many Loves of Dobie Gillis* and the Boston Celtics with all their championships, and she knew she could make money taking care of babies. The first time was for a family that owned two car dealerships in the state, and after that baby became a toddler, she became the nanny for a captain in the army and his wife, who had twins. Somehow she was even better with two babies at a time, but in another couple of years she was ready to move on. It wasn't that she didn't love the children once they could walk or say her name, but babies turned into children who wanted to know why the sky was blue and why fire was hot, and as they got older, they wanted to know why you weren't married and where were your mother and father?

Maeve had never told another story after her father died, and keeping that so had become important to her, though she knew how disappointed he would have been. But not having him as an audience, or a reader, would have taken any pleasure out of the telling. Anyone could make up things, she reasoned. She wasn't interested in impressing people she didn't know or would never meet. And as he had said, there was another gift she had, and that had taken her far away, after all. In recent weeks she had even begun to wonder if it could take her as far as the White House.

Delaware

Edwin had wanted a pool in his backyard for as long as he could remember. He was only an average swimmer, quick to get breathless, and when he turned his head out of the water, it had a ruinous effect on his stroke; his legs began to sink, his arms went quickly outward, and yet he was able to regain himself when his face turned back in once more. Mostly he preferred soaking or floating on a raft. He wanted a pool not for the exercise but for the status of being a pool owner.

In his richest fantasy, the pool resembled the Clampetts' luxurious, statue-lined oasis in *The Beverly Hillbillies.* In his more modest visions, he pictured the kind Rock Hudson and Doris Day were always luxuriating beside in their movies: rectangular but generously sized, outfitted with a stiff diving board, with a small pool house for changing. But Edwin worked in the payroll department of the sanitation department, and Lolly worked as an X-ray technician at the local hospital. Their combined salaries allowed them a two-bedroom ranch house that was small by most measures, though it managed to suggest a particular, if shabby, charm.

Edwin still drove a 1958 green Mustang that was unlikely to make another summer's trip to Rehoboth Beach, where he and Lolly rented an oceanfront hotel room at the Sands for one week a year. Even in the extreme temperatures of August, the water at Rehoboth was frigid — too uncomfortable for Lolly — and the appeals of the boardwalk pavilion had worn thin for her over the many years they'd been going. Without children of their own to accompany, she had become too self-conscious to ride the bumper cars or the Saturn 7, which rocked its passengers up and down with jerky, terrifying thrusts. Lolly had come to think, with some resentment, of their time at Rehoboth as more Edwin's trip, a chance for him to play arcade games and sit next to kids a third his age on rides and to play in the ocean with the abandon of a child. What she liked to do most was shop for antiques, or rent a bike or search out a garden tour, but these excursions held little interest for Edwin.

Affording a cement pool was no more realistic for them than buying a seaside cottage, but Lolly had gotten a significant raise earlier in the year, and they could, she said, consider an aboveground one, if they would also put their funds for this year's Rehoboth trip into it. It would be a way to celebrate her raise.

"You can still have pool parties with an aboveground," Lolly said. "It's still a real pool." They were sitting in their backyard patio chairs for the first time that spring, and they could hear the rustle of birds once again flying from branch to branch. "They're probably a little less maintenance. Anyway, something to think about."

"Above ground," Edwin said, inflecting the words with exotic wonder. Their feet were perched on the ottoman, and Lolly gave his foot a slight tap.

In late May, Edwin bought a model called the Galaxy from the one pool company in town. When completed, it would be eighteen feet long and fifty-two inches tall. In the pool showroom, there was a cardboard cutout, life-size, of a woman in a peach-colored bathing suit standing in the middle of the pool, one hand on her hip, winking.

"Let the Galaxy take you to the moon!" she said in a little white bubble.

After all the materials were delivered, Edwin spread everything out across the back lawn. Their yard was small, and there was little question of the pool going any-where but in the middle, which Lolly could now see would further dwarf the space. Edwin set himself the task of assembling the Galaxy in a week's time, as the pool salesman assured him he could.

He went about the construction with a meticulousness Lolly had never seen in him before. He marked out the pool's circumfer-ence, drawing a line through the grass with a piece of chalk as thick as a candle. He removed all the sod from the circled area, and then he laid out the pool's frame by uncoiling the wall into a track. That Wednes-day he mixed equal parts cement and vermiculite for the pool bottom and smoothed it and packed it with a trowel until it was well past midnight.

"There's a man building his dream by hand," Lolly said. "But do you know what you're doing?" She had brought out some lemonade, which he drank down in two gulps.

"This Saturday," Edwin said. "That's our day. I'm going to have it ready. The ques-

43

tion is, will *you* be?" He then put down his glass and gave Lolly a playful smack on her behind. "Get your suit out. In fact, get yourself a new suit. I thought we'd invite Ted and Georgia over to help us break it in. Have our first pool party. Maybe I'll barbecue chicken. We'll get a big beach ball, a couple of rafts. We'll just float the whole summer away."

During his lunch breaks at work, Edwin studied the manual's instructions about chlorination, the importance of keeping a pool slightly alkaline, and keeping up the condition of the pool filter. He learned about the right balance of calcium and magnesium needed so that the water would not appear cloudy. He jotted notes in the margins of the thick manual, and sometimes he would read a passage and then look away from it to see if he could recite it back to himself.

As far as he knew, no one on the street had a pool. On one side of the Rupps were the Gregsons, who were in their seventies, their children grown and living in other towns now. On the other side were Linda and Harry Pyle and their twin girls, aged nine. Linda Pyle made pottery in her basement that was shipped to art galleries all over the East Coast, and Harry, as far as

Lolly and Edwin could tell, spent most of his time playing guitar and was always trying to organize a rock-and-roll band. Harry spoke often of once having played with the drummer from Jefferson Airplane, and to hear him tell it, that brief encounter had been the apex of his life.

Edwin imagined Harry and Linda and their twin girls splashing around in his pool. He could see Harry stretched out on one of the rafts, his long ponytail trailing behind like a snake, and Linda's clay-soaked fingers trailing through the water, the clay crumbs melting off and floating to the surface.

They were his neighbors, but that didn't mean they got to swim in his pool.

The Rupps had tried for ten years to have a baby. When they got married, both twenty-five, they had imagined that by thirty they'd have their first child, first of several, perhaps. Despite the lack of success, they held off consulting a doctor. For the first three years, Edwin insisted that their luck was about to change, but already he had decided privately he was to blame. The doctors would do tests, and they'd confirm it. It occurred to him that Lolly might leave him when this became clear. She was still young and attractive. She could find a new husband and get pregnant. But Edwin kept telling her not to give up hope.

When more time passed, Lolly insisted that they submit to doctors' tests to identify the source of their problem. When the tests revealed that Edwin was sterile, he wept for two days out of shame. He begged Lolly not to leave him, and every time she said, "I would never leave you," he begged harder, as if she had said nothing.

Edwin had felt something more than guilt. For the first time that he could remember, he had kept something from her — not quite a secret, but a hunch, a dark suspicion. And she had never detected it. Occasionally, it made him wonder what else he could get away with.

WASHINGTON

It was Maeve's first time staying in a hotel, and before she went out for the day, she liked to sit on one of the couches in the lobby and watch all the goings-on. The bellboys at the Churchill were no older than she was, and even in their first hour of work they generally loaded guests' luggage onto their carts with their mouths downturned and their eyes squinting in monotony. Sometimes the manager swept through, a strikingly tall, bespectacled man whose pants swished like flags in a stiff wind, and the bellboys quickly found what they passed off as smiles. "Good morning, Mr. Whetton," they said in unison, and then just as quickly their faces slid to the floor.

Two modest chandeliers hung over a dark marble floor that captured ghostly reflections of the guests and hotel employees as they crisscrossed. The elevator bell rang out so loudly and frequently that it was easy to imagine that a trolley careening through was part of the daily bustle.

Maeve worked as a nanny for the lieutenant governor, and he had insisted on putting her up in the Churchill — that's where he stayed when he came to Washington; otherwise she could not have afforded it. But the concierge was the only employee she spoke to, if she could help it.

"I can see it's a busy morning already," Maeve said to him that morning. Her voice ran up and down like a flute, and when she had stepped out of the Churchill Hotel for the day, Mr. Hinton spent the rest of his shift trying to recall the sound of her. As a concierge in Washington, he had, he believed, heard just about every accent one could hear in the world, but he never ceased to be delighted by how many ways the English language could be vocalized.

Until Maeve and her mother and sisters left Ireland, she had never seen a black man in person. Living in the western part of Massachusetts for the next few years, she barely saw one there, either. But at twenty-two, after four years of working as a nanny in town, she had landed a job taking care of the lieutenant governor's baby boy in the family's large home in Boston. While pushing the baby's stroller through the Boston

Common in the mornings, she liked to stop at the fountain and watch the Negro boys, who, stripped to their shorts, splashed and yelped with a disregard she could only marvel at, until a police officer chased them off again.

Maeve was in Washington for a second interview for the nanny position; the latest Kennedy baby was due in December. The lieutenant governor, who had since become state attorney general, was friendly with the Kennedys, and he had helped her land the first interview, which took place when the family was in Hyannis. This past week had been her first true vacation in America.

She had enjoyed imagining herself in the midst of all the Kennedy children — their loud whoops and shrieks of laughter and angry screams playing like sirens all around her. "Maeve, what are we going to play *now?*" Christopher might demand of her. One child would be throwing Mary into the pool. *Was she just pretending or was she really in trouble?* It would all be a remarkable but beautiful chaos, Maeve had decided, and it had been all she could think of lately. But now she realized that possibility had most likely drained away on a kitchen floor in Los Angeles.

Despite all the turmoil here — and the

fact that she was completely unfamiliar with it — Maeve had decided that Washington was an ideal place for her to start over, even though the work would have been more or less the same. She knew enough that a flood of young people swept into Washington when there was a new administration. When she told her mother over the phone about the job possibility, her mother said, "Are your sisters and I still too close to you, being on the other end of the state — is that it? Working for the Kennedys would be an honor — I grant you that — but I don't know why you have to keep picking up and moving farther away. And to *Washington,* with all the violent shenanigans going on there. But then, Maeve, I've never understood what goes through your mind, have I? Never once."

Maeve liked the busy pace of cities, but she was eager to leave Boston. She had grown tired of being around so many young Irish men and women with backgrounds so similar to hers. And too many people had become bent on getting her married. At mass at Saint Clement's each week, the old widows and the mothers whose children had just moved out of the house circled around her after the service like a gang of thieves, telling her that they had just met the most interesting young men they knew she would enjoy talking to. And wouldn't she come over sometime for tea and just give Robert or Mark or Daniel a chance to say hello? It was getting so that even Father Frances, if left alone with her, might say, "Maeve, I thought of you the other day because I met a most intelligent young man who I think you would appreciate."

At the Kennedy house in McLean, Virginia, Maeve was expected to meet with Ethel Kennedy herself, who was scheduled to come home for a couple of days after the California primary. Now, with the unbearable news of the senator's death, Maeve felt paralyzed about what to do. She had called her mother for counsel, but her mother's heavy sobs had distorted everything she said.

"And what do you have in mind for today, Miss Maeve?" Mr. Hinton said. He had sent her to the Lincoln Memorial, the Thomas Jefferson Memorial, the National Portrait Gallery, the National Gallery of Art, and the Museum of Natural History — where she stared at the Hope diamond through the glass safe for twenty minutes — to a musical called *Promises, Promises* at the National Theatre, and also to the department store Garfinckel's, where she purchased scarves for her youngest sisters and a blouse for the older one. And each morning she had given him detailed reports of her impressions. It was unusual for her to be so animated with him; generally, Maeve preferred the company of children, but she had noted that Mr. Hinton was about the age her father would have been, and his smile reminded her of the way her father was so quick to reveal his happiness — which often came as easily as blinking.

She liked the gleaming white marble of Washington, in contrast to the redbrick facades of Boston, she had told Mr. Hinton. He had given her such reliable advice — there wasn't anyplace she had visited by which she felt let down — and she had decided that he would have the answer to her predicament.

"Today I'm a bit muddled," Maeve said, and already the lilt of her voice buoyed him. "You see, I was supposed to have an interview at Senator Kennedy's residence for a nanny position, if you can believe it. For the baby to come. Of course, I don't expect anyone to still meet me, but should I taxi over there and leave a note? I'm due to go back home tomorrow. I don't want to bother anyone there on the day of the funeral about a *job* — of all days. But I also don't want them to think that I didn't keep my appointment. Maybe Mrs. Kennedy and the children won't even live here anymore."

Mr. Hinton shook his head, and he had shaken his head so much since Kennedy had been shot that his neck had become sore from it. "I see your dilemma," he said. "That's very delicate, no question." But even this response made Maeve feel hopeful.

"I hate to burden you," she said, "but it would be splendid to know what you'd recommend."

Mr. Hinton put his hand to his chin, as he often did when he wanted to assure a guest he was about to arrive at the right piece of advice. There was an elderly couple from Michigan standing behind her, and Mr. Hinton said, "Let me see how I can help these folks, and I will get right back to you on that." The couple wanted to know the best entry point into Rock Creek Park, and Mr. Hinton, who preferred drawing his own detailed maps to the faded, blurry ones the Churchill printed, immediately set to his careful work. When he finally handed his map to the couple, the man regarded the piece of paper with awe, like a child given a picture of a clown or a horse.

"You should go into the mapmaking business," the man said, to which his wife heartily agreed.

"I do get my practice," Mr. Hinton said, and the compliment had made him feel so good that he had to let out a small laugh. In fact, he had been told that almost every day for the two years he had held the concierge position, but it never failed to bring out the smile that stretched almost unnaturally wide across his face. Some of the other black employees of the hotel, who watched his interactions with the overwhelmingly white guests and white staff and had decided that he smiled too broadly and too often, called him Pops — one of the nicknames for Louis Armstrong.

"Look at Pops over there drawing his little doodads for the white folks," Lanetta Jackson had said one morning to her fellow chambermaid Rosie DeBerry. "They tell him thanks, and he gets to grinning like one of those little lawn jockeys."

"Aw, he's nice," Rosie had said. "And he's old. I guess that's all he knows to act around white folks. He sure likes his job, always smiling."

"That's what I mean, always smiling," said Lanetta. "That's what I'm talking about."

After the couple from Michigan strolled away, Maeve stepped back in front, twitching slightly. "There's always a solution," he told her.

"Yes," she said.

"Do you have a number to call at the Kennedy house?"

"I've the number in my purse."

"Well, see, I'm sure there is someone whose job it is to answer the phone and receive all the condolences that are coming in, and so forth. That phone is probably ringing off the hook from leaders all over the world."

"Right," Maeve said eagerly.

"So I would recommend calling and say that you're here, but you know you'll have to come back at a later date. Without Bobby, Ethel Kennedy is going to need more help with those children than ever before. That poor woman. It's just such a tragic shame it *hurts.* All of it."

"Indeed," said Maeve.

"I'm just saying what you *might* do," Mr. Hinton said.

Maeve felt foolish that she hadn't worked all this out herself. "To call over there, you mean?" she said. "Yes, yes, I'm sure you're right. I'll run back up to the room, then, and see if I can get someone to answer."

"Have one of the operators connect the call for you," Mr. Hinton said.

55

Back in her room, Maeve stared at the phone, unable to pick it up. She paced around, then lifted the blinds over the air-conditioning unit. A silly thought came to her: Wouldn't it be lovely if Mr. Hinton could just call for her? Whoever would answer at the Kennedy house would understand immediately, the way he would have explained it. She had no intention of asking such a thing, of course, but she couldn't get past her nervousness.

"Just get on with it, then," she told herself. But this had little effect. She went to the bathroom mirror and examined her face. She had gotten some sun the last couple of days. "Yes, I was to come over today for an interview for the nanny position, but of course I know that is canceled. I'm ever so sorry.

"I'm ever so sorry." This didn't sound right to her. "I'm so bloody sorry. Incredibly sorry. I'm so terribly sorry.

"I'm truly sorry — for everyone."

NEW YORK

Lionel was studying his uniform in one of the station's bathroom mirrors. He had never been so full of right angles. When he had stepped out of his bedroom that morning, his mother put her hand to her mouth in astonishment. He looked exactly like his father did in the snapshots from his first days on the job.

"She always did like the uniform," Lionel's father said. He was sipping his coffee at the kitchen table, the sports page in front of him.

"Well, it's just a uniform," Lionel said.

"Son, that's not just a uniform," Maurice said, and the sternness of his voice made Lionel realize what would come next. "No, sir. Not that one. The guard at the bank, he's wearing a uniform. Man who sells tickets at the box office, that's a uniform. You're working for the railroad; you're in the brotherhood, son. And that's not just

57

the Pullmans. That's all trainmen. Nuh-huh. That's more than a uniform you have on."

But to Lionel it was a job — a summer job cleaning up after mostly rich white slobs all day up and down the East Coast and doing everything possible to make sure they didn't have to lift a finger for themselves. Yes, it paid particularly well, and he was grateful for that. (Maurice had only to make a few calls to get Lionel straightened away with the Penn Central Railroad.) But he wouldn't be grateful for having to be on his feet for sometimes twelve hours straight at a time, and he wouldn't be grateful for too many days of his first summer after his freshman year in college in a thickly starched shirt and jacket and a hat that cut into his scalp by the fourth hour of his shift, or for wearing shoes as stiff as toolboxes.

For Lionel, it was hard enough living back at home after enjoying so much freedom down in North Carolina for two semesters, at Winston-Salem State. He could handle only so much forced reverence being slung his way between now and the middle of August.

"What you have on your back is about tradition," his father had told him, as Vera set down the sausage and eggs. His mother tried to offer Lionel a sympathetic smile that said, *There's nothing you can do but let him talk.* "It's about respect. The union. Men who knew the only way they could get respect themselves was to say, 'Here is who we are, here is our service to you, and here is what we are going to demand for a job well done.' Pullman porters are, or were, the only union black men had in this country, and you want to know what's so special about the uniform? Boy, learn your history. Don't go in that first train car like you don't understand what I'm saying, because you do."

"I've been listening," Lionel said, and began to eat.

"All right, then."

"*Most* of the time," Lionel said, and smiled, revealing his first mouthful. Maurice then folded the sports section and hit his son over the knee with it.

"It's an honor and a privilege for any man to be on that train, and I know you understand that."

"Yes, sir."

"Senator Kennedy," Maurice began, but then he hardly knew where to start. "Bobby Kennedy stood up for the black man when no other white man would."

"Yes, sir," Lionel said.

"Your father always likes to sell President

Johnson short," Vera said. "LBJ has done a lot for Negroes, too. And don't you forget that, either."

Maurice shook his head. "You can't mention LBJ in the same breath as Bobby," he said. They had this conversation over and over.

"Well, we're not going to talk about all that this morning," she said.

"No, no, we're not," Maurice said. "But you're on a train carrying the man who was well on his way to being the next president of this country. *Well* on his way, winning California like that. The Golden State. The *big* prize. And a damned important president he was going to be — for all of us. Not just black folks. Like Dr. King, Bobby Kennedy looked into the soul of this country and —"

Vera put down her coffee and raised her eyebrows in a way that made clear that this morning was not the time for sermonizing. Maurice smiled and waved his hand in the air. "Anyway, son, if you see that coffin, you say a prayer for Bobby Kennedy, you hear?"

WASHINGTON

The room's troubled air-conditioning unit rattled like a farm machine, and Maeve was happy to step back out again into the hallway. It was still and quiet there, and she stood in front of her room without moving until she was startled by a family of five spilling out of the door just across the hall. She moved past them quickly and waited for the elevator man, whose generally twitching mouth and roaming eyes made her fondness for Mr. Hinton even stronger.

In the lobby she waited behind a rotund man in a pin-striped suit who was asking about the dinner menu at the Old Ebbitt Grill.

"Would you know if they serve rack of lamb?" the man said in a wet voice. "I would most enjoy a good rack of lamb before I leave, and I haven't found a place yet that serves it."

After Mr. Hinton had coached him, Maeve

stepped up and said, "That was exactly the thing to do, Mr. Hinton. I reached someone, finally. They didn't reschedule, of course — not with everything that's happened, but I didn't expect that. Now I just have to wait and see if they'll call. Maybe it will be some weeks. They didn't know."

"I certainly hope that they do," he said. "The Kennedy family would be very lucky to have you."

Maeve blushed and let her eyes dart across the room before she could look back at him. "Well, that would indeed be an honor," she said. "All those children, so heartbreaking, it is. And wee Douglas but just a few months. But I won't count on it. I don't want to get my hopes up. I do really love it here."

"Washington is a wonderful place," he said. There was so much more he wanted to say — about Washington; about sitting in the Griffith Stadium bleachers on a Sunday afternoon with the sun pouring across your shoulders, despite knowing the hapless Senators would find a way to lose again; about fishing for perch in the Anacostia River on a summer evening or walking over to the glorious Howard Theatre for a concert by Bo Diddley or Smokey Robinson or Sarah Vaughan, or standing on the steps of the Lincoln Memorial and trying to recite the words inscribed on the south wall: "Four score and seven years ago our fathers brought forth on this continent a new nation . . ."

But as a black man serving white people, he could never forget himself, even for a moment. There were already plenty of people, he knew, who questioned a black concierge in a hotel like the Churchill, in downtown Washington, of all places. Since he had held the job, by and large the hotel guests had treated him with politeness, but he was the most relaxed around the guests from France or England or Spain, guests who had no memory of lynchings and who were quietly appalled by a country that had only a few years ago made legal equal accommodations for black people. Mr. Hinton had worked at the hotel first as a janitor, then as a bellman. He had always been a favorite of the manager's — Lawrence Whetton, who had been raised by a black woman he loved more than his own mother. For many years Whetton had watched with admiration Mr. Hinton burdened with so many suitcases while smiling as widely as if he were carrying home all the cash he could put his arms around. Hinton's attitude at work had always been stellar, and he had been dependable in every way — during snowstorms, he never failed to arrive early to sweep the sidewalks when other, younger men complained of their aching backs. There had never been an electrical problem he couldn't fix or a room's television he couldn't set right again. There had been frequent occasions over the twenty years Whetton had run the hotel when he observed guests belittle Hinton. (Once, he had watched Mr. Hinton bend over to get a purchase on a man's suitcases, and the man said, in an accent long baked in Mississippi, "Boy, those bags cost more than your house, so watch yourself." The comment so upset Lawrence Whetton that the next day he brought Mr. Hinton into his office and increased his salary by three percent.) When the longtime concierge had died of thyroid cancer, Whetton didn't hesitate to appoint Mr. Hinton to the job. When the bell captain asked him privately, "Is that really such a good decision, sir, about Hinton? Is that the public face we want for this hotel?" Lawrence Whetton said, "Well, I'm not hiring his face. I'm hiring the whole man."

"Yes ma'am," Mr. Hinton said again to Maeve. "I think you'd really like it here. Nothing against the Bay State. I know it's special up there, too. But *cold*. No, you're at the center of the world when you're in Washington. I know it would suit you fine."

"That it would," Maeve said. "That it would. Do tell me what you would think of this, Mr. Hinton: I know the senator's body is coming here by train, and I know they expect a large crowd, but do you think it would be too much for me? I've seen so much already, and this was a day to be devoted to the Kennedys, anyway. I'd like to be there, but would it be too much, do you think?"

Mr. Hinton stroked his chin some more. "No, I don't think so," he said. "Not too much at all. It's true they're expecting quite a crowd, and I can't say for sure what you'd be able to see exactly. But I think anyone who thought highly of Bobby Kennedy and what he was trying to do for this country — especially anyone from Ireland — should go if they can, by all means. I would go myself if I wasn't working. Saturdays are the big day for me, the long shift, but I'll be thinking about Robert Kennedy all day — and his family — and that's the truth. No, I think that's a fine idea, as long as you can handle being in a crowd like that. You're going to be just like me — you're going to be standing all day."

"I can try," Maeve said. "I've never really

done anything like that. But I think I'll try it. My mother would be especially proud of me for seeing the train like that. It's all so terrible, isn't it? Sometimes I feel like I don't understand this country at all, and I've lived here for more than ten years. The leaders get killed here, and I don't understand it at all."

Mr. Hinton threw his head back, his eyes closed for a moment. "Well, I've lived here all my whole life," he said, and then he lowered his voice. "And the problem is, I understand it all too well."

PENNSYLVANIA

Delores King sat in Angela's newly decorated nautical-themed den, paintbrush in hand, while on the television Ted Kennedy was finishing his eulogy. He was reading from a speech his brother had given in South Africa two years earlier.

". . . Our future may lie beyond our vision, but it is not completely beyond our control. It is the shaping impulse of America that neither fate nor nature nor the irresistible tides of history, but the work of our own hands, matched to reason and principle, that will determine our destiny. There is pride in that, even arrogance, but there is also experience and truth. In any event, it is the only way we can live."

"I wish they'd show Ethel again," Delores said to the television.

"They just showed her," Angela said.

"How can you be pregnant like that and bury your husband?" Delores asked. "How in the world is she supposed to get through this?"

"She's a Kennedy. They just have a way of coping. But it's beyond me. Remember our Pekingese, Ringo? He got run over over a year ago, and I still fall apart about it."

Delores looked at the wet red paint on her posterboard. It read: "Our prayers are with you, Ethel," but now her choice of red filled her with regret. It was blood red. How could Ethel see this sign and not think of blood? It was just three and a half days ago that Ethel had cradled her husband's bloodied head in her lap in the kitchen of the Ambassador Hotel, where a busboy named Juan Romero had managed to put a rosary into his hand.

"I need to start over," Delores said. She looked over at her daughter, Rebecca, who was not yet five. Rebecca was moving a paintbrush back and forth over her paper, the blue paint long drained from the brush. "You're doing a good job of painting, Rebecca. I like your pretty blue."

Rebecca nodded vigorously. She was much paler than her brothers, since there weren't any outdoor activities she particularly enjoyed. Her nose came to a sharp point, like a ferret's, and before she answered a question, she often tilted her head back, which made her look as if she were sniffing out the possibilities of food.

Delores removed another sheet of poster board and began anew. "I'm going to pick blue, just like you, Rebecca," she said. Then her eyes went back to the television.

"Faye and Betty Jean are going to meet us there," Angela remembered. "Faye's really busted up about it. You should have heard her on the phone."

On screen a camera panned across the congregation, which showed Jimmy Durante sitting a few rows back of a bespectacled Cary Grant.

"So many people are going to be on that train, they're saying," Angela said. "Ethel's going to feel like she has to entertain them all. What she'd probably like to do is just ride the whole way with the casket and not have to focus on anyone else."

"But she's going to want to be with her children, too," Delores said quickly. "Kathleen is almost seventeen, and she can maybe help."

"I have two kids, and my husband is alive, and I still don't know how I make it through the day," Angela said. Her girls were ten and twelve, and she and her husband had just sent them off to their first summer camp, a hundred miles away.

"Where did you say the boys were again?" Angela asked. "Or did you tell me?"

"They're with Arch's mother," Delores said. "I had to make up two big —" She mouthed the word "lies." She had a small laugh at this — at the very idea — but then glancing back at the television, she quickly fell back to her somber expression.

"What did you tell her?" Angela blew on her paint. Delores glanced over at Rebecca, who had now discovered the baby bottle filled with green.

"I just said that R had an early B-I-R-T-H day event in the morning and the boys would make it miserable if I had to drag them to it, and that in the afternoon I was signed up to deliver meals for the church, and the boys would go crazy if they were cooped up in the car like that on a Saturday. I ask that kind of thing of her so rarely, and you should see her —" Delores let her mouth drop, and she narrowed her eyes to little slits. " 'Well, I guess if you don't have any other option.' She's always talking about *options.* As much as Arch works, I have about as many options as I do fur coats."

Angela might have laughed at that, but lately she had grown worried about Delores, who seemed to constantly be making some reference to her difficulties or unhappiness.

What Angela knew was that in the last year, Delores's boys had both been suspended from school — Brian, eleven, for fighting, and Greg, twelve, for writing "Fuck Face" on the blackboard when the teacher stepped out of the classroom. She knew, too, that Arch was increasingly bothered by her spending time with Angela — and Faye and Betty Jean. All three friends' husbands were members of the Rotary Club. They all belonged to the local country club, and all of them went to the First Presbyterian Church, and once a month one of the couples would throw a barbecue. Delores and Arch were always invited, but they almost never attended. Arch called the group the Cocktail Club, and with that name he believed he had picked out a particularly despicable moniker.

The four families all lived within a few blocks of one another — Delores and Arch were the latecomers, having bought the house five years ago. Only Arch hadn't attended college, but he had grown his modest tire business, which he started when he came back from the Korean War, into the town's biggest tire supplier and service center. Tire King, he called it, and that's how everyone referred to him. The company's three tow trucks all had the logo emblazoned on the side, with Arch's grinning face painted underneath.

Once a year, in the summer, Delores could persuade him to come out for an afternoon on the lake — Faye and her husband had bought a lake house an hour or so outside of town — and she could count on Arch to be polite and hold an expression of contentment for most of the day. He wouldn't shy away from small talk, since there was common ground enough around the Pittsburgh Pirates, and Arch sometimes had insights into automobile manufacturing that the other men were interested in. But before he and Delores would climb into bed that night, Arch would quietly work himself into a litany of complaints about them.

"They've got everything all figured out," he was fond of saying. Though only one of the husbands had gone to an Ivy League school, Arch referred to their Harvard degrees and their "perches from their ivory towers," and he was fixated on the generally soft-looking appearance of their hands.

Lately, when Delores did mention that she had been with Angela or Betty Jean or Faye, Arch made it a habit to ask what they talked about.

The night of the California primary,

Delores said, "What? Do you want to be in on our makeup tips?"

"I just know how they like to talk, is all. Life is more complicated than they like to believe," he said. "There's a lot going on right now in this country, and more and more people are going to have to choose sides. And all I'm saying is, don't let them fill your head with their revolution talk. And all that baloney."

The day after RFK's assassination, Delores stayed fixated in front of the television. Because there was a gun involved, Brian and Greg were modestly interested, and only complained of boredom by the mid-afternoon. They wanted her to take them to the Moose Lodge to go swimming, but Delores couldn't tear herself away. For dinner she ordered fish plates from Captain Jim's, and as Arch and the children ate at the table, Delores ate from a TV tray in the other room.

There was no uncertainty about what Arch thought of Kennedy. Over the last year, as Kennedy had gone from downplaying any interest in the presidency to actively campaigning that spring, Arch had called him "a mama's boy" and "arrogant," and when Kennedy began to more sharply criticize America's policy in Vietnam, Arch said he wouldn't mind "taking a swing at those big Kennedy teeth of his." Now, after he had the children help clear the table, he threw a leg over the easy chair in which Delores was sitting and squeezed his arm around her. "An Arab," he said. "A stinkin' Arab, of all people."

"So what if Arch asks little R about the birthday party?" Angela asked. "How are you going to keep from getting caught?"

"I haven't figured that out yet. Do I tell R to L-I-E to him? Maybe. God, what have I gotten myself into?"

"Would his mother really have said no if you had just told her you were going to see the train, the same thing that *thousands* of people are going to be doing? Is she really that bad?"

Rebecca was done with her paints and had moved to Delores's lap. Delores was becoming frustrated with her friend's questioning. She stared at the television as she stroked Rebecca's hair. A camera set high above showed Ethel, her black veil flowing over her shoulders.

"It's him, not his mother. Arch would hit the roof, the way he feels about the Kennedys. No, today Rebecca and I are regular fugitives from justice."

Michael Colvert was lying on his bed, the rubber soles of his shoes pressed delicately against the wall, and he pulled back the leather pouch of his slingshot once more. He had sent nearly a hundred imaginary stones through the air.

He was glad to feel the smooth wood handle in his hand once more. He had tried to explain what a good shot he had become to his father, but his father hadn't seemed much impressed. Michael wondered if his father thought he was a little old for slingshots and was, instead, ready to have his own gun — for hunting, though his father hadn't said anything like that. To his friends' bewilderment, Michael wouldn't shoot at birds or squirrels, and used the slingshot only for target practice — soda bottles, old gasoline cans, school crossing and speed limit signs by the road — and now he could hit small targets from fifteen yards away.

None of his other friends could make such a claim.

In the kitchen, he could hear the soft drone of his mother's voice. In the last week, since he had returned home, she had spoken in hushed, halting tones every time someone called to see how the boy was doing.

"Well, we're just taking it slow and easy," she would say.

"We're not really talking about that very much right now, to be honest."

"A little quiet, but that's to be expected, considering all that he's been through."

In these moments she was quick to turn to see if he was listening, which caused him to direct his attention out the window at the neighbor across the street, who was forever mowing the yard, or if he had a copy of *Boys' Life* in his hand, he would read the headline "A Sailor's Knot Saved This Scout's Life!" — letting his lips move for effect — for the tenth time without reading any further.

James Colvert and his wife had separated nearly a year ago; he then moved to Michigan, where an old college friend had offered him a partnership in a shipping business. Michael had spoken to him a few times on the telephone since then — on Michael's birthday, at Christmas, and when the Knicks made the playoffs. He promised to have Michael come visit him once he got settled into his new home, his new job, but mostly Michael's mother had done what she could to erase him from their lives. Their marriage had been marked by long stretches of silence in between too many cruel arguments, and in a relatively brief spate of years they arrived at a general state of shock that they could have ever loved each other at all. There were no pictures of his father in the house, except for a snapshot Michael kept in his drawer of the two of them on a Ferris wheel at the state fair, with Michael holding a candy apple nub and his father flashing his crooked grin as the bright lights beneath them swam like colored fish.

Three weeks earlier Michael's father had pressed his face against the narrow pane of glass inside the thick oak door, his eyes scanning the classroom, and Michael watched him for several seconds before recognizing him. Before Michael could say anything, the man gently opened the door, and Mrs. McCauley, the sixth-grade math teacher, walked over to him, her powdered face squeezed into an expression of concern, as he whispered into her ear. She nodded once and said, "Michael, your father needs to see you." Whether any of this seemed unusual to Mrs. McCauley, Michael could not tell. He nodded and bounded out into the hallway, his heart racing.

"Well, here he is in the flesh," James Colvert said. "Let me look at this fine-looking young man." He put his warm, heavy hand on Michael's shoulder, and at that moment Michael thought he might collapse from the weight of it.

"Now that's what you call growing," he said. "How tall are you now?"

"Fifty-seven inches, exactly," Michael said quickly.

"I'll bet you're a hundred pounds, too," James Colvert said.

"Almost," Michael said.

His father nodded, and then turned to look over his shoulder.

"Well, let me explain the plan we've got going here, and then we can skedaddle. I've got a carload of fishing equipment out there in the car waiting for us, and all we have to do is hop in and take off."

"Where are we going?" Michael said. He was aware of his voice bouncing off the lockers in the empty hallway.

"The Great Lakes State, where else?" James Colvert said. "Fishing, hunting, camping, whatever we like. But we have to go now is the thing. I talked to your principal all about it, so we're all square there."

"What about Mom?" Michael asked. He looked back in the window to see Mrs. McCauley drawing a pie chart on the blackboard.

"Mom knows all about it," he said. This was a lie, and James Colvert was surprised at how much he enjoyed saying it. "She's just kept it a secret, like I asked her. She's good at keeping secrets, your mother. Case in point. But like I said, we have a whole heck of a lot of driving ahead of us, so we should get started."

"What about school?"

"Yeah, your teacher's in on it, too," James Colvert whispered, but this wasn't true, either. "It's all right for you to miss the last few weeks, since you're doing so well." Earlier in the spring, he had called the school's secretary for the date of the last day of classes, but by the time he booked their cabin, the available dates didn't mesh with Michael's school dates. That morning, after he watched Michael head off to school from his car parked down the street, then saw Michael's mother drive off to work, he left a postcard in the mailbox explaining that he was taking Michael camping and that he would have him back by the end of

June. He left no telephone number, and didn't say where they would be — omissions he particularly relished.

James Colvert began walking down the hall, and Michael noticed the scuffed boots under his father's khaki pants, which were severely worn, with a hole in one of the back pockets. Michael looked once more to his classroom, but Mrs. McCauley was out of view, and then someone said something to cause the class to laugh before she could quiet them down. Michael raced to catch up.

"Wait, my books," he called out.

"You won't need them," his father said. "Your teacher will take care of them."

There was a sparkling red Mercury Monterey out front, where the school buses would start to line up in the afternoon. Michael watched the bald spot on the back of his father's head and tried to remember if it had been there before.

"Now was I lying about the fishing gear?" his father said, his arms held out like an eager salesman. There were at least four fishing rods that Michael could make out, and a large metal tackle box that sat on the vinyl seat. There was a net and a pair of adult-size waders lying on the floor.

Michael smiled — for the first time, he realized. "That's a lot," he said. "You could catch a whole lake with that."

James Colvert snorted. "The car's brand-new, too. I flew in a few days ago and picked it up for the trip."

Michael felt light-headed; it was as if he had stepped inside one of his Richie Rich comics.

Traffic on the Garden State Parkway was light, and the stubby pines that had been planted just a few years earlier were towering over the roadside signs. When a truck carrying fruit out of the state and, some miles later, a truck carrying steel pipes passed, Michael was sure that the drivers were craning their heads to admire the beautiful car.

Later, when they were about to cross the New Jersey state line, Michael thought of giving a small cheer. He thought his father might appreciate that, but then it came and went, and no other sound he could think of over the low moan of the motor seemed particularly right.

Jamie took a bath these days, though he still referred to it as a shower, and everyone had made silent note of this. Joe had become tired of trying to catalog all the things that were different now for his son, but at the end of every day Ellie and Miriam talked about how Jamie seemed to be, what daily tasks he seemed to be getting more comfortable with, which tasks he seemed to avoid altogether, what he did and did not like to talk about. They saw themselves as caseworkers, and when Joe was not listening, they filled each other in on any new observations or insights.

When the water shut off, rattling for a moment the thin walls of the kitchen, Ellie looked out the back window toward the train tracks. The grass already had suffered from a hot stretch in May, and the blooms of the azaleas — lining the edges of the yard — had been spectacular this year, but now they were withering. The funeral was over, and on the radio the announcer was talking about Robert Kennedy and his publicized skirmishes with union organizer Jimmy Hoffa. Ellie tried to imagine if a train carrying Robert Kennedy's coffin would look any different from the ones on the C&O line that passed by twice a day usually — a forty-to-fifty-car train carrying lumber or coal or sometimes automobiles. How long would the Kennedy train be? Would his children be on board? she wondered. What would they think of all the people who would be lining up to stare at them as they passed? What sense could they make of any of it?

Lionel had come with his mother plenty of times to Penn Station — to say good-bye to his father and then go off in the city together, or sometimes to meet him after his train had come in and take the subway back home together. As a child, Penn Station had felt overwhelming, and he clung to his mother's or father's hand so tightly that they had to laugh.

"What's the matter?" Maurice said, after a twenty-hour ride to Savannah, Georgia, and back. "You afraid you're going to lose us and end up on a train to Bangor, Maine? Or Richmond?"

"No," Lionel said.

"Or Chicago?"

"No."

"Ending up on a train to Chicago wouldn't be so bad, now," Maurice said. "Be a little hard you navigating the South Side by yourself, but a man could do worse than to end up in Chicago."

"I'm not a man," Lionel said.

" 'Course you're not," Vera said, rubbing a gloved hand over the back of his head.

"Chicago. Philadelphia. St. Louis. Boston. Detroit. The trains have taken me just about every place I want to see in this country. And some I don't ever need to see again."

Lionel and his father had always strolled through the original Penn Station with dizzy wonderment — the intricate patterns of the iron-and-glass ceiling like metallic spider-webs, the marble columns thicker than redwoods — before most of it was demolished in 1963 and reconstruction began. He remembered the way his father shook his head when they first stepped into the new station together, after construction was complete. The new ceiling seemed as low as the one in their apartment, and the grand columns had been replaced with stumps that held the dull glimmer of tinfoil. The fluorescent lights looked like they had been lifted from a cafeteria.

"If this is modern," Maurice said — to his son and anyone else who was listening — "then I don't want nothing to do with the future."

Lionel checked in at the Penn Central office, where he was directed to the Kennedy train. Stepping outside toward the rail yards, he had his head down, trying to fix the zipper on his bag, and when he looked up again and saw the immense crowd on the opposite track, he was startled. They were packed in together like gumballs. There were men in light business suits and straw hats, and young women in brightly colored slacks cradling cardboard signs that read: "We'll Miss You Bobby" and "Rest in Peace" and "God Bless You RFK." Several young mothers had children on their hips, and some of the women's faces looked swollen from crying. There were a dozen young white men in their plaid shorts and button-down Oxford shirts, their faces pink from the body heat all around, and elderly black men and women hunched over, trying to will their knees to hold firm.

Just below the crowd, on the tracks, was a flank of stony-faced police officers positioned twenty feet apart, soaking up the blinding sunlight and sweating through their blue short-sleeved shirts, the handles of their pistols pinned against their ribs. Their arms were crossed, when they weren't wiping the sweat off their cheeks, and they stared straight ahead, not talking to one another or to the crowd above. Lionel couldn't remember when he had seen so many black police officers at once.

Several Secret Service agents were talking with crew members in front of the train, and when they broke up, Lionel approached, flashing his new badge to them for inspection, as he had been instructed to do inside the station. One of the agents removed his sunglasses and studied Lionel's photograph. "First day on the job," he said. "How about that?" He then indicated with a turn of his jaw that Lionel could keep walking.

"I'm looking for Buster Hayes," he said to the porter whose shoulders were as broad as a linebacker's. "I'm assigned to his crew."

Buster Hayes was counting something on his clipboard. He let a little time pass before he looked up and took Lionel in. "Well, you're in luck," he said. Lionel nodded and jutted out his hand. Buster Hayes considered the hand first and could see that Lionel had done little manual labor in his life. Hayes nodded once and took Lionel's hand in his, showing him the strength of his grip. "What do you say, young buck?"

"Fine, thank you."

"No, my question was, *What* do you say?"

"Excuse me?" Lionel said, his hand still being crushed by the older man.

"I'm just checking to see what kind of

listener you are, young buck," Hayes said. "I said, 'What do you say?' — which was not my way of asking you how you were, and yet you told me anyway. A porter has to *listen.* At all times. I ask you to go get me a crate of Cokes, I need to know you're not going to come back with a box of M&M's. If a man says, 'I'll take my coffee with sugar,' then you need to not come back to him with cream. Do you understand what I'm saying?"

"Yes, sir."

"Okay, then. Welcome aboard. This is a hell of a first shift for a young buck like yourself. Do you know everything about this train today, and the important trip we're about to take?"

"Yes, sir."

"Of course you don't, young buck. I just asked if you knew everything about this train, and you just told me you did. You don't know about the tender wheels or the poppet valve or how to locate the compressors, now do you?"

"No, sir," Lionel said.

"You got me worried already, young buck," Hayes said. He looked over at the crowd across the way.

"No, you don't know this train," Hayes said. "And this ain't a day for me to teach you anything about trains, neither. The best thing you can do on this day is to stay out of the way and watch and learn. You Maurice Chase's son?"

"Yes, sir."

"That's a long-timer right there," Hayes said. "Pullman porter. Yes, sir. Men like your father made the brotherhood. Of course, the Pullman brotherhood has pretty well come to an end, and that's a sad development. But that's all I'm going to say on that today. Senator Kennedy's coffin is scheduled to arrive in half an hour, but you don't have anything to do with that, and that's for a reason. First day on the job, you need to stay as far away as possible from that coffin. No telling what you'd do, you so green. I'm going to take you to the car you're going to be serving today and get you situated." But first Hayes stepped back and held out his hand in the direction of the train, as if it were a prize on some game show. "And welcome to the Pennsylvania Central. You see where it says Penn Central?"

Lionel studied the glistening coaches and took a step back, not finding anything that helped him.

"The reason you don't is because it's been blacked out by request of the Kennedy family," Hayes said. "Maybe they wanted the train to resemble a hearse. Makes sense to me, though. We got twenty-one cars, and the last two are where the Kennedy family is going to be, so no one goes in there. Not me, not the conductor, nobody wearing this uniform. Unless they ask for somebody."

"Yes, sir," Lionel said.

Buster Hayes took another look at the new employee, crinkling his eyes for effect. "You ready to work, young buck?"

"Yes, sir."

"All right, then, let's get to it." Buster Hayes led Lionel down the narrow aisles of the train, letting his hands bounce softly over the tops of headrests, whistling a tune he surely whistled all the time. Here and there he slowed to lower his head so that he could survey the crowd out the window. "No, not like any ordinary day, and that's true for every one of us on this train. This day is some history."

"FDR had a funeral train," Lionel said. His father had ranked Roosevelt highest among all other presidents during his lifetime. "And Abraham Lincoln."

"Whoa, young buck knows something about the history of funeral trains," Hayes said. "Young buck knows something after all."

The train smelled of vinyl and aftershave,

90

and every surface had been scrubbed until the cleaning crew was satisfied that each car looked like it had just rolled off the assembly line. As they headed toward the rear they met a porter whose hair was the color of marshmallows.

"Mr. Chalmers," Hayes said, and they shook hands. "Mr. Chalmers, this here is Lionel Chase. First day on the job."

"They put a new man on the job on *this* train?" Mr. Chalmers said. He hadn't looked over at Lionel, but he arranged his face in a show of utter dismay. "Lord Almighty."

"They must have confidence in him," Hayes said. "He's Maurice Chase's boy. So maybe they know what they're doing after all."

Mr. Chalmers offered his weak hand to Lionel. "How's he getting along, son?"

"Doing very well," Lionel said.

"Good, good. That's a good man, Maurice Chase."

"I'm taking him to his car," Hayes said. "Mr. Chalmers can assist you in any number of ways because he knows this train. Young buck tried to tell me *he* knew this train."

At this Mr. Chalmers shook his head, his face reset in amazement.

They kept walking, and after Hayes stopped to straighten a doily on the back of a seat, they stepped into a car featuring a miniature bar on the far end. The passenger seats were replaced by long couches and four round, elevated tables for passengers to use while standing up.

"This is your car today, young buck," Hayes said. "And the man behind the bar over there we call Big Brass, but you will call him Mr. Trent. You're going to be helping Mr. Trent serve drinks and snacks and whatnot. We're expecting maybe a thousand people on this train, and I figure seventy-five percent are going to stay in the snack cars. There's three of them, but you stay assigned to the one."

Hayes introduced the two, and he told Big Brass the same story he told Mr. Chalmers about Lionel's supposed knowledge of the train, and Big Brass appeared equally troubled. But Lionel knew there was no point in offering a defense. He could see that this was all part of the experience for the new man. "You do your job the way you're supposed to, and you can count on your crew members for *everything*," his father had told him. "Porters always have to have each other's backs."

Lionel planned to save virtually all the money from his paychecks, since he was staying with his parents. At night he would focus on his artwork, not spend his money at the bars or jazz clubs or on women. Adanya was in North Carolina, and they might go the whole summer without being able to see each other.

"You're in Mr. Trent's hands right now," Hayes said. "I got to go to my own station, but you give Mr. Trent your full attention, and he'll take care of you. Remember this, young buck: you're going to have a few hundred bosses today, in addition to Mr. Trent. And by serving them, you are doing your small part to serve your country today. Am I overstating things, Mr. Trent?"

"No, sir," Big Brass said. "That's Senator *Kennedy* we're talking about. And God rest that man's soul."

Hayes stuck out his hand, and Lionel grabbed it and tried to squeeze harder than before, but this time Hayes's grip was twice as hard, as if he had anticipated Lionel's impulse. Hayes smiled broadly — for the first time. As Hayes walked back, he was whistling the same tune as before, though more fully this time, so that it swept through the car, ringing off the glass windows. Then he stopped abruptly and headed back in their direction. "Mr. Trent, you hear the news?"

"What news is that?"

"They've arrested the man they think shot Dr. King."

Big Brass barely let his lips move. "Well, that's good. What's it been, two months now?"

Hayes said that was right.

"How long did they take to nab the Kennedy assassin — about two *seconds*?" Big Brass said.

"Well, Sirhan didn't even try to get away," Hayes said. "Dr. King was killed by a sniper. It's a little different. They caught him in London, in fact. This just came over the news a little while ago. They said the name, but I can't remember."

"London," Big Brass said. "The American authorities couldn't catch him, but the English could, huh? The only question I have is, what shade of white is he?"

He and Hayes let out a knowing laugh as Lionel looked on. He hadn't heard the news, either, but Buster Hayes wasn't exactly sharing it with both of them, and Lionel wasn't sure if he was supposed to pretend to not even be listening. He had felt the ache of King's death like any other black American, crowding into a dorm room with a dozen other students as they whaled and pounded the plaster walls with their fists. Lionel certainly knew what it was to be called *nigger,* to be followed by sales-clerks as he shopped for a present, and he knew the fear of being passed by a car full of white men craning their heads at the sight of him, the brake lights suddenly blooming in the night air. But he understood that as men of an earlier generation, Hayes and Big Brass shared a history of indignities, injustices, and probably far worse than he was likely to ever experience.

"Anyway, just wanted to pass that on," Hayes said, and ambled back through the cars.

"I thank you," Big Brass called out, and then he looked at Lionel as if he wasn't sure what he was doing there. Then he said, "Okay, son. Here's what I need you to do."

Michael's mother appeared in the doorway, and Michael quickly let his feet come off the wall. He looked at her upside down.

"So you want to play with your friends, then?" she said. She was trying to sound carefree, but both of them could hear the flutter in her voice.

"We're just going to go to the field," he said.

"Walt and Ty?" she asked.

"And Daniel."

"Right, I spoke to his mother earlier in the week."

She sat down on the edge of his bed and ran her fingers through his fresh haircut. His hair was what she noticed first when the police brought him to the door. Like a hippie, she thought, with his overgrown cowlicks.

"What do you boys like to do in that field, anyway?" she asked.

"We climb trees," Michael said, hoping that would suffice. That Friday morning Ty Weldon heard his father say to Ty's mother that the train would be passing right through town, and Ty knew that meant it would first bisect their field; when no one was looking, Ty studied the little diagram in the newspaper that showed the train's route from New York to Washington. During lunch, he told Michael, Daniel Gregory, and Walt Pluncket that they should go see it, but not to tell their parents. "If they think we're interested in seeing it," he said, "they might want us to go with them or something."

"Well, just don't climb too high," Michael's mother said, and wished she hadn't. But she also knew that Michael wouldn't hold it against her.

"Okay," he said.

He waited on the steps of his front porch for his friends. Next door he watched a man climb a ladder, a cigarette clinched in his lips, to inspect the shingles on the roof. Every time the man reached over to tug on a piece that concerned him, he paused first to mop his brow.

"You wouldn't catch me up there," Ty called out as he strolled up the walkway. "Not on a hot day like this. Black attracts the heat, you know. Like a thousand times."

"I don't mind the heat that much," Michael said. "I like being up high like that. Gives you a good view."

Ty sat down next to him and looked over his shoulder to be sure they were alone. "We're going to get a good view where we're going."

"Yep."

"My parents were watching the funeral on TV," Ty said. "They didn't say anything about seeing the train, though."

Both of them sat and tried to imagine what was ahead of them. In a few minutes Daniel and Walt arrived. Michael's mother looked out the screen door and came over to stand with them. "They say this might be the hottest day of the year so far. You boys be careful not to get overheated. Stay in the shade as much as you can."

They offered a low murmur of polite response.

Michael stood up and said to the ground, "I guess we'll be going." He began to move toward his mother to put his arms around her before he caught himself, but the other boys didn't seem to notice. She did, though, and smiled. She squeezed his shoulder and said, "Don't get into any trouble over there."

Ty looked at Michael quickly, wondering what else he had told her, but Michael didn't acknowledge him.

Out by the street Ty said, "Does she know we're going to see the train?"

"Yeah, a dead body," Daniel said.

"He's in a coffin, dimwit. It's not like you're going to see his flesh rotting off or anything."

"No," Michael said.

"Hey, my mom's been crying ever since he got shot," Walt said. "She goes for hours and keeps saying, 'What is this country coming to?'"

"Tell her to ask Michael the professor," Ty said, not with resentment, but pride. "Michael always knows the answer, don't you? Mr. Honor Roll Hotshot."

Michael could only smile. He was so grateful to be back among his friends that nothing else mattered.

MARYLAND

Roy Murphy was looking at his three ties, trying to decide which might look best with his pale-striped seersucker suit. He had worn the yellow tie the previous day, but no one from the office would see him, except the weekend editor, and Roy hadn't seen him yesterday, so he chose the yellow one.

As he tied it, he studied himself in the mirror. He studied the way his cheekbones failed to rise, the way his ears jutted out too low on his head, the handsome green of his large eyes, his brown, wiry hair cut short. He wondered what Jamie West would make of his face now and whether Jamie would think that Roy looked more like a man than when they saw each other last.

They weren't friends in high school, but Roy was a close confidant of Jamie's high school girlfriend, Claire Payton. In this arrangement, since Roy and Claire were such close friends, Roy knew a great deal about

Jamie, and Jamie knew little about Roy. Claire understood early into their courtship that Jamie didn't like to hear much about Roy — or any other boy, for that matter. She also understood that Jamie seemed to dislike Roy, perhaps only because he was another boy who knew Claire well, but also, Claire believed, because Roy and she had much more in common. They both liked to write — poetry and also editorials for the school paper. They both loved J. D. Salinger and Robert Frost and had a fondness for music, for string quartets and Benny Goodman's small combos, and preferred the Kinks over any of the other British bands. They liked looking for constellations up in the night sky, and they compared notes on the various birds — mostly yellow warblers and red-winged blackbirds and orioles — they saw in any given week.

Roy appeared scrawny next to Jamie because he was. And Jamie didn't trust Roy's intentions with Claire. How could a guy spend that much time with Claire and not want to kiss her?

Claire was at the University of Virginia, and Roy had heard that she had since become pinned to a student there from Richmond. He wondered if Jamie knew, or cared. He wondered how much they would talk about Claire, if at all. Roy was no longer in touch with her.

As a reporter, Roy was already becoming confident. His first week, when one of the sheriff's deputies tried to dismiss him by saying there was nothing the paper needed to report about an arrest made that night on a local arson case, Roy replied, "With all due respect, Mr. Tillman, we'd like to be the judge of what there is to report." Roy reenacted the encounter for his parents that night at dinner, and he replayed it in his mind for the better part of that week, when he was back to covering a Boy Scout Jamboree and a property dispute story between two dairy farmers.

The drive to the Wests' took just a few minutes, and he parked his car — his mother's sedan — in front of the neighbor's house. He was running early, as he always was, but it helped him relax and let him review in his mind how he wanted to start. How long would he talk to Jamie before bringing up the matter of being on the record? Would he ask that he and Jamie have some privacy, in case the parents wanted to listen in? What if the sister, whom he only vaguely remembered, thought it would be neat to watch?

He'd keep it simple with Jamie in the

beginning. How did it feel to be back? What were his plans now? Had he gotten fully used to his injury? And then, depending, he'd attempt to more fully explore Jamie's psychological state. How did he see his life now? In what ways did he feel changed, besides missing the leg? He'd also ask him, since the funeral train was passing right through town, did he have any thoughts on the Kennedy assassination — perhaps as a way to gauge Jamie's view on the politics of the war. Kennedy had made passionate arguments for America's withdrawal from Vietnam, and Roy wondered what Jamie thought of that. That summer Roy had already learned that questions that weren't obvious could have their own payoffs, and he had become skilled at moving a subject into offhand lines of questioning with little difficulty or awkwardness.

On the Wests' front door — dark green and peeling — was a little wooden plaque that said "Welcome," the lettering slightly crude; Roy wondered if this was something Jamie had done as a kid with a wood-burning set. He knocked once, then stepped away.

Mrs. West pulled the door back, balling up her apron. "Hello, hello," she said brightly. "Come in. I'm Ellie West. Welcome."

"Roy Murphy," he said, putting his hand forward. "Nice to meet you, Mrs. West." By the way she turned her head, he could see that she recognized his face. He let her study him as he stepped in, and before he could speak again, she said, "You look very familiar. I don't know if I've seen you in town before or what it is. You're not new in town?"

"No, ma'am," Roy said. "In fact, I went to Burton." He took a moment to scan the long hallway. He could hear someone listening to the radio in one of the back rooms.

"Well, how about that?" Ellie said. "Then you know Jamie? And his sister, Miriam? She's four years younger. She'll be a senior next year."

"I did know Jamie," Roy said. "I mean, I knew him just a little bit. We didn't have any of the same classes, I don't think. I was a friend of Claire Payton's."

"Oh, Claire," Ellie said in a wistful tone. "Pretty Claire. We were so fond of her. We were just heartbroken when she and Jamie broke up. We loved Claire to death."

Roy smiled in a way that said that he wouldn't offer anything more about Claire, and when he could see that Ellie was done

104

thinking about her, he moved his notebook to the other hand as a way of reminding her why he was here.

"Well, come on in," she said, finally. "Jamie's here, Mr. West is here. I know Miriam'll come out at some point."

As she walked toward Jamie's room, Roy studied the framed photographs lined up on the wall. Here was Jamie in his early teens, his hair worked into a ducktail. Here was Miriam in pigtails and an unself-conscious grin of snaggled teeth. Here was the family portrait around the same time, Mr. West and Mrs. West standing behind their children, their hands firmly clamped down on their shoulders, Mrs. West's hair swirling upward as if part of a science project. Perhaps the photograph for the church directory, Roy thought.

Roy could see Mrs. West leaning into Jamie's bedroom, but her voice was suddenly hushed. She looked peculiar leaning her head so far in, and it occurred to him that if she leaned any farther in without moving her feet she might topple forward. Then she turned and smiled — a smile of some relief, Roy thought. Roy could hear the sound of wooden crutches, and when Jamie moved out into the hallway, he seemed to consciously look away from Roy, conferring quietly once more with his mother. She nodded, then eased toward the young reporter.

"Let's have you and Jamie move into the backyard for a while," she said. "Miriam has the radio on so loud, it might be a distraction. I know it's already so hot out, but we have plenty of shade out back." She took him gently by the arm, as he watched Jamie let himself out a side door.

"That sounds just fine," Roy said. "Whatever is convenient for everyone."

From the kitchen window Roy watched him now as he settled into a lawn chair under a large oak tree whose trunk bore the faint traces of an old rope swing. Jamie put his crutches on the ground next to him and pushed himself out of the chair once to better adjust himself. He was still looking away. There were two other chairs next to him, and at the end of the spacious lawn Roy saw two big archery targets pocked with holes.

Mrs. West led Roy out. "Here we are then, Roy," she said, and turned one of the chairs to face Jamie. "Well, how about this as a little Burton reunion? You two don't even need any introduction. Jamie, did you know that Roy was working at the paper? Roy says he hasn't seen you since graduation. Isn't that what you said, Roy?"

She had confused what Roy had said about Claire, but there was no need to correct her.

"Yes, ma'am," he said. "Hey there, Jamie. It's good to see you." Roy jutted his hand out again, as if sprung from a coil. Jamie studied Roy's small, delicate hand for a moment before shaking it, and when he stuck his hand out in return, he let a sly smile spread across his face. It looked out of place on him, Ellie thought, and in that moment she barely recognized him.

"Murphy," Jamie said.

Roy had consciously not glanced at the missing leg since Jamie had stepped out into the hallway, and he was careful not to now, though it was much harder standing over him like this.

"Do sit down here," Ellie said to him, and when he did, she couldn't yet bring herself to step back into the house.

"How about this," she said again. Her eyes eventually drifted past them, and when they went to the railroad tracks she said to Roy, "Oh, did you know that the funeral train is going to pass right by?" She pointed out past the edge of their yard, where there were a few more weathered lawn chairs, to the gravel-lined tracks. Beyond the tracks was

107

an expanse of woods, spindly pine trees mostly, half of which were bare.

"There are a lot of people who'd loved to have a view like that today," Roy offered. He looked over to the neighbor's yard for comparison. A good part of it was taken up with liriope, and there were clothes drying on the line, rippling in the breeze like ghosts.

"It's all so terrible," Ellie said. Roy thought that if he didn't reply, she might have no choice but to leave them alone. He nodded once quickly, then glanced back over to the tracks.

"Well, I'll let you talk, then," she said, and she squeezed Jamie's shoulder before excusing herself.

Roy opened a page of his notebook and took in Jamie's face for the first time. There was a watery sharpness to the lines of his jaw now, and he was broader through the shoulders. His hair was growing out from his military cut. Even Jamie's hands looked bigger, meatier.

"So, thanks for agreeing to talk to me," Roy said.

Jamie's sly grin had faded, and for the first time he appeared to Roy the way he had back in high school. Handsome, confident, unimpressed by everything around him.

"So how's Claire?" Jamie said, in a voice

meant to convey his indifference.

"Oh, you know, I really wouldn't know," Roy said, and tried to make a laughing sound. "I haven't talked to her in over two years, probably. Yeah. After high school, we just kind of fell out of touch, really. You get into different colleges, and it's just harder to keep up. And, too, you get into college, and, well, you're different, you know? Or maybe it's just that you're older. I don't know if she's the same girl anymore. Maybe."

"War tends to change you a little bit. Look at the great change I got."

Roy looked at Jamie's leg — or at what wasn't there. Jamie was wearing a pair of khaki shorts, and the leg ended just a few inches past the cuff. It was perfectly rounded off — like a watermelon, Roy thought. He had seen this type of injury before, but not up close. He could see the purple traces of scars from the amputation surgery, but they were disappearing already. In most ways, the leg looked as if it had never extended any farther.

"I really am sorry about that, Jamie," Roy said. "I know that must be really difficult. I just can't imagine."

"I guess a missing leg makes a newspaper story around here."

"Oh, I don't think we were thinking of it like that. Not at all. But what do you think? Can I turn this on?" He held the little microphone between them, and he was embarrassed to see that his hand was shaking slightly. Jamie stared at it for a moment, and it reminded him of all the times he had passed Murphy in the hallway — Murphy keeping his head down, always averting his eyes. Murphy couldn't have weighed any more than Claire back then. Murphy the pencil. Now here he was these years later, but who had the upper hand? Jamie glanced out beyond the fence and could feel that old resentment toward him once more.

"Sure."

"So here's how it works," Roy said. "If there's anything you don't want to answer, just say so. Otherwise, we'll say that everything you say is all on the record. Which just means that would be part of what I could consider using for the article. Quotes."

"So college has changed you, too, you're saying. You mean you're not still that All-American listener? That's what Claire used to say about you. What a good listener you were."

"Yeah, that was me," Roy said. "The man on the sidelines."

110

"I guess you knew a lot about me through Claire."

"Not really," Roy said. "Sock hops. Proms. Doesn't that feel like a long time ago to you?"

"Yep." Jamie swatted at something buzzing near him.

"We were talking about changing. Besides the injury, how would you say that being in Vietnam has changed you? Or do you think it did at all? Or maybe you feel like it's too early to know."

Roy leaned over the tape recorder to make sure the cogs were spinning.

"I wrote Claire when I was over there," Jamie said, "even though I'd heard she had a boyfriend. She wrote me two letters back. The first one was all about the classes she was taking, her sorority, how hard she was studying. Like I was some kind of pen pal or something. Guys around me are getting sexy pictures of their girlfriends, letters about how they're waiting for them to come home. I guess I was kind of hoping for something more than reports from Biology 101 and English Literature."

Roy offered a nod of compassion. He understood he wasn't going to get answers to his questions until he let Jamie say everything he wanted to about Claire.

111

"You probably saw all that coming, didn't you?" Jamie said. "You probably saw it long before I did, Claire finding some slick Joe College after high school."

"Well, Claire was complicated," Roy said quickly. He realized his mistake too late and shielded his eyes from the sun, though they were sitting in the shade.

Jamie almost smiled at Murphy's nerve. What Murphy said was true, but Jamie knew it must have brought some satisfaction for Murphy to be the one to say it. Murphy probably *had* spent more time with Claire, in the end. But she had dropped him, too. In most ways, it was like she didn't exist anymore — no one had seen her, no one had heard from her. There was another guy from their high school who had gone off to Vietnam — Barry Yarborough, nose tackle on the football team, always singing Beach Boys songs, his little brother killed in a school bus accident — and as Jamie had heard it, no one knew whether he had been captured or killed, or whether he had simply run off. The last anyone had seen him, according to Sutton, he was with his platoon in Hue. Missing in action. That was how he thought of Claire now.

Delores would meet her friends and possibly their husbands just a mile from Arch's shop. Until then, Delores would have to entertain Rebecca in out-of-the-way places.

Delores put her sign and Rebecca's pictures in the backseat of their car. Rebecca sat in the passenger seat and clutched her one-eyed doll named Millie. Delores backed them out of the long driveway without knowing where they were going.

"Was that fun?" she asked. "Did you like painting?"

"Yes," Rebecca said.

"We're good painters, aren't we?" Rebecca nodded. "Your brothers used to like to paint, too. Now if it's not a football or a BB gun, I can't get them to touch it." In the last six months Delores had lost all inclination to censor herself with Rebecca. She talked about how difficult Rebecca's brothers had become, how intolerant Rebecca's

113

father could be of the things that Delores wanted to do or believed in. She even told Rebecca when she had insisted that Arch sleep on the couch, which on average was about once every couple of months. Once she told Rebecca that deep down her father was a good man, but that he could be oppressive, and then she explained what that word meant. On such occasions Rebecca had learned to arrange her face in some pensive expression, which Delores willed herself to see as sympathetic comprehension. Rebecca had learned to nod at the right moments, say, "Yes," when Delores finished her thoughts by asking, "So do you see how that would make me feel?"

Delores thumped her fingers against the rubber-covered steering wheel.

"You and I are going to see a train today, sugarplum. Would you like that?"

Rebecca studied her mother. In truth, Rebecca had no particular fondness for trains — or for anything with wheels on it — but to her mother, and she shook her head vigorously.

"Well, good. It's going to be going really fast, and it's not going to stop for us, but we can wave bye-bye to all the people on board, and maybe they'll wave to us. But that's not for a while. Not until after lunch.

114

Meanwhile, we just have to decide what we want to do. Today everything we do is going to be our secret."

New Jersey

In the days since he had been back, Ty, Daniel, and Walt had not asked Michael about his time with his father, since their parents had drummed it into them to treat Michael as if nothing unusual had happened. But they very much wanted to know the story. In the early days of his absence, they knew only that he was missing. From the way their parents shook their heads with concern while saying so little in front of them, the boys came to wonder if they would ever see their friend again. When their mothers said, "We just have to hope," the boys took that to mean the situation was beyond hope.

By the end of that first week, the tone of discussions had shifted. The rumor was that Michael's father had taken him, and now when the subject of Michael came up at the dinner table, there was a brightness in their parents' voices.

"Sooner or later, they're going to find that

father of his," Ty's mother had said. "And Michael will be just fine."

"I'll bet Michael has no idea of all the trouble his father is in," Walt's mother said.

"Michael will be home soon," Daniel's mother said. "And then his father can get what's coming to him for putting his mother to such worry."

As the four boys walked through the tall grass, Daniel looked at Walt, and then both of them looked at Ty. Michael was whistling the melody to "Walk, Don't Run." When they reached the group of trees they intended to climb, they surveyed the freshly cut grass and stared up at the potential branches on which to perch themselves.

"Here it comes!" Daniel called out. "Here comes the train!"

The boys looked down the tracks.

"Made you look," Daniel said.

"Hey, I knew it wasn't," Walt said.

"Hey hey hey," Ty said. "Don't be such morons." He spit convincingly, the way his older brother had taught him. "It's hot as hell. We should be swimming."

"Well, they're not bringing his body by *boat*," said Daniel. He had a new strategy lately of countering Ty's insults with his own, but this didn't seem to have any discernible effect.

"They're going to bring *your* body by boat," Ty said. "A tugboat. I was just talking about the heat."

"Hey, you want to go to the pool later and see Marianne Lassiter?" Walt said.

"Why would I want to see her? With those hairy arms. Her arms are hairier than a gorilla's."

"Then her bush must be like a jungle," Daniel said.

"Like you know about her bush," Ty said.

"I know it's hairy," Daniel said.

"You don't know crap," Ty said and flicked Michael on his forearm to make sure he was not the only one incredulous that Daniel could know anything about any girl's privates. "She doesn't even know who you are. You swim in the kiddie pool, anyway."

"I was just playing around that day," Daniel said. "I wasn't swimming in it."

"Michael, we were at the pool the other day," Ty said, "and Daniel was over there trying to swim laps in the *kiddie* pool with all these moms and their babies all over the place, and the lifeguards told him to get out."

Michael offered the obliged snicker. He had not been to the pool yet and wondered which of the lifeguards were back from last year.

"Hey, what are we going to do?" Walt asked. "This is boring, just waiting around." He checked his watch. They were expecting the train to come by at one-fifteen.

"All right, I know what," Ty said. "I'm going to be Sirhan Sirhan, and someone be Kennedy."

"I will," Walt said.

"Okay, Walt's Kennedy in the hotel, and he's coming through the kitchen of that hotel."

"Who are we?" Daniel asked.

"You be the guys that grabbed Sirhan and wrestled the gun out of his hand. Rosey Grier and Rafer Johnson."

"Who's Rafer Johnson?" Daniel asked.

"Some athlete who won a gold medal in the Olympics," Ty said.

"Oh. I'm Rosey Grier," Daniel said. "Michael, you be Rafer Johnson. But other people got shot, too."

"Well, do you want to be the woman instead?" Ty said. "A woman got shot."

Daniel pulled his T-shirt out at the chest and sang in a girlish voice, *"I've just been shot in my boobies."*

"Shut up," Ty said. "You're Rosey Grier." He paced around, trying to conjure up what he had heard Walter Cronkite describe on the evening news that Wednesday.

119

"Okay, I'm here in the corner," Ty said, crouching. "You don't see me, though."

"Hey, we won California," Walt said. "Whooooo." He strutted with his arms stretched above him. He then put them down to shake someone's hand. "Thank you, thank you."

Daniel and Michael walked uncertainly behind him. "Congratulations, Senator," Daniel said at last.

"Blam!" Sirhan Sirhan had taken fire, and Kennedy collapsed to the ground, clutching his head. "Blam!"

"Who's shooting?" Daniel called out. "Over there! Get him!"

Ty got off another two shots before standing up and running from Daniel. Michael quickly followed. Ty eventually curled his body against himself and froze, holding out his shooting hand while Daniel tackled him and reached for the weapon.

"Get the gun!" Daniel cried. "Johnson, help me. Get the gun."

Michael climbed on top of the two and grabbed Ty's hand, which was shaped with his pointer finger out and his thumb cocked back as the gun's hammer. When Michael wrestled the gun free, Ty's other fingers sprang to life, trying to reclaim it.

Michael stood up, his hand now the gun,

and looked around uncertainly. Walt lay on the ground, watching the scuffle but otherwise admirable in his posture of death.

"What do I do with it?" Michael asked.

"I guess you hold it," Walt offered, "until you can give it to the police."

Daniel was still wrestling with Ty, but Ty was ready to get up and pushed him off. "Let's do it again," Ty said. "Only this time, both you guys need to come get me at the same time. Michael, I could have shot you, too, if I wanted to. You're supposed to charge me as soon as I shoot."

"Okay."

In the second effort, Walt relied on more theatrics, drunkenly staggering before slumping to the ground, and once on his back, he rolled around, moaning at the pain. Daniel got the jump on the assassin faster this time, as did Michael, but Ty managed to keep the gun out of their reach by holding it inside his belt as they pried at his arm. In the third attempt, Ty got off a shot at Daniel, which brought the insurrection to a brief pause when Daniel pointed out that Rosey Grier wasn't, in fact, shot.

"You're too technical," Ty offered. "He could have been. Besides, we're just playing. Doesn't have to be one-hundred-percent accurate. I don't look like an Arab, but that doesn't matter."

"Actually, you kind of do," Daniel said, and Walt laughed.

"Blam!" Ty said and shot at Daniel again.

After another assassination it was time to switch roles. And then they switched again. When they had exhausted the possibilities, they generally agreed that Michael had been the best Kennedy because of the way he managed to collapse so violently, his arms flying behind him as if he were a bedsheet being snapped into the air, and on the ground he managed to be completely still, indifferent to the capture of his assassin. Walt had had trouble tackling anyone as Rosey Grier or Rafer Johnson, and Daniel had a particularly good turn as Sirhan because he had remembered what the shooter was overheard to shout while being pinned to the ground: "I can explain! Let me explain!"

DELAWARE

The water in the pool was turquoise, and the smell of chlorine was strong, but to Edwin it was thrilling, like smelling a woman's perfume in the first minutes of a first date. All his life he wanted the smell of chlorine to fill his backyard. Lolly wore her one-piece swimsuit under a pair of terry-cloth shorts and her long T-shirt with the Beatles' Yellow Submarine on the front. She had not purchased a new suit, much to Edwin's disappointment. For the last two years she had settled for her green one-piece, with black stitching on the side and unusually wide shoulder straps that made Edwin think of overalls; the suit had turned almost purple from the years of washing. She had become too self-conscious to wear a two-piece; her stomach had been flat all her life, but by her early thirties it had curved outward, and sometimes in profile she thought it looked like she was hiding a small dinner bowl under her shirt. Edwin had gained exactly five pounds since she married him, and they had settled mostly into his behind without much fanfare. He wore a pair of black-rimmed glasses that at first glance resembled a mask; Lolly sometimes kidded him that they made him look like the Lone Ranger. But his blond hair had remained the same, parted to one side, longer over his ears and collar in a way now that Lolly found slightly unbecoming.

Between the two of them, Lolly had dated more and had more romantic flings before they got married. She had been a pretty bride, and even now it wasn't uncommon for men at parties, when Edwin stepped away, to flirt with her and make suggestive comments. The flirting made her feel sexy, and she wasn't rude when she let men know she wasn't available. Sometimes she lifted her ring finger and said in a playful voice, "Ring-a-ding-ding," then walked through the crowd knowing the man was taking a last, lustful gaze at the swing of her derriere.

But that attractive spark she could sometimes feel about herself dimmed around Ted's girlfriend, Georgia, who, with her overflow of auburn hair and Amazonian curves, could have been a Raquel Welch impersonator. That morning, as Lolly got dressed, she could already imagine how slight Georgia's bikini would be, and she knew that at all times of the day Ted and Edwin would be staring at her.

In the kitchen she began chopping vegetables when the smell of chlorine drifted through the back-door screen — sharp and acidic. Edwin came in and surveyed the preparations. The train would be coming through town at three-fifteen, but Edwin was only thinking of the party.

"Music!" he said. "We gotta have music. I'll get the eight-track out there."

"Let's just not play it so loud, though," Lolly said. "We don't have to play it for the whole neighborhood."

"Lol," he said. "Please don't bum me out."

Seven hours after they had left Michael's school, his father had found the radio broadcast of the Tigers–White Sox game. "Tigers could use a win," he said. Michael was resting his head against the cool glass of the window, his eyes too heavy to keep open. It occurred to him that he should say something to his father's remark, or just nod, since he was unsure of what passed for an acceptable silence between them. In almost everything his father had said during the long drive, Michael had worked hard to show him that he couldn't agree more, or that his father had just pointed out some colorful fact that Michael would surely make use of at some time.

"Priddy has two men on and two men out, and he's not out of this yet. Now he steps off the mound. He wants to think over this first pitch to Oyler."

"Hey, sport," James Colvert whispered.

"Sport, wake up. We're going to pull in here for the night." Michael was aware of the neon lights before he opened his eyes, the vibrant red turning his darkness into spots, and he thought he heard the crunch of gravel. He righted himself and put his head against the vinyl headrest.

"Okay," he said, squinting into a motel's dark-paneled office, where he could see a man leaning over a desk, flipping through a magazine.

"We're still a few hours away from the cabin," his father said. "I'm going to go in and get us a room. You stay put." Michael nodded only after the car door shut and watched his father's long stride to the office. The man at the desk reached over to turn a knob on his transistor radio and waved him in. The man glanced out at their car as James Colvert spoke. When he came back out, key in his hand, his lips were puckered, as if he intended to whistle.

"Okay, one room for two weary travelers," he said, holding the car door open. He went back to the trunk and pulled out a leather suitcase. Though Michael had wondered about it in their first hundred miles, the idea came to him now with some alarm: he had no extra clothes. He had no toothbrush, no pajamas to sleep in, no change of underwear or socks. As he got out, he said, "I don't have any luggage."

James Colvert smiled. "Well, that's a temporary problem," he said. "Nothing we can't fix. I did pick up an extra toothbrush for you, and tomorrow, when we get to where we're going, I know a department store where we can pick up what you'll need." He held the plastic key in the light of the sign. "Room seven."

They followed a pathway made of smoothed stones, and when he got the door open, James Colvert reached for a switch on the wall and, not finding one, crept to the shadowy outline of a lamp on a desk. A dim, orange light revealed two small beds with brown bedspreads and a painting between them of Indians on their horses, one with his tomahawk raised over his head. James Colvert put his suitcase down and closed the door. "Well, it's not the Taj Mahal, but it will do," he said. All these hours later, his voice still wasn't entirely familiar to Michael.

James Colvert flipped open his suitcase and retrieved a tube of toothpaste and a toothbrush still in its clear packaging. "That's for you," he said.

Michael took it in his hand and contemplated its particular shade of green. "Thank you." He brushed with more effort than he could usually summon, since he didn't want to appear ungrateful, and spit with a fierceness that surprised him. He sat on the corner of the other bed with more uncertainty than he had felt all day.

"Well, go ahead and hit the hay," James Colvert said. "You're not used to being up this late, I guess."

"Sometimes," Michael said, but he didn't find the convincing note he had intended.

He then unbuttoned his pants, suddenly self-conscious, and slipped off his socks, placing them neatly on top. He got under the rough sheet and blanket and turned to face the wall, studying the lines in the wooden slats. He knew it would be long after the lights were turned off before he fell asleep.

DELAWARE

Edwin was giving Ted and Georgia a tour of the pool. Ted had been a friend of Edwin and Lolly's for five years, from when they lived in the same apartment complex. When they first met, Ted was married to a Chinese student named Mai; three years later they had an infant daughter named Ling-lee. This was during Ted's "days of haze," as he called them now, when he was often drunk or stoned. Ted was generally a happy drunk, but when he passed out, he slept through the better part of the next day. When the baby was asleep, Mai berated him for the groceries he had forgotten to pick up, the soiled diaper he hadn't detected, the money he'd squandered, the nights he had failed to come home. A week after Ling-lee's second birthday, Mai moved back to China with her.

Edwin and Lolly didn't know Georgia as well, and Georgia's beauty — she had once worked in the Chicago Playboy Club as a cocktail waitress — made Lolly feel more reserved. Georgia had been seeing Ted for nearly six months; she worked as a beautician and was ten years younger than the rest of them, though she looked even younger.

Edwin stood up on the last step of the ladder and narrated how he had put it all together. "And you, my fine friends, have the honor of helping us break it in."

"Groovy," Ted said. He wore a T-shirt with a cobra sprung to life over snug-fitting jean cutoffs, with a red bandanna around his neck. His curly hair piled upward, and since growing out his sideburns, he liked to run his fingers down the length of them when he spoke. Georgia wore flip-flops underneath her red-painted toes and a tie-dyed T-shirt that she had tied above her belly button. Her blue jeans flared at the tops of her ankles.

"Everyone in the neighborhood is going to want a piece of this," Ted said.

"With good reason," Edwin said.

Ted ran a finger through the water. "It's like your own private oasis, the way it's just *here*. When can we jump in?"

Edwin nodded. He wanted to be the first one. "Anytime, I guess. Lolly's in the kitchen. I'll get her to take a picture." He went to the back door, half singing the Doors song they had heard that morning. "Lol, company's here. Party's started." He stuck his head in. "Hey, can you get my camera? Everyone's ready to jump in, and I was thinking we would capture it on celluloid. Can you come out?"

Lolly retrieved the camera from the bedroom. "Do you want to take out some of this stuff?" she asked, pointing to the trays on the kitchen counter.

"Not yet. Let's just get in the water. It's going to be unbelievable."

"Really, no one will believe it?"

Edwin stepped all the way in. "Come on, Lol. Already you're not making it fun."

"Okay, okay. I know you're excited. All right, here comes the Pool Party Queen right now, ready to document this important moment in history."

When Edwin stepped back out, he was stunned to see Ted waist deep in the pool. Edwin jerked back so violently that he almost knocked the camera from Lolly's hands.

"Holy crap, Ted! You were supposed to wait. Shit, man. What the hell?"

Ted's smile drained from his face. "What's wrong?"

"You were supposed to wait," Edwin said. As he approached the pool, the sight of Ted and his hairy chest bobbing in the water was so painful he had to look to Georgia, who quickly turned away in embarrassment. "Lolly was going to take a picture," Edwin finally thought to say.

"Let's all get in, then," said Ted. "Come on. Hey, bro, I didn't mean to steal your thunder. But this pool is *happening*."

"It's just, you know," said Edwin. "I put the thing together. I kind of wanted to be the first one in."

"Everyone in the water," Lolly said. "Let's get this poor man wet before he has a breakdown."

Lolly winked at Georgia. "Hi, honey. Do you want to come in and get changed?"

Georgia, still a bit unsettled by Edwin's outburst, grabbed her canvas bag and stepped quickly inside.

Lolly put the camera down. It was time to strip to her bathing suit, and as she looked at some distant point beyond their fence, she could feel Edwin and Ted watching her while pretending not to. The light coming through the trees was bright and unforgiving. When Lolly was done, Edwin took his glasses off and held them between his fingers while removing his shirt. In the sunlight his hairless, white chest looked like a giant egg. He climbed the steps of the ladder and paused for a moment.

"No diving, remember," Lolly said. This was a further irritation to Edwin, who knew exactly what the safety guidelines for his pool were. It was only five feet deep, and Edwin was six-foot-two. Of course he wasn't going to dive. Instead, he inched his toes to the edge of the ladder, his arms firmly clutched to his sides, like a tin soldier, and fell cleanly through the water, making almost no splash at all. He collapsed his legs when he hit the cement bottom so that he could be fully submerged. But instead of pushing back up, he stayed in that position, knees bent, for so long that Ted and Lolly eventually locked eyes in concern. Ted pushed himself off from the side, and as he got within arm's length Edwin rocketed violently upward. After he ran a hand across his face, he let out a raucous whoop of approval. "In my own backyard!" Edwin shouted.

Ted laughed and gave Edwin a splash. "This is heaven, man," Edwin said. Slowly he drifted around the perimeter of the pool. "Feel that beautiful water."

"It feels good, man," Ted said. "Come on in, Lolly."

"Let me get a picture of King Neptune first," she said. Edwin waded over to her and offered two peace signs, his eyes tiny slits in the sunlight.

"What was that yelling?" Georgia called out. She let the screen door slam harder than she meant to, then put a finger to her lips as an apology. She was wearing a white bikini that featured three large silver rings, one that connected the fabric over her breastbone, and the other two joining the fabric at each hip. She walked toward them a little sheepishly, smiling but avoiding their gazes. Even Lolly couldn't help staring so unabashedly. Georgia's full breasts swung with the precision of windshield wipers, and the curve of her waist made both Edwin and Lolly think of a guitar. Georgia was used to being stared at like this, and when she went swimming in public she was relieved when the first seconds of stunned silence were over. She let out a small laugh, as if everyone was so silly, and went up the ladder and slid in before anyone had time to recover.

After she swam to one side, Edwin turned his gaze from her and said to Lolly, "Every one in, Lol." Ted, Georgia, and Edwin watched as Lolly stood atop the little platform. Before she could jump, she saw the faces of the Pyle twins, Norma and Nadine, pressed against the chain-link fence.

"Hey, you two," she called out.

"Hi," they said in unison. "When did you get a pool?" Norma asked.

"We just got it," Lolly said. She could feel Edwin trying to get her attention, and she knew what he was thinking: *Don't invite them over.* "We'll have to have you over for a swim sometime."

"Today?" Norma asked.

"Not today, honey," Lolly said. "Today we have company."

Georgia waved at the girls, and the girls eagerly returned it.

"So we'll see you later," Edwin said. But the girls didn't move.

"It's fine, Ed," Lolly said, and then made her splash, which, as far as she could tell, was the biggest one all day.

WASHINGTON

After a quick run-through of the Botanic Garden, Maeve took a bus to Union Station. The train was scheduled to arrive around four-thirty, but even now, inside the cavernous hall, underneath a shimmering, barrel-shaped ceiling that caused Maeve to fall into a neck-craning waggle, there was a steady line of people without luggage weaving in and out between a multitude of police officers and scampering down a flight of stairs; after recovering from her awe of the place, she quickly followed. Eventually the line came to a halt, and after a few minutes she tapped the man in front of her on the shoulder; he had an earplug connected to his transistor radio and took a moment to realize.

"This is the line to see the funeral train, is it?" Maeve asked.

"I hope so," said the man. He chomped an unlit cigar.

The line took a few steps forward and stopped again. Maeve fished out a postcard she had gotten that morning — of a Venus flytrap said to be one of the biggest in the world — to send to her sisters. She had never sent a postcard before and stared at the empty white space on the back with trepidation. In the picture the plant's "teeth" were as long as nails and terrifying, its "mouth" deep crimson inside and sprung open like a bear trap. Seeing Mr. Hinton each morning had made her think of her father more frequently than usual that week, and she was remembering how he had encouraged her to write her stories down. Maeve gripped her pen until she could feel it press against the bones of her fingers. Finally she wrote: "I was at the U.S. Botanic Garden this morning — quite lovely! — until this horrid creature nearly swallowed me whole."

The girls would laugh at that — she could see their faces now, turning the postcard over after getting to the end of that first line and then shrieking at the insidious plant. They were all old enough not to believe it, of course, but they would be grateful for the joke all the same. "Maeve!" they would shout in gleeful surprise.

"They say the train has just left New

York," the man said, and held up his radio to explain his source. He wasn't quite ready to turn back around, but Maeve showed no interest in chatting. "What a train ride that must be," he said before giving up.

As stories went, the idea of a giant Venus flytrap seizing her up was a trifle; she was more imaginative than that when she was still learning to write her name. But she still tingled — how long had it been since she had even *thought* anything outlandish? She leaned against the wall and continued.

"Luckily, I had my Polo mints, and nothing burns a Venus flytrap more than mints. Spit me out halfway down the hall, it did, before keeling over. All the ruckus forced the place to shut down, and now I'm wanted by the authorities for killing the bugger. If they try to contact you, tell them I'm back in Ireland as far as you know . . . and that my career killing the giant Venuses has just begun. Love, Maeve."

It was silly business, what she had written, but at that moment Maeve could feel herself shaking slightly. Was it relief? Anxiety? She wasn't even sure, but she knew she liked the sensation. And she wondered if she could have even had such a thought if she was still in Massachusetts, where she had carried her grief around like a trunk. For the next few minutes she let a rush of emotions wash through her, and then she fell sad once more, thinking of how close she might have come to starting over here in Washington.

The line trudged forward a few steps down toward one of the train platforms — and stalled again, then started up again and stopped, and everyone resigned themselves that this was how it would be for who knew how long.

PENNSYLVANIA

On the edge of town, Delores pulled into the parking lot for Weir Park. A week earlier she had read in the paper about a local soldier who was killed in Vietnam, and the man's mother was quoted about what a good father he had been to his two little boys, and that one of his favorite things to do had been to walk with them down the street to Weir Park. The paper said he had stepped on a land mine.

Generally Delores took Rebecca — and the boys, when they had become too restless — to the park a couple of blocks from their house, though increasingly it was becoming a hangout for teenagers who smoked and wore bright scarves in their hair and were perpetually barefoot. Delores had noticed how Brian and Greg would watch them, and then pretend to be looking at something else if they caught her noticing. Once, as the four of them were walking home, Brian said, "Those guys are hippies. I bet I could knock their teeth out."

"What in the world kind of talk is that?" Delores said. "You do *not* talk that violence."

"All they do is sit there and act weird," Greg added; lately, a potential scolding from his mother did nothing to prevent him from speaking his mind.

"Peace, man!" mocked Brian. He then took a puff on an invisible cigarette.

"Who do you two think you are to make fun of somebody else? Do you think you're better than those young people because they dress differently? Have they done something to you to make such a violent threat like that?"

"Far out, man," said Greg, though he had, if anything, voiced something closer to a foreign accent.

"They're hippies, Mom," Brian said. "What do you care about hippies for?"

"I'm trying to understand how you've decided that *hippies* are somehow unworthy of basic respect. What do you even know about hippies, anyway? What do you even know that makes you so informed?"

"Dad doesn't like hippies," Greg said. "He says they're lazy and all they do is do drugs and hang around doing nothing."

"Well, that may be true of some of them

142

— *some,*" Delores said, "but you can't make those kinds of sweeping statements about a whole group of people. That's ignorant. Besides, we don't make violent threats against *anyone.*"

Now, as Delores and Rebecca took in the unfamiliar park, they saw there were just two mothers with their children — a boy and two girls. One woman wore cat-eye glasses in a shade of green and smoked as she talked to the other woman, who was heavyset but appeared younger. Both wore pale sundresses, and their faces looked damp in the stifling heat. Delores and Rebecca stood on the edge and contemplated the monkey bars, a once yellow balance beam, and the sandbox, which was framed with dull, rotting boards. There was also a modest slide with glistening aluminum that looked scalding to the touch, two toddler swings — one broken — and two regular-sized swings. The other women turned to them and smiled quickly before resuming their conversation.

"Okay, Rebecca, what do you want to do first? Do you want me to push you in the swing? It's nice to be at a new park, isn't it? Isn't this fun?" Rebecca was watching the two older girls atop the monkey bars. They seemed about eight or nine years old,

Delores thought. The blond girl was stroking the other girl's ponytail. The ponytailed girl seemed to belong to the woman in the glasses, since both of their chins disappeared immediately from under their mouths. The girls were giggling, and the one stroking her friend's hair was trying out an adult voice as she counseled the girl on what to do with her hair. Rebecca, who spent too much time in the company of boys punching one another on the arm and calling one another "idiot" and "retard" and generally expressing themselves in sudden barks of excitement or rage, was transfixed.

Delores whispered, "You're watching the big girls, aren't you? They look like they're having fun." Delores gave her another moment, then scooted her along and swept her up into the one swing that fit her.

The boy had worked up a respectable pile of sand in one corner of the sandbox, and his tongue stuck out one side of his mouth as he worked.

"Big push," Delores said. In the air Rebecca's neck twisted so that she could keep watching the girls, who seemed not to notice. Delores pushed a dozen times until she felt slightly foolish. "Well, we can do something else," she said. She let the swing come to a stop, then lifted Rebecca out and set her down. Rebecca continued watching the girls, and finally Delores said, "Let's go see what they're doing, then. Come on." Rebecca moved in small, hesitant steps until she and her mother were at the bottom of the monkey bars.

The girl whose hair was still being worked on was saying, "I'm going to keep growing it until it reaches my waist."

The other girl nodded, focused on her work.

"Hello," Delores said cheerily. She noticed that the mothers paused their conversation when they heard Delores's voice. "This is Rebecca."

The girls said hello with little interest. "Do you want me to put you up there?" Delores asked. Rebecca could not speak.

The girl with the ponytail regarded Rebecca for the first time now and asked, "How old is she?"

Delores said to Rebecca, "How old are you?" and got no answer. "She's almost five," she said.

"Oh," the girl said, and seemed to do some calculation. "She can come up. This is our beauty salon."

"A beauty salon!" Delores said. "How about that. Rebecca, would you like me to take you to the top floor of their beauty salon?" Rebecca nodded once, her mouth tucked into a tight line. Delores lifted her to the top rung and helped her get steadied on one of the bars. She let her hands go for a second, then put them back under Rebecca's shoulders. "Are you hanging on?" Delores asked, keenly aware that she was now the prime focus of the two girls and their mothers.

"Yes," Rebecca said, with some impatience.

"Well, hold on good and tight, okay?" she said, and began to back away. In the sandbox the boy was making a grinding, mechanical noise, but otherwise the playground had become hushed. Delores stepped toward the edge, a short distance from the two women, and waited for the conversations to resume.

"She's a cutie," the woman with glasses said.

"Oh, thanks," Delores said. She felt conspicuous for having to stand.

"She looks like you," the other woman said.

"Not like her brothers," Delores said. "They look just like their father." The women smiled and nodded.

"Molly, it looks like you have a new customer," the woman with glasses said.

"Can you say hello to your new customer?"

"I'll be with you in a minute," Molly said sharply. The idea that she was getting backed up was rather appealing to her.

"That's nice — thank you," Delores said. "She just loves older girls. Her two brothers are older, but they don't hold the same fascination. Not by a mile."

"That's her brother, Lee, over there," Molly's mother said. "She barely acknowledges him, but he doesn't seem to mind. He's always in his own little world."

"We haven't seen you here before," said the other woman. "We come here all the time. You didn't just move into the neighborhood, did you?"

"No," said Delores. She had to think about what she was going to reveal. "We just happened to be out this way."

The women nodded. It was unclear if they would go back to their conversation now. Finally Molly announced to her client, "Okay, I think we're done," and the girl pulled her ponytail forward for inspection.

"It looks very nice," she said in an adult, unconvinced voice. She then moved alongside Molly, becoming one of the salon workers herself, and said to Rebecca, "We're ready to take you now."

Delores took a few steps when Rebecca

147

didn't move or speak, but then Rebecca began to inch herself into the same position the other girl had occupied. She wasn't used to being up this high, and she studied her fingers' grip around the bar for assurance. Delores started to offer her some assistance, but she was also grateful for the brief reprieve, since she would have Rebecca the entire day.

"You can buy little girls all the dolls and doll dresses and whatnot, but in the end they like to play with hair as much as anything," Molly's mother said. This got a polite laugh.

"She's a quiet one, your little girl," the other woman said. "Is she shy?"

Delores often heard this question about Rebecca, and she had come to resent it. Why did Rebecca's reserve seem to bother people? Weren't there enough children talking endlessly and asking every variation of tedious questions? She admired Rebecca's quiet manner; she believed Rebecca was taking in everything around her when she was so quiet. If others considered Rebecca to be a little dull, Delores had decided that she was smarter than any other child her age. Even Arch had wondered out loud about Rebecca. That spring, he and Delores were watching an episode of *Family Affair* that centered around Buffy and her strong attachment to her doll, Mrs. Beasley. After it was over he stayed in his chair and mulled over what he wanted to say. "Sometimes I worry that Rebecca is a little slow. Do you ever think that?"

On the monkey bars Rebecca sat with her back to Molly, as Molly ran her fingers through Rebecca's short bob. "We should be able to do *wonders* with this," she said, which felt too shopworn a sentiment even to her.

The other girl reached over to Rebecca's hair for her own assessment. "Let's wash it first," she said, and held her hand above Rebecca, as if holding a spray gun, and began making a hissing sound. Rebecca was alarmed at first, but she sat still until Molly said, "Okay, it's all clean."

The little boy had wandered over to the bottom of the monkey bars by now. "What are you doing up there?" he asked. He was a couple years older than Rebecca, but his voice had retained a high-pitched, soft pronunciation of the hard syllables.

"You can't come up," Molly said. "It's only for girls."

The boy put his hand on the first bar to test that idea. "I can if I want to."

On the bench the two women resumed

their conversation about the local elementary school, only in quieter voices.

"No you can't," said Molly, who stopped combing Rebecca's hair with her fingers. "No."

"You can't boss me," he replied.

"Just go *away*," said the other girl, who was used to helping Molly deny her brother. "Go swing."

"What are you doing to that girl?" he asked. Now he was on the level just beneath them. Delores took a couple of steps closer.

"Nothing. We're fixing her hair," Molly said. "Now *go*."

Delores turned to see if Molly's mother might intervene, but she was not paying attention to the disruption at the salon.

"Did she ask you to?" the boy said.

"You're *annoying* us," Molly said.

The boy reached out and tugged on his sister's foot once. Then she kicked out at him, hitting a bar instead.

"Missed!" the boy cried out.

Delores began walking over, her eyes trained on Rebecca. Before she could reach them, the boy climbed another rung and grabbed his sister's leg, and this time he held on. Molly gripped the bars on both sides of her to get more leverage, then swung her leg back and forth, trying to shake him. Delores saw what could happen, and she quickened her steps, her hands out in front of her.

"Rebecca —" What she had intended to say was, "Rebecca, let's go explore this balance beam over here," or "Let's say goodbye to the salon now," or some variation of an exit line that she, as a mother, had said countless times in so many situations over so many years. Instead, Molly's leg swung fiercely, and she broke free of her brother's grip at last, sending her leg upward and into Rebecca's side, and Rebecca toppled through the space below. Delores was ten feet away then, and even as the toe of her open sandal dug into the grass, she knew she could not catch her. The monkey bars had four levels, and Rebecca fell cleanly through the top two, sailing past the boy, who watched in horror — less for the girl than for the punishment he was sure to receive for his role in all of this. But her body turned as she descended, and the side of her head knocked against first one bar, and then, as she twisted further, another on the level below, this time striking the back of her skull. The two impacts rang out in a way that defied how anyone there might have imagined the sound of a child's head against a metal bar. There was a musical pitch in the blows, as if what had struck the bars was another piece of metal or a mallet. She hit the ground not all at once, but in a blur of stages, like a dropped marionette. One arm landed first, then a leg, then the side of her face. The weight of her torso followed last.

What came out of Delores's mouth as Rebecca hit the ground was a sound so shrill that the birds in the trees on the playground perimeter turned their heads in curious admiration. Since Rebecca's body was within the narrow confines of the bars, Delores had to dive under and crawl in. Rebecca's eyes were closed, but her lips were moving, and Delores could see that in a few seconds Rebecca was about to release a torrent of pain and upset. One side of her face was already starting to turn deep plum.

"Baby girl," Delores whispered, straining to breathe herself. She scanned Rebecca's body — making sure her arms and legs were moving — and then reached carefully behind Rebecca's head to feel for blood or a deep cut. At the touch Rebecca let out a remarkable howl, and Delores gingerly tried to scoop her off the ground and into her arms. Only then did Delores feel the eyes of the boy and the girls, looming over them. Rebecca's scream came in waves, each more forceful than the one before. The two mothers were in front of Delores now, panting.

"Oh my God!" Molly's mother said. "The little sweetheart. She just fell the *whole way* down."

Delores had no intention of responding. If they had been paying attention to their goddamn children, this wouldn't have happened. Molly knew that being this high up, away from her mother, was to her advantage, and she showed no signs of coming down. The boy jumped down and watched from a distance.

"Is she going to be all right?" he asked quietly, because he knew he should.

Delores whispered, "Tell me all the places it hurts, honey. Can you do that? Do your arms hurt, or your legs?" Rebecca's face was swelling, the colors churning underneath the skin. Delores began to slide out on her backside, cradling Rebecca with one arm. When Delores could stand up, Rebecca's body still limp in her arms, all the things that were supposed to occur to her, as a mother, swirled around in her head like a high-speed merry-go-round.

"Poor, poor *thing,*" Molly's mother said. "You might want to take her to the hospital, just to get checked out. I know she hit her head. Oh, so awful." She then remembered

Molly up top, watching. "Come down right this minute," she said to her, and Molly scrambled down.

"She's going to need ice on that," the other woman said. "She did, she just hit her head so *hard.* There's a grocery story just around the corner. You could get ice there."

Delores wanted to get away from them as quickly as she could, but Rebecca's shrieks were making it difficult to make a decision. She was worried about broken bones, the blow to Rebecca's head. She had checked her teeth, which were unharmed. She rebalanced Rebecca in her arms and broke into a trot to their car, the women trailing behind.

"You're going to be all right, honey," Delores said. "Mommy's right here. Mommy's always right here."

"Are you sure we can't do anything?" Molly's mother called. "I'm *so* sorry. Molly didn't —"

Delores opened up the passenger's side of the car, and Rebecca crumpled toward the steering wheel. The women watched Delores get in, and they both offered delicate half-waves as she pulled out, as if to say, *No hard feelings?*

"Okay, let's just think now," Delores said when she got to the end of the street. She put the car in park and tried to hold Rebecca's wet face in her hands. She had seen the grocery store on the way in, and now she tried to remember if it was left or right. "Rebecca, can you move your hands and your feet for Mommy? Do you think you can?"

Rebecca curled her fingers inward, then resumed her crying.

"Okay, that's good, sweetheart. I know. I know. And your arms don't hurt? You can move them around? I'm worried about your sweet head, too." Delores thought about the hospital more clearly now, and then just as quickly she wondered how she would explain to Arch what had happened. She couldn't make up anything more about a birthday party because he might want details — *Who was in charge? Why wasn't anyone watching her?* She knew the explanation to Arch should be the least of her worries, but she had built the day around lies, and everything felt more tangled up.

"Rebecca, we're going to get you some ice for your face, to keep the bruise from getting so bad. Now I just need to remember which way." She thought for another moment. Then: "Rebecca, how old are you, honey? Can you tell me how old you are?" Delores repeated, and Rebecca nodded without saying anything.

"How old are you, Rebecca? Mommy forgot for a moment. Can you remind me?"

Rebecca could feel another wave of sobbing coming on, but she managed to stifle it for the moment. "Four and three-quarters."

"That's right! That's exactly right. That's a good sign. I think we're going to be okay."

DELAWARE

Georgia was floating on one of the two rubber rafts, and Edwin and Lolly were tossing the beach ball back and forth. Ted kept swimming underneath Georgia and tugging on her feet, which made her giggle. It was time for lunch, and Edwin dreaded having to step out and put the chicken on. Even in the water the extreme heat of the day was draining their energies.

"So Lolly wants to go see Kennedy's funeral train later," Edwin said.

"Oh, I want to go," Georgia said. "Can I go?"

"Sure, whoever wants to go," Lolly said.

"I still can't believe it," Georgia said. "Did you know that his wife is pregnant with his *eleventh* child? How do you even have eleven children?"

"You're asking the wrong girl," Lolly said. Then she went under to avoid looking at Edwin.

"I don't want Nixon in the White House, that's for sure," Ted said. "He gives me the creeps, man. That guy is Lon Chaney."

"Who do you like, McCarthy?" Edwin asked.

"I guess," Ted said. Then he jumped onto Georgia's raft. When she shrieked Edwin watched her long leg kick into the air, the tendons as clear as stems in a glass vase. Ted was on top of her, and as they kissed, their wet lips smacked in the air. Georgia settled her hands on the top of his shorts before Ted made the raft capsize.

"You think there's anything to Humphrey?" Edwin wanted to know.

"It's hard to tell with a vice president," Ted said. "I just really liked Kennedy. Kennedy told it like it is, you know? He was the one talking about ending the war long before the others. Kennedy gave a fuck. I liked how he was always talking about the Indian. I thought that was cool, saying how much the white man had let the Indian down. And that's the truth, man. Those Indians, they have it tough. On the reservation, no jobs, no food. Because we screwed them. They're the poorest people in the country, the Indians. Now that Kennedy's dead, Humphrey, McCarthy, they're kind of the same to me. Kennedy was about hope, you know? What are they about?"

Edwin arched his eyebrows. "When did you get so up on things? I didn't know you followed politics."

Ted shrugged.

"I think he was going to win it all," Lolly said. "A lot of people feel like that. He might have even been a better president than his brother. Remember how he went into Indianapolis the night Martin Luther King was killed, and that was the only big city that didn't have a riot? He came in there, talked to them, and in just a few minutes they just went home. That's what he could do. He could touch people like that."

"What time is the train coming?" Georgia asked.

"The paper said soon after three," Lolly said.

"It's going to be crowded," Edwin said.

"We should probably get lunch started," Lolly said.

"All right," Edwin said, and he floated over to the ladder. Immediately the beads of water on his back and shoulders began to melt away in the intense sunlight. Ted followed and dried his shorts with his purple towel, then dug around in Georgia's bag.

"Who wants to get high?" Ted asked. He

held a marijuana cigarette above his head.

Edwin glanced quickly at Lolly. "Sure," he whispered.

"I do, I do," Georgia said.

Ted lit the joint, and his face fell into a tight clinch. He nodded his approval and sauntered over to Georgia. He held the joint between his fingers while she took a drag.

"Is that from Elliot? From Jamaica?" Georgia asked.

"No, I bought it off Iggy. Elliot's stuff was never from Jamaica, Iggy said."

"Oh," Georgia said. She thought about this a moment, looking to Ted for the significance of that.

"How about you, Lolly?" Ted asked. He started toward her, but Lolly shook her head.

"Lolly doesn't smoke anymore," Edwin called out. Lolly paddled over toward the ladder.

"It's no big deal," she said. "Who cares, Edwin?" She wrapped her hair around her finger.

"No one," he said. "I'm just saying."

"Well, you said it."

Ted took another toke and, holding the smoke in his mouth, reached over and kissed Georgia full-on. This immediately sent her into a coughing fit. Her eyes were streaming tears.

"Jesus, I wasn't ready for that," she said.

"I'm sorry, babe," he said. "I thought you liked that."

"I don't," she said. "Just let me get my own smoke." She coughed again, a deep, ragged screech, and when she swung her head away she saw the Pyle twins next door watching her through the fence. They had Barbie dolls in their hands, a yellow plastic bucket filled with water at their feet. The Barbies were trying out their new pool. The coughing had alarmed the girls, but they didn't look away once Georgia caught sight of them.

"The chlorine smell is kind of strong," Ted told Edwin. "Are you sure you don't have too much chlorine in there?"

Edwin was picking up the chicken pieces with tongs and placing them onto the grill. "I'm sure," he said.

"I thought it was kind of strong, too," Lolly called. "You checked it?"

"Of course," Edwin said. "And the pH level, and the alkalinity. I checked it all."

"I don't know. It sure is strong," Ted said.

"You're already stoned," Edwin suggested.

"Maybe," Ted said. He ran a hand across his chest, running a finger through the ringlets of chest hair. "Maybe." He sat down in one of the patio chairs and went back to his joint.

"I'll bring out the rest of the food," Lolly said in the voice she reserved to show her annoyance — low and from her gut. Edwin nodded, and when the screen door closed behind her, he discreetly turned the grill so that he didn't have to crane his neck to watch the swimming pool. Georgia had her arms stretched along the rim, her head thrust back and her eyes closed against the sun.

"So you and Georgia are getting pretty serious," Edwin said softly.

"I guess. It's cool, though. No pressures, nothing too heavy. And she's young, you know."

"She's a free spirit," Edwin said. "I like that about her. She's a cool chick."

Ted released the joint from his lips and turned toward the pool. "Hey, baby, Edwin says you're a cool chick," he called out.

Georgia opened her eyes and shielded them from the sun. "What'd you say?"

"Shut up," Edwin told him. "God, be cool, man."

"What?" Georgia shouted once more.

Ted was laughing. "Nothing."

Edwin closed the grill and glared at Ted. What was so special about Ted that he could get a girl like Georgia? he wondered. Ted sold stereos for a living and had no particular hobbies, other than listening to music and getting stoned. Edwin thought about how sad Ted had been that first year after Mai took their daughter back to China. After an ordeal like that, Edwin considered, maybe it was only fair that he ended up with a girl as stunning as Georgia. Still, it was hard for Edwin not to resent Ted, or to despise him, even, when he was in the happy couple's presence.

Lolly backed carefully into the screen door, then spun around, her hands full of plates. "I agree with Ted that the chlorine feels too strong," she said. "It's overpowering." She was still using her annoyed voice.

"You're just not used to it," Edwin said as he lifted the grill cover and flipped over the chicken.

Ted stood up and handed the joint over to Edwin. It had shrunk so that Edwin could barely pinch it between his fingers. A month or more had passed since Edwin had smoked, and as he inhaled he could feel Lolly watching him as she spread out the plates. They used to get high regularly. Now she was content to drink wine, but Edwin never developed a taste for wine. He missed the days when he could roll marijuana joints on the kitchen table, when Lolly might sit in his lap and he would reach his hands up the back of her shirt and fiddle with her bra strap until she had to undo it for him. Making love with Lolly on a Saturday or Sunday afternoon, both of them stoned, the sunlight pushing through the blinds of their bedroom windows — these were some of the happiest memories Edwin had, and lately he had been thinking about those first two or three years of marriage with increasing frequency. There wasn't any real worry over Lolly not yet being pregnant back then, and there were no other tensions between them. Go to a folk club, maybe drive to an art gallery in Wilmington, get together with friends. Now nothing felt the same. How, Edwin wondered, had their relationship become such a struggle?

But at least he had the pool. And maybe Ted and Georgia would come over like this all summer long. He didn't want to be jealous of his friend, but even so, if Ted and Georgia hung out here on weekends, with Georgia in her remarkable bikini, didn't that already have the makings of a good summer? At least better than the last few?

Georgia climbed slowly out of the pool, and as Lolly spread out the plates on the small patio table, Edwin watched Georgia dry off. Then, behind her, he saw the twins again. They had their faces against the chain-link fence, their Barbie dolls in little scarlet skirts, their Barbies' hair wet and combed back. Couldn't their parents come up with something for them to do besides spy on Edwin's first pool party? Edwin waved the tongs toward them in stiff recognition, his mouth set in a pouty sneer, and they removed themselves from the fence.

"Looks good," Georgia called out. As she got closer, Edwin could see that the skin around her eyes and nose was bright red and flecked with tiny bumps. When she came closer for a peek at the chicken pieces, Edwin saw that the whites of her eyes were also inflamed.

"Go ahead and help yourselves," Lolly said after laying out the cut vegetables. When she saw Georgia's face she put her hand to her mouth. "Honey, your face is breaking out! You're red all over."

Georgia traced her fingers all around her eyes. "Oh my God! It does kind of itch," she said. "It's really red?"

"Edwin, there's too much chlorine," Lolly said. "Look at her — she's having some kind of reaction." Edwin came over, and Georgia tilted her head back so that he could see for himself. Edwin could make out even more

165

tiny bumps in the sunlight. Georgia kept her eyes closed as he listened to her nervous, shallow breathing.

"Oh, man. Maybe I have too little pH," he muttered. "But I don't see how. Are you sure it's not sun poisoning?"

Lolly turned Georgia's chin gently so that she could look again. "That's not sun," she said. "You've got to fix the water before anyone goes back in."

A charred smell exuded from the grill. Edwin flung the cover open and was besieged by a dark mass of smoke, which he tried to fan away while flipping the burning pieces over. He let out a small moan and tried to think what he could do.

"This has never happened to me before," Georgia said.

"Hang on, Georgia," Edwin said. "We'll take care of you. I just want to get this chicken before —" He reached for a knife and began slicing off the blackened skins. Ted put his hands on Georgia's shoulders from behind and turned her around.

"Wow," he said. "My baby is all blotchy." Georgia made a pitiful face, which caused Ted to pull her close. "Oh, my sad little bunny. Come here."

Edwin turned to watch Georgia press against Ted's hairy chest, and when he saw

Lolly looking at him, he turned back to the chicken. "Okay, we're recovering over here. I'm just going to do a little artful surgery. Who needs the skin, anyway, right?"

He flipped the pieces over once and said to Ted, "Here, turn these over again in one minute. I'll take Georgia in and see what I can find for her face."

"I'll do it," Lolly said, which was what Edwin was afraid she would say.

"No, I'll handle it. My pool, my problem." Edwin held the screen door for Georgia and led her to the bathroom, where he opened the medicine cabinet, though he had no idea if there would be anything there he could use. "Are you in any pain? I tried to be so careful with all the chemicals. I studied and studied the manual. I don't get it."

Georgia reached for the cabinet mirror, putting her face an inch away from her reflection. "It mostly just itches, but I look so terrible."

"It would take more than a little reaction to make you look terrible. That's for sure."

"Poor me," Georgia said.

"I mean it, though," Edwin said, and picked up a tube of something he didn't recognize. He scanned the small print and put it back. "Ted is one lucky guy. I don't know if he knows how lucky."

"You're sweet," she said. The cabinet mirror was still between them, and it gave Edwin an ideal opportunity to stare at her cleavage. When he glanced back into the cabinet, he saw a tube of A+D ointment.

" 'For minor skin irritation,' " he read. "Here, this should work." He closed the cabinet and leaned into her. "Now close your eyes, and I'm going to rub this in. Then we wait for sweet relief."

The smell of chlorine had even permeated the small bathroom, but Edwin could still breathe in the scent of Georgia's skin, which smelled faintly like peaches. He put a generous dab on the tip of his finger and rubbed it across her nose and under her eyes. She showed a little smile as he traced his finger.

"Does that tickle?" he asked.

Georgia nodded.

"Yeah, tickling is a good thing." He kept rubbing and reapplying, and finally Georgia opened her eyes.

"All done?" she asked.

"Well, that depends," Edwin said in a new, childlike voice. "Do you *want* me to stop?" He surprised himself with that, though he had imagined himself saying some variation of that line almost as soon as they had met. He had generally conjured up rubbing suntan lotion into her shoulders, not rub-

168

bing ointment on her broken-out face, but he had seen his opportunity and taken it. Georgia took a step back, her wide eyes narrowing and her beatific smile crumpling into a face he hadn't thought possible.

"That should do it, I think," she said.

Edwin's heart quickened immediately, and he was aware of a sound like the muted thud of boxing gloves against a punching bag. Could she hear it, too? He could feel the first beads of perspiration forming on his forehead. "I just meant, do you think I have it covered enough?" he said. "I just wanted to be thorough. Since I feel so bad that this happened." He looked down at the tile floor, not wanting to swipe at his moist skin, but equally concerned that drops would start running down his face.

"Well," Georgia said, "maybe the chicken is ready."

"Right, I'll bet it is," Edwin said, but he couldn't look at her again. Only when Georgia turned to walk back through the house could he look up, but this time he kept his eyes trained on the walls.

MARYLAND

From the kitchen window Ellie watched Jamie and Roy talk. Joe came up behind her and took a look for himself. They could hear Miriam's radio.

Roy was writing something in his notebook, his head bent down but nodding to show Jamie he was still listening. Jamie held one of the crutches out, the foam cushion tucked under his arm, his other hand fastened to the grip so that it felt like a machine gun.

"Did he say he wanted to talk to us, too?" Joe asked.

"I wonder what they're talking about. I hope Jamie's okay."

"He's faced a lot worse than a reporter's questions. I think he can handle himself."

"Well, it's different," she said. She watched Joe tie his shoes, wondering if he was going somewhere. She decided then that she didn't want him to be interviewed.

"He went to school with Jamie," she said. "We didn't really know him, though. He wasn't a friend of Jamie's. The Murphys. Do you know any Murphys?"

"Not that I can think of," he said. "Irish. Sad day for the Irish. Kennedy. Murphy."

"It's a sad day for everyone."

"Well, not everyone wanted him to be president," said Joe. "But he didn't have to die trying, that's for sure."

Outside, Roy was switching the tape over. "Sutton is supposed to come over in a while," Jamie said. "You remember Bill Sutton?"

"Sure, I remember Sutton," Roy said. "What's he up to these days?"

"Not a lot," Jamie said. "That knucklehead wishes he could go to 'Nam. He and I are a hell of a pair now. Gimp and Limp. He even went over to the draft board and wanted to take the physical, show them what he could do. That was before I came back. When he saw my little souvenir, suddenly he piped down about that."

"Well, let me ask you, if I can: You went and fought for your country in Vietnam, and there are a lot of people who say we have no business over there, that it's not our war. And don't think we should be there. Do the politics of this war enter into it for you at all? I guess what I'm trying to ask is, do you see your being over there in any different light than when you first got there?"

Jamie watched two squirrels chase each other across the trunk of a tree. "You a war protester, Murphy?"

"No," Roy said, and it was the truth. Increasingly, the journalism majors were becoming some of the most vocal student leaders in protesting the war on campus, and their familiar, image-laden editorials and grotesque cartoons of Lyndon Johnson in the weekly student newspaper had become as ubiquitous as the ads for Coppertone or Planters peanuts. But Roy had mostly stuck to his beat: covering the latest announcements from the school's president and developments between faculty and the administration. He wrote a little-read regular column called "The Blackboard Report."

Jamie stared at Roy, wondering whether he believed him. "To that question, I think I'm going to say — what do I say, no comment? Off the record?"

"Either. Off the record means you'll answer it, but I can't use it. It's up to you. Whatever you feel like."

"I don't pay attention to politics. I killed the enemy. That was my job. When you're shooting at gooks who are shooting at you,

you're not thinking about anything else but how to survive. It's when you're not dodging mortar fire or tossing a hand grenade that you have a little time to think about what you're really doing there, and how badly you want to get home. And what you have to get home *to.* I mean, I've seen shit that most people can't possibly imagine.

"You know, I wasn't really recruited by schools, not really. I always thought I could have played college football, played for Loyola, or University of Delaware. On that level. But nothing like that worked out. And I wasn't exactly the college type, so . . . not like you. Not like Claire. So I'm working over at Jurrel's Garage, and my number comes up. I'm over there a year, then rolling into two years, and that's when I'm in Than Khe, and we're getting serious fire. And the next thing I know, my future as a one-legged pirate is totally secured. A few months later, I'm getting interviewed about life without a leg by the second-chair clarinet in band who wants to know what's it like, and what's next for me, the brave soldier whose life now is basically for shit."

Roy could feel himself not blinking. He was not going to nod his head, as if he understood, and he wasn't going to offer a half-smile, which might say, *Well, it will be all right.* All he could do was let his gaze go to the grass between them and listen to the different ways they were breathing.

"So, you know, what the hell?" Jamie said at last. "Sure, if someone asks me if they should go fight for their country, go over there and just keep your fucking head down. But guys like you, you don't have to worry about that, do you? College guys — you guys are the real geniuses, with your deferments. Can't be touched. Unless you want to be one of those little war correspondents running around. But that's probably not your thing, either, is it?"

"No," Roy said. "That wouldn't be for me."

When the interview was over, Roy drank the lemonade that Mrs. West brought out for them, and made exaggerated little moans of enjoyment. The thing to do, he decided, was to pretend that the interview had gone splendidly, and with an eagerness that came close to being suspicious, he asked Jamie about his archery. Jamie agreed to demonstrate and maneuvered onto his barrel chair, stacking his arrows next to the wooden table Joe had built for him.

"I hope you all had a nice talk," Ellie whispered to Roy. She had come out with the pretense of checking whether she should set a sprinkler to the dry lawn, and Roy was standing away from Jamie, giving him the space to set up.

"I think we did," Roy said. "I'm still hoping to interview you and Mr. West, if that's okay."

"You can certainly ask me questions," she said, "but I have to warn you, I'm biased toward the subject."

"Of course."

"I don't know about Mr. West's availability today, though," Ellie said. "I know he has some things he's trying to get done before the train comes past. So Jamie is going to show you his shooting, then. I think that's wonderful. Maybe that will make it into your article, how much he practices his archery. Did he tell you he wants to try to get into the *Guinness Book of World Records* someday? The record for most consecutive bull's-eyes is what he and Mr. West keep talking about."

"He didn't mention that," Roy said. "Maybe I could get him to tell me about that. That would be good for the story."

"Of course, of course. Well, he'll tell you. Or if he's too modest, which he usually is, I'll get Mr. West to explain it to me, and then I can tell you."

"Okay," Roy said.

"Well, if he's going to show you his shooting, I'll get out of the way. That would make a good picture, by the way — Jamie with his bow. Not that you all won't have your own ideas. I'm just the mother."

"Yes, ma'am. In fact, all our photographers are on assignment today, with the funeral train. I've got a camera in my car, and they asked me to see what I could do with it. So I'll see if he'll let me take his picture in a little while. And I like your idea, with the bow."

Jamie began lining up his arrows.

"So," Roy said, "we can maybe sit down in a little while, then."

"Yes, good." Ellie went over to Jamie and surveyed the worn targets as he put on his arm guard and tested his bowstring.

"Everything okay?" she asked in her innocent voice.

"Yep," Jamie said.

She looked over at the train tracks. Ellie thought of Rose Kennedy then, and tried to imagine what she must be going through, the shock of the last few days, the loss of a second son to an assassin. *At least I have my Jamie,* she thought. *He'll never be quite the same, but at least I can still look at him. I can still listen to his voice. I can still tell him I love him.*

The four boys sat on the ground, breathing heavily into the warm air, as Walt inspected a place on his arm where someone had stepped on him during the shooting melee. They listened to a small flock of magpies that was roosting in the trees above them, and Ty checked his watch again. If the train was on schedule, the wait was about over.

"My dad said he thinks someone is going to kill Sirhan Sirhan, just like they did Oswald," Ty said. "He said the only difference was that Bobby Kennedy was *about* to be president, but that basically it's almost as bad. He said he thought Bobby Kennedy would have been a better president than John Kennedy because he was tougher."

"My dad said he was going to vote for him," Daniel said proudly. He tried to recall what else his father had said, but his mind was blank.

"Hey, my mom liked him," Walt said, "but

my dad said Bobby Kennedy had everything handed to him his whole life."

"Why did he do it, anyway?" Daniel said. "Why did he kill him?"

"They don't know," Ty said. "Not really." Michael was looking down at the ground, following an ant. The others looked at him, and then at one another. Walt shrugged.

"Michael, what did your dad think about Kennedy?" Ty said. Walt and Daniel looked at Ty in vague disbelief, and then turned to Michael. Michael shook his head without looking up.

"I don't know," he said. "We never talked about that kind of stuff. He wasn't shot yet when I was with him."

"Hey, so what did you guys do together all that time?" Walt said. "What were you doing in Michigan, anyway?"

Michael lifted his head and considered Walt's red face. "My dad rented a cabin there, by a lake," he said. "This little log cabin. It was small, but it was made of these giant logs."

"Cool," Ty said.

"We fished a lot," Michael said. "And he showed me how to prepare the fish, how to cut their heads off and take off the scales with a paring knife. And a couple of times he let me shoot his pistol at some tin cans.

Have you guys ever shot a real gun before?"

The boys said they hadn't. "Not a real one," Daniel said.

"He's not talking about squirt guns, doofus," Ty said.

Daniel said, "Duuuh."

"They're loud," Michael said, "and it knocks your arm way back when you fire." He then demonstrated, his arm soaring over his head.

The three boys tried to imagine.

"Did you know everyone thought you were dead at first?" Daniel said.

"Shut up," Ty said.

Michael watched one of the magpies fly to a lower branch. "No."

"Hey, only in the beginning," Walt said. "Then your mom figured it out, I guess."

Ty looked at Walt and rolled his eyes.

"We knew you'd come back," Daniel said.

"So you're a college boy, then," Big Brass said.

Lionel said he was.

Big Brass nodded, though this was not an indication of his approval. He poured himself a half-cup of Coke and took a glance out the window, where he caught sight of factory workers leaning out the windows of a building the color of gums.

They were standing behind one of the vents, the air cool and pleasing on the back of their necks, and when it suddenly cut off, both men turned around, as if the vent would explain.

"That ain't good," Big Brass said, and within a minute they could feel the car warming up.

Lionel was getting used to the rumble under his feet, the sudden thrust that threatened his balance at any moment. Big Brass had been watching him, and after

Lionel reached for the soft-paneled wall to steady himself, he told him, "Always be connected to something. If I'm not pouring a drink, my hand is holding on to this little surface right here." He indicated that Lionel should look at his hand. "If I'm pouring a drink and I need to steady the cup, I'm moving my feet a little wider apart. If you keep them together too close, it's easier to fall. Your weight's not distributed. The wide stance is your friend on this train, always."

Lionel had been taking the subway his whole life, but he showed the older man how he would do it from now on, his feet apart in a way that felt unnatural. Big Brass took his time before responding. "That'll work," he said.

A man with a press badge leaned over to order a hot dog, and Lionel watched Big Brass lift one of the wieners, pinch it into a bun, and then close it into a small convection oven underneath. He then wrapped it in tinfoil and dropped it into a cardboard box. "That's hot, sir, so do be careful," Big Brass said, and the man put his coins on the counter, grinning and unwrapping it to apply ketchup.

Big Brass began to tell Lionel a few things he should know about the temperamental convection oven when another train soared past — a distance in between that felt like mere inches. The force of the other train's speed sent a little quake through the snack car, and Lionel gripped the edge of the counter.

"Huh. I'm surprised they're not holding trains until we pass," Big Brass said. "Seems like that's what they ought to do." It took him a moment to remember what instruction he was giving when their train ground to a dramatic slowdown, so much so that the tip jar traveled the length of the counter.

Lionel looked to the older man for an explanation, but Big Brass wasn't ready to speculate. He crouched down and looked outside, as several of the passengers had thought to do as well. But what he saw offered no clues.

"Something's going on," he said. "Where was that we just passed through? Was that the Elizabeth station?"

Lionel hadn't noticed.

"Yeah, that was Elizabeth," Big Brass said. "But something's wrong to slow the train down like this. We were cooking at sixty miles an hour, thereabouts." He waited, taking a calculation as only a man who had ridden trains his whole life could. "This, this is twenty-two miles an hour right now. Something is most definitely *afoot*."

MARYLAND

Miriam had wandered out to the backyard, feigning interest in Jamie's shooting. Roy was standing a few feet away from Jamie as he aimed his bow, and she could hear Jamie talking in a low voice. He was most likely talking about his technique — his release and follow-through. She watched Roy as he wrote in his notebook, and stepped closer to them. When Jamie released another arrow — this one hitting just to the right of the yellow circle, she called out, "How's the interview with Robin Hood going?"

Roy turned, already smiling politely. She was older-looking than he was prepared for — for some reason he had clung to the image of the girl in pigtails and braces from the picture in the hallway. Miriam was wearing tight-fitting jeans and a loose madras top that revealed her narrow shoulders. Her hair was clipped by a yellow barrette, and she had a mischievous smile that Roy didn't see in Jamie or her mother. She could have easily passed for a sorority girl, he thought — a Maryland Tri-Delta, or Alpha Delta Pi. When Roy realized that Jamie wasn't going to make the introductions, he told her his name and stepped over to shake her hand, which made her giggle.

"So are you raking him over the coals yet?" she said.

Roy laughed uneasily. "Oh, I don't know about that. Your brother's pretty tough."

"I guess," she said, walking over to the back of Jamie's chair. "But there are ways of making him talk." She ran her hand through his hair once. She never liked how the high-and-tight had looked on him, but she was sorry now not to feel the prickly sensation of it. "So am I in the way of official business?"

"Ask Edward R. Murrow here," Jamie said.

"He's just showing me his shooting," Roy said, "which, of course, is highly impressive. Do you shoot, too?"

"I shoot my mouth off," she said. "But I don't shoot arrows. So you went to Burton. You would have been a senior when I was a freshman, but I don't remember seeing you. Do you remember me?"

"I don't know that we ever met," Roy said.

"Murphy was a close friend of Claire's," Jamie said, aiming his bow once more.

"Oh wow, Claire the Fair. So you and Jamie were friends, then?"

"We didn't actually hang out together too much," Roy said quickly.

Jamie made a sound in his throat, but Roy pretended not to notice.

"Huh," Miriam said. She could see that Jamie was in a mood — irritated, remote. She figured it to be an awkward situation for Roy, and she was surprised to feel more softhearted to him than to her brother. She could see that Roy was someone Jamie wouldn't like — mannerly, physically unimposing, perhaps a little too brainy.

"So are you going to ask me some questions? I'll be a good interview. I'm a serious blabber, though, so just be warned."

Jamie put down his bow and glared at her, but she was having too much fun now. She thought of what she had said at the breakfast table that morning, trying to be Jamie's protector, and now she was surprised by how much distance she had from that feeling. Since he had come back home, they had spent plenty of time in each other's company, but mostly Jamie was content to be silent. Miriam and her mother had assured each other that this was to be expected, given Jamie's injury, the trauma of war. But Ellie had also come to wonder if for Jamie, home had become Vietnam.

"Here," Miriam said, and she walked over to remove some arrows from the targets, whose color was conveyed only in fragments now. When she had tugged the last arrow out, she said, "You should move the targets back. This has gotten too easy for you."

When she put the arrows back in Jamie's hands, she said to Roy, "So, what, you're interning at the paper?"

"That's right," Roy said. "I'm at Maryland."

"I might go there," she said. "Or Penn State. How do you like it there?"

"I like it," Roy said. "Good classes, good journalism program. The campus isn't much to look at, if that kind of thing is important to you, but it's a fun place. You'd like it there, I'd bet."

"And that's not where Claire goes, right? She went to — where did she go? Virginia?" She looked down at Jamie, who had no intention of answering.

"Right, Charlottesville," Roy said. "I was telling Jamie I don't really hear from her. She hasn't come back here during the summers. The last I heard she was studying psychology. But who knows?"

"Claire's going to be a shrink?" she said. "Gosh, I always figured Claire as more of a poetry teacher, or teaching English literature at some girls' school. She had that air about her, you know. That way."

"You talk like you two were pals," Jamie said.

"Well, you dated a long time. She was always at the house. I don't know, I felt like I knew Claire pretty well, actually. I don't know her now, obviously. I'm just saying —"

"Now you see my sister wasn't being modest when she talked about her ability to blab."

"Touchy about the old flame, are we?" Miriam said.

"I'm just saying, whether she's a psychology major or an English Lit major or whatever the hell she is, it doesn't have a lot to do with me, does it? You and Mom with your 'Oh, Claire.' Do you think her parents don't know about what's happened to me? In a town like this? Have I gotten a phone call from her or a letter? Anything that says she could give a damn? So all this mooning over Claire is, you know, is . . . I don't really need it."

Roy had been looking down during this time, too embarrassed to look at Miriam,

188

too nervous to look at Jamie. Finally Miriam turned and walked back toward the back door.

"So what else do you want to know?" Jamie said.

PENNSYLVANIA

Delores and Rebecca sat sipping their Cherry Cokes. They were at Stribe's Drive-In, and on the tray attached to Delores's door was an empty carton of crinkle-cut French fries and the balled-up wrapper of a cheeseburger. Rebecca held half of her cheeseburger in its wax paper and sometimes tried to smile, which she saw put her mother at a little more ease. On and off for an hour Delores had managed to hold ice to Rebecca's face, but still, from a few inches above Rebecca's eye to just above her jawline, her skin resembled the sky at twilight. She had managed to walk a little outside the grocery store without noticeable difficulty, and the way she gripped her doll and the fact that her crying had dwindled to sniffling made Delores believe she had suffered no serious injuries; they didn't need a doctor after all.

When the boys got badly scraped or

bruised, they were engaged in activities Arch entirely approved of — football or climbing a tree or wrestling. He was particularly cautious with Rebecca, though, calling her his "little plum," and he could quickly fall into a rage if either of the boys was being rough with her. He was just as protective of Delores. He didn't like her getting on ladders or handling hammers or carving the meat with sharp knives. In the early years of their marriage, Delores had found this attitude rather endearing, and she was amused when he gently removed such things from her hands and sometimes kissed her on the cheek as he sent her off so that he could handle the task in question. But with three children that habit had became at first impractical, then irksome. For much of their young lives the boys had needed two pieces of wood nailed together or sawed in half, or airplanes made of balsa wood rescued from tree branches, and since no one ever turned any lights off except Delores, bulbs constantly needed replacing. These little jobs had become the heart of Delores's days, and Arch's ideas about what Delores should and shouldn't do had lost all significance.

Delores peered inside Stribe's — at an older man and woman tucked into a booth, the man's head hung low toward his cardboard plate, the woman trying to make conversation with him despite his wish that she stop. Delores reached over and gripped Rebecca's knobby knee like a gearshift. "Maybe today we'll have two lunches," she said. "What do you think about that?" When Rebecca didn't answer, Delores pressed the button on the speaker box and waited for someone to respond.

NEW YORK

The laggard speed of the train allowed the faces of the mourners to come through distinctly, and many of them waved when they saw anyone from the cars looking out.

"Sure are a lot of people out there," Big Brass said. "And all of them hot. 'Course, we're in a train that's already lost its air condition."

Buster Hayes made his way through the crowded car, and even before he could reach his crew members his expression had indicated grim news.

"Let me tell you what I know," he said when he got to Big Brass, and he spoke into the man's ear. Lionel could see that he should focus on the bar. A few passengers had taken notice of Buster Hayes when he came through, and the room grew quieter.

"We don't want to excite anyone," Hayes said. "But that train that just blew by, the Admiral, ran straight over some folks back

193

in Elizabeth. The crowd didn't know other trains were running — *I* didn't know that, either — so they were all over the tracks. Conductor's just trying to get a sense of how bad it is."

"Good God Almighty," Big Brass said. Buster Hayes agreed, then said, "Two of them just got pulled right under, they say. And listen to this: one of them was a woman holding a little girl at the time. But the report I got said the girl got thrown into the air and landed in the crowd, if you can believe it."

Big Brass was not yet ready to.

"So we're slowed indefinitely until they can work this mess out," Buster Hayes said, and he became aware that half of the car's passengers had trained their eyes on the two men. "Kennedy family about to have a fit."

"With good reason," Big Brass said. "Lord, Lord."

"Anyway, I need to check in with the others, and I'll let you know more when I get an update. They're radioing back and forth like crazy, trying to make sure all the other trains get held as we pass."

"Well, that's the first thing I thought when that train just went by us. I knew that wasn't right."

"No, it wasn't," Buster Hayes said. "It's a

major fuckup is what it is. Conductor was pulling the emergency brake, apparently, but it didn't slow him down enough."

"No," Big Brass said. "Mercy."

Buster Hayes pulled away from Big Brass then and clapped Lionel on the shoulder. "You all right, young buck?"

"Yes, sir," Lionel said. He had heard everything, but he tried to hold himself as if he was surprised that Buster Hayes was still in the car.

"Mr. Trent will fill you in on what's happening. But let him do the talking with passengers. This is a situation, right here. And we want everyone to be as calm as can be, considering."

"Yes, sir," Lionel said. Buster Hayes moved carefully through to the next car, and after the passengers watched him go, they turned to Lionel and Big Brass.

"This is something else," Big Brass whispered.

New Jersey

The train was nearly forty-five minutes late, and Ty put his ear to the railroad track.

"Hear anything?" Daniel asked.

Ty shook his head and checked his watch again. "Not yet."

Michael balanced himself along the rail as Walt piled some stones on top of a wooden plank. Daniel stretched out lengthwise over the tracks, his hands together under the small of his back. "I'm tied up," he said.

The boys studied him and were pleased with the new idea. Ty walked over. "Well, I warned you and your gang," he said. "I told you there'd be trouble if you didn't leave town. Now it's curtains for you."

Then: "No one will save you this time," Walt added.

Ty lay down on the tracks, putting his ankles together and his wrists over his head. "Michael, try it," he said.

In the distance, Michael could see a man

and a woman walking hand in hand. "Here comes someone."

Ty and Daniel craned their heads from the tracks. Walt shielded his eyes from the sun.

"I didn't think we'd be the only ones here," Ty said. "I'll bet you they don't climb any trees, though. Michael, get tied up."

Michael brushed away some pebbles before easing his back onto the tracks. He lifted his head off the rail several times before he could find a suitable angle.

"You've rounded up the whole gang," Ty said to Walt.

"That's right," Walt said. "All of you varmints are going to pay now." He wanted to say more, but he felt out of his element as a ruthless sheriff. "That's right," he finally added. He caught sight of a few more people approaching the tracks. "Hey, where do you guess they're all coming from? You think they parked over by Webber Street and walked along the stream?"

Ty lifted his head again. "I was thinking most people would just go downtown to watch. Train's passing right over Dunlop Road. Doesn't matter much to me, though."

"Well, let's go ahead and climb up and get ready," Daniel said. "It's going to be here soon." He got up and dusted himself off. "Now I'm stiff."

Walt and Ty followed, as Michael watched from his position. "You bums!" he called after them. "You left me tied up."

"Come on," Ty said, not looking back. Walt and Daniel looked up at the tree they had chosen and waited for Ty to climb first.

"So it looks like I'm done for," Michael called out.

Ty looked back quickly and saw that more people were approaching the tracks. "Michael, come on up."

Michael wiggled his feet, lifted his chin. "No one untied me. I'm doomed."

Ty pulled himself up the lower branches, with Walt pushing off next. For the moment they concentrated on their path, as Ty tested a branch with his hand and said, "That will hold." He stopped when the branches began to fan out — and were thinner — and then repositioned himself. Since he had to stay closer to the trunk than he had planned on, the view was too obscured to fully suit him.

"I wish I could cut some of these damn branches," he said to his friends below. He looked down to check on Walt's progress, then looked out again at Michael. "What is he doing?" he asked. "Michael, you're going to get hit by the stupid train if you don't get up. Come on."

Michael lifted his torso, then sank back down. "I'm tied up."

Ty watched a man and woman dressed in black, a flaxen-haired girl in a dark summer dress between them, at the edge of the field. The girl pulled impatiently on the woman's arm. "It's getting crowded," he said.

Walt had settled on a branch directly beneath Ty and contemplated the safety in that. "Hey, don't fall on my head," he said.

"Okay, I'll just fart on you instead," Ty said, but his agitation with Michael didn't let him enjoy it the way he should have.

Daniel climbed up past Walt, finally, and tested the branch across from Ty.

"You're right," he said. "The branches *are* kind of in the way. I wish I had a machete or something." Now that he was settled in, he looked out at Michael, then craned his head expectantly farther down the tracks. The crowd that had been gathering over the last half-hour was fifty yards away. Daniel could see that one woman had a poster board sign by her side, but he couldn't read it. The sun bathed the mourners in a yellow wash, which made him grateful for the shade. "What are we going to do about Michael?" he asked. "We can't just leave him down there."

"It's not like he *is* tied up, you idiot," Ty said.

"Hey, it's weird," Walt said. "He's barely said a word all day, and now he's acting like a big goof. Of all times."

"Michael, get your butt up here!" Ty yelled. "You're going to get flattened."

"Don't worry, I'm not afraid," Michael called out in his attempt at a melodramatic voice.

"Brother!" Ty said. "What a pain."

Daniel inched himself a little farther out on his limb and looked out over the tracks in restless anticipation. "What time is it now?" he asked.

"It's way past time," Ty said.

"When I was a little girl, I had a bad fall, too," Delores said. They were outside the city limits, meandering a wide, circular course. There were cornfields beside them that already looked like they would expire before harvest time. "I was just about your age, and I was on my daddy's tractor. Did you remember that Grandpa was a farmer for most of his life? He had a big tractor with big wheels, and I used to love climbing on them. They were about twice as tall as I was. One day I climbed up to the tractor seat because I loved the view from up there, and when I was coming down my dress got caught on one of the gears, and when I tried to get it off I fell all the way down, just like you did. And I got a big boo-boo on my face, just like you have. I cried so loud, and my mother came running out to find me, and she scooped me up just like I scooped you up and took me inside and put ice on my face just like we did. And she gave me kisses on every part of my head that wasn't bruised. You don't remember Grandma Fern, do you? You were so young when she died. You were just a toddler, just barely walking."

Rebecca turned away from the cornfield and shook her head. "Did you get better?" she asked in her weak voice.

"I sure did. I got all better in no time. Just like you will."

They were passing a dairy farm now, and a field so green it looked like it had been drawn in Magic Marker was dotted with cows. Rebecca was fidgety and gingerly rubbing her eyes, careful not to touch the bruised side of her face. Delores had picked up a bag of jelly beans to improve her mood, but Rebecca mostly just stirred her finger around in the bottom, moving colors.

"So many cows," Delores said. "I know a cow goes 'Moooooooooo,' but I'm forgetting how a sheep sounds. How does a sheep talk, pumpkin? Hmmm?"

Rebecca shook her head to let her mother know that she could do a reasonable bleat some other time, but that she was not in the mood to perform now.

Delores brought the car to a stop. "They're all looking at us, aren't they?

Those cows are wondering, *What are you two doing out here?* And that's a good question. A very good question."

WASHINGTON

Until Maeve started working for the lieutenant governor's family, she had not paid much attention to politics, despite her mother's worshipful affinity for John Kennedy, who was still a Massachusetts senator when they arrived from Ireland. And, as she pointed out repeatedly, a Roman Catholic. The lieutenant governor was a Republican, and in the speeches Maeve heard him make and in the few conversations she had with him that weren't about the baby, Maeve was moved by his efforts to deliver welfare services to the state. After his term as lieutenant governor ended, he became state attorney general, and some months later, when Robert Kennedy announced his bid for the presidency, Maeve followed Kennedy's campaign with keen interest. She couldn't fathom that a man who wanted to do so much for this country had found the time to have so many children, and when pictures of his family showed up in *Life* magazine and in *The Boston Globe,* she liked to imagine herself taking care of baby Douglas, who was just a newborn, and feeding him at the table while Bobby and Ethel, amid the rest of their children, ate breakfast and talked about the busy day ahead.

It was early May that Maeve had taken the bus to Hyannis for her initial interview for the Kennedy nanny position. Maeve had never seen a house so big — in every way it looked to her like three houses put together. The head nanny, Mrs. Bernard, was waiting for her between the enormous columns framing the front door. Maeve had hoped that at some point she might get a chance to hold Douglas in her arms and demonstrate immediately her special way with babies. And after she was escorted in and seated, somewhere in the large house she could hear the faint sounds of a baby shouting out, babbling.

After asking about Maeve's trip down from Boston, she said, "The lieutenant governor tells us that you have been excellent with his young son." Her skin was dark, and she spoke with a Spanish accent. "But he is still so young. And I'm wondering why you would be ready to leave him for another child?"

"I love him dearly, I do," Maeve said. They were seated in the sunlit living room, on two avocado-colored wingback chairs, and there were framed photographs on the shelves that Maeve wanted to look at but knew that she shouldn't. Beyond them, she could see through the glass doors sailboats bobbing past, like low clouds, not far from the edge of the lawn. "And I love children of all ages — boys, girls equally. But I think it's probably true that I'm the very best with babies, and so when a baby becomes a toddler, I sometimes feel ready to get back to another baby. I can't say why, really. Maybe babies and I just understand each other — daft as that sounds."

The nanny looked at Maeve without smiling, and Maeve, understanding that the Kennedy children weren't to be deserted like this, said, "It's been like that since I was caring for my three sisters, you see. I could get them to settle down or to take their milk or to fall asleep when no one else could, and everyone considered that a gift. And maybe that's true enough."

"I take care of baby Douglas right now," Mrs. Bernard said evenly, "but when Mrs. Kennedy delivers in December, we'll need someone to give full attention to the new baby. Mrs. Kennedy expects the family to be traveling quite a bit with Mr. Kennedy, and that means you would also need to be traveling — in planes and trains, hotels and cars. In foreign countries. So are you a good traveler, Maeve? We're looking for someone who can be extremely flexible and able to adapt."

Maeve nodded and lowered her voice to a solemn register. "I'm very easy in that way, yes, ma'am. I think if you would ask the lieutenant governor, he would say the same, I'm certain. I'm quiet. I'm easy to get on with. And as long as the baby is happy, I'm happy. And with me children are always happy."

NEW JERSEY

The three boys found it difficult to talk about much other than the lateness of the train and the possible reasons for its delay. (*It took the wrong track. Someone stole the casket. It collided with another train.*) Michael had remained on the tracks, and they shouted at him until they became worn out, and then went back to complaining about the train once more.

Finally, in the clearing, a black bead began to emerge. From that distance the train looked like a drop of ink slowly pouring out. Daniel's eyes stretched wide, and in his shock the branch beneath him shook. This caused Ty to whip his head around, and though his view was too obscured to see what Daniel had seen, he understood the train had come into view. He began his descent in a jerky, careless manner, stopping only for one second to see for himself the train's progress.

"Michael!" he screamed. "Get off the tracks! The train is coming *right now!*" He scrambled past Walt and moved his legs out of the way for Ty; whatever was going to happen, Ty would lead the way. Ty let the bark scrape against his legs as he moved down the last branches, accepting that there should be some amount of pain involved in a moment like this. He jumped eight feet to the ground, his body collapsing onto itself. As he ran to the tracks he turned and called for Walt and Daniel, who were scrambling down, and then he looked again to the train.

James Colvert quickly had established their morning routines. He liked to wake at dawn and fish for a half-hour from the shore. Michael wasn't necessarily expected to be out there, but on the days when his father's tackle box bumped against the door, or he accidentally let the screen bang against its frame, Michael got up and joined him. His father preferred silence when they fished, and if they had catches worthy of a meal, they'd cut and clean them on the back step before going in. Afterward, James Colvert liked to walk the mile to the drugstore in town for a copy of the *Detroit Free Press*, mostly for the baseball box scores he liked to pore over. On these walks he sometimes talked about his own childhood summers, the way his father taught him to fish and hunt and navigate a canoe through choppy waters. He had a few stories that briefly involved Michael's mother, but when Michael mentioned her in a story of his own, James Colvert's face tightened, as if he had just stepped on a sharp object. By the second week Michael decided not to mention her anymore. He would see her at the end of June, his father told him. Until then, Michael would have to be content to think about her when he got into bed, or as he swam in the lake by himself, or if his father had remained in town to watch a Tigers game in the one bar that held aloft a battered set in the corner, next to the kitchen.

On their last morning together, Michael was surprised to wake up before his father. The cabin was still, save the occasional flying insect, and he could hear his father's raspy breathing in the next room. Underneath the window shade he could see that the sky was the color of their one kitchen pot. He thought of taking his rod and reel out by himself and surprising his father with a catch all his own. Mostly they had gotten by eating channel catfish for dinner that his father had reeled in that day, but Michael had grown bored with the taste. And he was tired of being hungry in between meals, since there were almost never any groceries in the house.

His father had said the lake was also stocked with walleye and whitefish, but they hadn't pulled up anything like that. Michael imagined himself carrying a plate of whitefish that he had broiled, with butter and lemon juice flowing over the sides, his father seated at their shabby little table.

"Well, let's eat," Michael would say, his face suppressing any hint of vanity.

Instead, Michael was content to remain stretched out on his bed and puzzle through a dream he'd had about being in a canoe with Superman, who, while trying to catch fish with a net, had talked serenely about his days battling Lex Luthor. Before the dream was finished, Lex Luthor appeared in a canoe behind them but seemed little interested in causing any disturbance.

When his father did wake up, he moved in a slow, halting manner, and stared out the window as he sipped the coffee he had made. When he became aware that Michael was watching him, he said, "We might need to get us another fan. I couldn't sleep at all. Did you hear me rolling all around in bed?"

"No," Michael said. "I heard that raccoon scratching around by the front door,

211

though."

"Well, he's got his right. We're in his home, after all. We're the trespassers."

On the water they could see Mr. Ahrens, who had the skip out. He stayed in the cabin two doors down with his wife of forty-three years, Edna. "You know what Edna told me the other day — I ran into her in town," James Colvert said. "She said she didn't even care that much for the water. Said she preferred the mountains. And yet this is where they've spent every summer since World War Two. I said, 'Why do you keep returning, then?' And she said, 'Have you ever seen Lewis in the water? He's just like a little boy out there, he's so happy.' I guess that's true. Look at him." His voice was almost wistful, and it was the first time Michael had imagined his father to be lonely. The way he had talked about his days in Michigan — being captain of his bowling team, his neighbor friend who trained hunting dogs, the workshop he had built for himself in his garage — it hadn't occurred to Michael that his father was anything but happy to have started a new life for himself.

Michael put his face to the glass, but there was little he could see beyond the small white sail and the red hat Mr. Ahrens kept firmly clamped to his head. He watched as long as he thought he was expected to acknowledge the remark, and then he went back to the kitchen table. He wondered what his friends were doing in school. Was this the last day? He couldn't remember now. His father had told him that everything had all been worked out — the remaining tests, his homework — in a way that didn't make much sense, but he had decided not to think about it. He wondered, too, if his mother had explained to his friends when they had come around looking for him about his going away with his father. Except for the girl whose father owned the Castaway — the little diner in town — and who sat at the counter reading Nancy Drew books, he hadn't seen another kid his age. Surely there would be more kids who came to the lake for the summer, or who at least pulled up in packed-down station wagons with their parents to stay for a week or two, but he hadn't yet asked his father about that. He worried his father might think that he wasn't having a good time.

Michael was hungry but unsure what he could eat, and waited for what his father might say or do next.

"We need more bloodworms," James Colvert said finally.

"We could go into town," said Michael,

who was always relieved at the chance to get in the car and to possibly eat at the Castaway. James Colvert agreed.

When they arrived, they were seated in a corner booth, and before the waitress could refill James Colvert's cup of coffee, Michael had eaten all his banana pancakes — and all the toast that had come in a plastic basket.

"Somebody was hungry," she said, and winked at James Colvert. He watched the waitress as she moved a couple of tables down.

On their way back from the diner, less than a mile from their cabin, Michael spied a raccoon splayed at the edge of the road. Its insides had drained to the grass, but its head was undamaged, perfect. Both ears sat straight up. The tail was so flat it appeared as if someone had painted it onto the surface.

"I wonder if that's ours," Michael said. Most nights, as he lay awake in bed and listened to an animal crawling and scratching around the cabin, he could conjure up a vision of himself chasing after it. Now the worry that the raccoon on the road was the same one that hovered just on the other side of the walls of their cabin at night made him sorrowful. He could already hear the sickening stillness that awaited him when he got under his sheets that night.

"A one-way pass to Raccoon Heaven," his father said, watching his rearview mirror. "Where there are no more cars. No more worries. But I doubt our little friend comes this far into town."

Michael wanted to look back one last time before they rounded the bend, but he also didn't want his father to think he was concerned either way. With fish they considered too small to keep, his father got impatient with how delicately Michael removed the hook from the fish's mouth.

"Get it out and get him back in, or else your oils are going to rub off on him and he won't have anything on him to protect himself," he said one afternoon, taking the wriggling fish from Michael's hand. "He'll be dead."

When they got out of the car, James Colvert walked with the day's newspaper tucked under his arm past their cabin and down to the water, where they kept two metal fold-out chairs. The heavy chairs looked out of place, and Michael was embarrassed that they didn't have canvas ones, or the cheap, lightweight kind available at the Red & White store. These chairs belonged stacked up in a basement, or perhaps spotted alongside the road at a yard sale. They sank deep into the grass.

"Why don't you put the bait in the refrigerator," James Colvert said, having remembered he was still clutching the small cardboard container only after he sat down. "We can try them out in an hour or so and see how it is today. With the sun so bright already, they're going to be hitting top water mostly." He got out his keys and put them in Michael's damp hand and put the container in the other.

As Michael walked to the door he looked for any signs of the raccoon — tracks, signs of digging — but nothing looked different from the previous day. Inside he put the bait on the one shelf of the refrigerator. He held the door open and studied the few contents: three bottles of Pabst Blue Ribbon beer, a bottle of ketchup, a carton of milk, a full container of chicken salad they hadn't gotten around to eating. Opening the refrigerator made him long to be back home; he remembered the gleaming silver shelves of his mother's refrigerator, the fuzzy outline of shapes and dimmed colors in the fruit and vegetable bins at the bottom.

When he finally closed the door, he heard a muffled thump out front. It sounded like a car door, and when he went to look out the front window, he first heard footsteps by the side of the cabin. Then he saw the sheriff's patrol car pull behind the Monterey. He had seen the sheriff a couple of times at the diner, his hair shaved into a crew cut so shorn that his pink scalp shone through, like a large Band-Aid.

Michael cracked open the screen as the sheriff and his reedy deputy approached his father. But what were they doing here? Maybe the diner had been robbed, and they wanted to know if Michael or his dad had seen anyone suspicious before they left.

Michael saw them before his father did, and he thought he might learn more if he simply listened from the cabin. He had learned enough from the movies that when a kid suddenly appeared, the police officer would often cut off what he intended to say and pull nervously on the bill of his cap before shuffling off.

James Colvert was folding his newspaper in half when he heard the rustle of the equipment on their belts.

"Morning," he said, getting quickly to his feet.

The sheriff nodded curtly. "Morning. You James Colvert?" He looked around, back Michael's way, but didn't appear to see him.

"That's right. What can I do for you fellows?"

"Do you have a son named Michael Colvert?" the sheriff asked. He was squinting into the sun.

James Colvert considered what to say. "That's right."

The sheriff nodded again, and the deputy watched him, waiting.

"He inside?"

"What seems to be the problem? I'm the boy's father."

The sheriff motioned to his deputy and said, "Go have a look."

"Now hold on just a minute," James Colvert said, and when his eyes went to the cabin they found Michael staring back. "I'd like to know what this is all about. We've paid full rent on this cabin — in advance. I've got the paperwork somewhere inside."

The deputy didn't have to walk far before catching sight of Michael. "Hey there, buddy," he said. His voice was high and twangy, like the country singers Michael moved quickly past while fiddling with his transistor radio. "Is your name Michael Colvert?" Michael could see that the deputy's cheeks were pockmarked, his eyes watery gray.

"Yes," Michael said.

The deputy reached out to pat the boy on his shoulder. "Good, good. That's good." Then he said, "Hey, Sheriff."

Michael could feel his father's eyes on them, but he was not ready to look back at him. Michael was watching the sheriff, looking for the toothpick, but there didn't appear to be one.

"I'm going to have to take you into custody, Mr. Colvert," the sheriff said. "The boy's mother claims you've kidnapped him from her. There's a warrant out for your arrest." The sheriff removed his handcuffs from his belt, and the sunlight danced in a multitude of refractions in his hand. There was little shock in any of this for Michael — only in hearing the words said out loud, at last. That his mother hadn't packed a suitcase for him had seemed remarkable, and now everything else that seemed so unusual — his being taken out in the middle of class, no telephone calls, the very idea of his mother agreeing not to say good-bye — was clear enough. There had never been any arrangement.

"I'm the boy's father," James Colvert shouted at a volume that made the sheriff stop what he was doing. The deputy turned back and walked over, in case there was going to be trouble.

"It's a matter of law," the sheriff said gently. He had a thirteen-year-old son, and he could sympathize with a man who wanted to give his boy a summer by the lake. "Apparently you didn't work this out with the boy's mother, or some such complication. Anyway, you'll get yourself a lawyer and sort through it. But right now I have to place you under arrest and read you your rights." And he proceeded to do so.

James Colvert held his face in so pitiful an expression that the sheriff looked down at his boots as he spoke. His deputy took notice, and because he was a young man and did not know the joys of fatherhood, he could only wonder why his boss was in such a state. When the sheriff finished, James Colvert nodded once to let the sheriff know he had heard.

The sheriff considered the boy now, and smiled. He thought to wink but caught himself. He then slipped the handcuffs around his prisoner, carefully, the way he might have helped his wife on with a bracelet, and the click made Michael flinch, since it had otherwise become so quiet.

Then James Colvert said in a low voice that sounded as if it had been ripped from his throat, "*She's* the one that ruined our family. Whoring around." He was speaking to himself now and shook his head in resignation.

Michael knew vaguely what "whoring" meant, but it also didn't make any sense as a way to describe his mother. It was like saying she had a tail or slept in a cave. It had been so long since Michael had heard that voice — the low snarl, the name-calling through clenched teeth — but now it was so fully back in his system, and he started to back away. It was all clear now: this time was never about the two of them, father and son. It had all been a way to get back at his mother.

The sheriff turned to his deputy. "We're going to need Rusty. It's not going to do to take them in the same car. Call Rusty from the car. He shouldn't be far."

"You want me to take the boy on with me — to the car?" the deputy asked. James Colvert's outburst had made him nervous. The sheriff looked at the father in disappointment. "Yeah, go on," he said, and he let out a deeper sigh than he meant to.

Michael didn't look back at his father, and his father wasn't looking at him. Instead, Michael fixed his eyes on a distant spot over the water, where the sun poured across the top like a chemical spill. It was still and calm, and as the deputy put his hand around Michael's shoulder to lead him away, Michael caught sight of something breaking through and sending a spray of silvery drops ten feet or more, safe for another day.

"Come on, then," the deputy said. "Have you ever ridden in a squad car before?" The deputy's voice was more excited than was appropriate, given the circumstances.

Michael shook his head.

"Well, this is your lucky day."

PENNSYLVANIA

Delores pulled into the parking lot of her church, which had been freshly tarred over and gleamed in the intense sunlight. She and Rebecca sat across from the new fellowship hall, where volunteers picked up meals to deliver to the elderly. There were just a few cars parked out front, and once inside the hall, Delores and Rebecca could hear the scraping of pots from the kitchen. The basketball goals on either side of the floor had been cranked up toward the ceiling, and a banner still hung from one of the rims that read: "Welcome Bible Campers: Feel the Sprit!" Rebecca picked up a strip of red crepe paper off the floor.

"Look, Mommy," she said.

Delores smiled. She then pushed open the kitchen's swinging door, unsure if she would know anyone behind it. Usually she dealt with the church secretary for volunteer activities, and the secretary was known for never being there on weekends — including Sundays. Under the hum of dim fluorescent lights were three men cleaning up the kitchen.

"Hello," she said, too loudly for the space.

The men looked up but did not answer.

"I was looking for Mrs. Winters. She's usually coordinating the meal deliveries. It's not my day, but I have a little time I can volunteer —" She stopped when she noticed the men's eyes go to Rebecca, each of them grimacing. She scanned the room for someone who was not in a white apron, and then she grabbed Rebecca by the hand — harder than she intended — and led her back across the wooden floor. Didn't these men understand that accidents happened to little children? Or maybe they thought Delores was somehow responsible. Her shoes smacked across the wooden planks, filling the large hall with the sound of firecrackers. Rebecca was tired of getting in and out of the car and whined in frustration.

Outside they took a few steps toward the sanctuary, but already Delores could imagine the air-conditioned hush of the empty halls. Reverend Blake would surely be visiting members who were in the hospital this time of day, or possibly he was at home sanding that canoe of his to which he was always making references in his sermons. Some of the parishioners thought he tried too hard in his sermons, that he filled them with too many metaphors and made too many references to noted works of literature and paintings. "Why can't he just stick with the Bible?" Delores's mother-in-law had complained more than once. "Who's he trying to impress?" But Delores liked the broad script he unfurled each Sunday, and she willed herself to pay attention to every word, as if he were a professor back at Penn State, and she was to be quizzed on the material.

Without offering an explanation, Delores stopped and helped Rebecca back into the car, and Rebecca let out a deep puff of protest for the pointless visit. She was still holding the little strip of crepe in her fingers.

"I'm sorry," Delores said. "You're being so good."

As Delores turned the ignition, she saw one of the men from the kitchen approaching. He had taken off his small paper hat to reveal a scrub of jet-black hair that looked mismatched, somehow, over his deeply lined face.

The man appeared contrite with his hat off and his shoulders stooped; it occurred to her that the men had all realized their insensitivity and sent him out quickly to make amends. "I don't know if she needs any more drivers today," he said, "but I thought I'd just —" She noticed a white slip of paper in the man's hand.

"This is her home phone number, if you want to reach her. She's left the office for the day." He held it out, then stepped back after Delores reached for it. "All the day's meals have already been picked up." He began to turn back to the fellowship building but took a quick glance toward the passenger side.

"Is your little girl going to be all right?" he asked, pointing a finger toward Rebecca as thick and scratched as the end of a broomstick. "Do you all need any help?"

"She's going to be fine," Delores said, as if she couldn't imagine what he was talking about. "Thank you for the number." The man nodded and watched as Delores backed out. She pulled to the edge of the parking lot, stopping to steal a look in her rearview mirror. The man was still watching them, and now the other two had come out to join him.

NEW JERSEY

When he was close enough to reach Michael's tennis shoes, Ty heard the thud of Walt jumping behind him. Michael was watching the train bearing down on them, and he smiled at Ty in a way that made Ty remember the day when Michael was one of two students left in the class spelling bee. The other boy had just drawn the word "marquisette," and when Mrs. Nance called it out, Michael closed his eyes for a second, letting a drowsy smile grow across his face. He knew he was about to win.

"Get up! Get up!" Ty shouted, but the train's grinding churn made his words inaudible. Michael was surprised his friends didn't understand. The fun of it was seeing how close you could cut it. Why were they so panicky? At that moment Michael began — without urgency — to hoist himself up, but his friends didn't notice this. Walt was there now and grabbed Michael's arm; Ty took the other, and Michael said something that neither of the boys could hear. If they wanted to believe they were saving him, then he would play along, and he let his body go slack, his legs trailing behind like a gown. A man in a baseball cap came running over, followed by two younger men, but when they saw that the boys were safely away from the track, they stopped just in time to turn to the train, their chests heaving from exertion and fright. The train's horn ripped through, but even the conductor, at a hundred feet away, could see that there was not going to be another disaster. The conductor, who had seen the figure on the track too late to possibly stop, was shouting a prayer of gratitude — and wondering how much more peril he would be faced with before pulling into Washington.

Ty and Walt carried Michael partway down the slope; Daniel arrived too late, but when he got to them he kept his hand on Michael's shoulder just the same. They put him on the ground gently, as if he were mortally wounded, and then they turned to watch the rest of the train. The conductor sounded his horn once more, and the force of wind swept over the boys. The adult faces looking out the train windows ran together, like fresh paint sprayed with water. Michael got to his feet by the time the last car approached, and there, for a fleeting second, each of them caught sight of the American flag draped over the mahogany coffin of Robert Kennedy. It was elevated, set atop chairs, for everyone to see. And yet it wasn't what the boys had imagined, somehow. Minus the flag, the dark, mahogany coffin looked just like the coffin Ty's grandfather had been buried in the previous summer. Walt had thought maybe the casket itself would be red, white, and blue, and Daniel had thought maybe it would be solid gold, or have a bust of Robert Kennedy at the top of it, with eagles, or at least eagle wings, along the sides.

The four friends watched the train sail quickly from view. There was a man on the outside of the caboose, also in a dark suit, waving with the mechanical motion of a metronome. The train's whistle moaned once more in the distance, and then the stillness of the air gradually returned.

Some of the men and women now turned their attention to the boys. One man in a baker's uniform took a few determined steps toward them, but the woman next to him said something that changed his mind. The man shook his head — in bewilderment, the boys thought — and then turned and walked the other way. The signs the mourners had held up high now slumped over their shoulders as they walked away. A few of them kept watching the boys, but mostly they fixed their eyes to the ground, some of them wrapping their arms around each other in comfort.

Michael walked nonchalantly toward the tree, and the others followed quietly behind him. There were hours still to kill before they were due home, but for the moment they were content to walk through the grass of the field and think about what they had seen — and what had been averted. They were waiting for Michael to speak. Only after they passed the tree they had been in and moved in the direction of the creek did Michael, without turning to them, call out in a surprisingly convincing Middle Eastern accent, "I can explain! Let me explain!" And then he began sprinting. It took the others only a second to recover, and then they began the chase, their delicate legs running hard once more, their slick faces turned fierce and unrecognizable.

DELAWARE

Both couples were sitting around the patio table, the smell of chlorine now diluted since Edwin had added more pH. He had suggested that everyone could go back in, but no one trusted the water except him. He had been quiet since the incident with Georgia in the bathroom, and he was nervous that she might say something to Ted. But what could she say? Nothing had happened. Still, the joy Edwin had felt about the pool and the excitement of possibly seeing so much of Georgia over the summer had left him so fully, it was hard to believe he had ever let himself be that hopeful. Georgia might not want to come back. She had understood his intention, and her response was a clear rejection. The last thing he felt like doing was going to see the funeral train, which, they'd learned from the radio, was delayed by a couple of hours or more.

Georgia's face was still pink around her eyes and nose, but it appeared less irritated overall, and she said it no longer itched. She was resting her feet in Ted's hands, her legs stretched across so that the sun painted a lone white streak on her shin. Edwin alternately stared at her legs and looked away in misery.

Ordinarily, Lolly would have been more understanding toward Edwin about the chlorine mishap, but on this day all she could feel was contempt. He had ogled Georgia with no subtlety at all, and after insisting that everything was fine with the pool after Ted and she had complained, he was pouty and pathetic. As Lolly poured herself another glass of wine, she had the odd impulse to do something that would shock him. Take off her top and kiss Ted on the mouth? Make some crack about Edwin being sterile? She imagined piercing a small hole in the pool pump late at night, as he slept, and enjoying his frustration as he searched for the problem.

The twin Pyle girls were still in their backyard playing, their thin voices drifting over as Steppenwolf's "Magic Carpet Ride" came to an end on the radio. Georgia turned to make out what they were doing. The girls were still clutching their Barbies, who seemed to be in some disagreement about what they would wear that night to the drive-in.

"You know, I've never even gotten to meet Ling-lee?" Georgia said to Lolly. "I think it would be so fun to have her around and play with her, play dolls with her. Do all those girlie things. I think it's just so sad Ted never gets to see her."

Ted lifted one of Georgia's feet and kissed the top of it. He let out a deep sigh. "Yeah, I miss her, but even that sounds weird because I don't really know her at all anymore. I haven't seen her in three and a half years. I've gotten two pictures of her in all that time. I don't even know if she speaks English. That's fucked up. I don't even *know* if my daughter could communicate with me. And that's how Mai wants it."

Georgia put her hand to his cheek. "Baby," she whispered. Ted let his head drop to his chest.

"Sometimes I think about going to China, you know, but I don't speak the language, and I don't know if Mai would even let me see her. She hated me when she left."

"Well, it was a hard time for her," Lolly said. "And we don't need to get into all of that. You're not the same person now. But the thing is, as a father you have rights. By law, you could see her, I'm sure."

"I don't even know," Ted said. "I don't even know what the law says in China about that kind of thing. Mai took off so quickly. I should have gotten better informed about all of that stuff — my rights, the rules. My lawyer didn't tell me crap, you know? But I was really out of it back then. So I don't know what to think. I don't hate Mai for it. I don't hate her. I just flaked out on her. I was wasted so much of the time. The shitty thing is, I don't even know why. We used to have good times. The four of us would go out — those were good times, right?"

Edwin and Lolly nodded with appropriate vigor.

"Right, so why did I go and blow it?" Ted said. "That's the thing. We had good times. Mai. I loved her, and that's the truth. And I loved Ling-lee. But I pissed all of it away. And Georgia knows this is nothing against her. You know that, right, baby? I'm not saying —"

"Of course," Georgia whispered.

"I mean, without Georgia, man. Anyway, Georgia knows this is not about her at all. It's about Ling-lee. So what was I saying?"

"You were just talking," Georgia said.

"Yeah, I know, but . . . well, anyway. Yeah, I would love for Georgia to meet Ling-lee.

234

It would be great if she could just spend a whole summer here with us. Take her to the beach, the park. *Here,* in your *pool.* Whatever she wanted to do. Whatever she wanted." Ted looked into the sky, and it was unclear if he was past the point of starting to cry or on the verge of it.

"Why are you so sure that could never happen?" Lolly asked. "Seriously. Maybe it's time you look into what your visitation rights really are. I'm sure you have *some* rights. She's your daughter, too. Maybe the thing you're describing, a visit like that, could really happen. I would just say, Don't give up. She's still a little girl. You're still her father. You know how to reach Mai. Maybe it's time to see what's truly possible."

The four of them sat in silence for a moment. They could hear the tinkling sound of an ice cream truck. Georgia thought that maybe Ted didn't want to talk about Linglee any further, and she started to say something about the speakers he had been building from scratch when he said, "God, I feel like my heart is about to explode right now."

"Baby," Georgia said, getting to her feet. "What's wrong? Your chest hurts?"

"No, no, I feel something is opening up

235

inside me. Or something. It feels beautiful. Lolly is so right. I'm Ling-lee's father. What am I doing just *dreaming* like this? I should be able to see my little girl. Oh my God, Lolly!" Ted stood up and came around the table. He put his arms around Lolly and squeezed until she squealed in laughter.

"Lolly! You are a savior. I swear to God. I'm going to do it, Lolly. I'm not going to just sit around thinking about her anymore. I'm going to figure out what I can do. Even if I have to go to *China*. Thank you, Lolly. You've done something really deep for me!"

Ted wouldn't let go, and Lolly finally had to squeeze back. "I've just been talking — that's all," she said. "One friend to another. You deserve to see your little girl. I know you love her. You could still be a good father to her. It doesn't have to be too late. Seeing her would be good for you. And good for her, too."

Ted released her, but his entire body was vibrating. "Oh my *God*," he kept saying. Georgia took his hand, and then he leaned down and hugged her just as hard.

"You're going to be a good daddy," Georgia told him. Ted took her face in his hands and kissed her on the mouth for a long time. Lolly and Edwin looked at each other, and Edwin tried to smile at her.

"I just feel it, you know," Ted said. "I've been so *stuck*. About Ling-lee, I mean. Like there was nothing I could do, and Lolly's right. I have rights. Regardless of what Mai says, I know I have some *rights*. Maybe she could even come this summer, you know. Why not?"

"Well, first things first," Lolly said, "before you get too ahead of yourself. You have to find out how to contact your lawyer."

"Yeah, I know his name. That won't be a problem," Ted said.

"So start there," Lolly said. "One step at a time."

"You're right," Ted said. "Just gotta take that first step."

Edwin finished his beer. He couldn't remember being so unsure what to do with himself. He knew he had made Georgia uncomfortable in the bathroom, and Lolly was focused on everyone *but* him. Was it still because of the chlorine? Or was she suspicious about his insistence on trying to help Georgia? Without lifting a finger, Lolly had suddenly made Ted the happiest guy in the world. But Ted should have felt like that without anyone even mentioning Ling-lee, Edwin thought. He had Georgia! Now maybe one more piece of Ted's life was going to come together. Who could say? He and Georgia and Ling-lee might end up a regular family. And they might end up coming over to his pool all summer long. Georgia would be wearing her wondrous bikini, and she might find a way to say as little to him as possible. Ted would fill his pool with his tiny chest hairs, and Lolly would stay moody all summer. It was early June, and everything Edwin had dreamed about for the summer felt shattered into oblivion.

"You're a special person, Lolly," Georgia said. "You really are. I've never thought to encourage Ted like that. We haven't really even talked about Ling-lee that much." Ted shook his head in agreement. "I know he's sad about never getting to see her, and I didn't want to make him more sad by bringing her up," she said. "But I just heard those little girls playing next door, and I don't know. I just thought of her — and mentioned her."

"But don't you see?" Ted said. "You're the one that started this. If you hadn't mentioned Ling-lee, Lolly wouldn't have thought to say what she did. Don't you see, baby? It all started with you."

"That's right," Lolly said.

"Oh my God, I guess that's true," Georgia said, and she smiled brighter than she had all day. "That makes me happy."

"Yeah, of course," Ted said. "You both have done this amazing thing for me. It's like this *harmonic convergence,* or something. Everything feels so opened up right now. No, you helped, too, baby." Ted sat down and held out his hands in an invitation for her to sit in his lap.

Georgia wrapped herself around him, tucking her head under his chin. "It's funny," she said. "This is a sad day for the country, but for us it feels like a celebration, suddenly."

"That's right," Ted said. He looked over at Edwin, who looked faint. "And we owe it all to Edwin and his pool."

"Hardly," Edwin said.

"I'm serious — think about it," Ted said. "If you hadn't invited us over, Georgia wouldn't have seen those little girls next door, and she wouldn't have thought to say what she did about Ling-lee. At least not in front of Lolly like that. So all of *that* happened because you wanted us to be here to help kick off your new pool. Forget the chlorine. It's a great pool, Edwin. It's a damned great pool. Thank you, brother."

"Thank you, Edwin," Georgia said. She flashed her flawless teeth at him, and there didn't seem anything false or begrudging about it. Immediately Edwin's mood began

239

to lift. He was probably never going to touch Georgia again, but he still wanted to be around her. He worked up some hope that she might come over and hug him the way Ted had hugged Lolly, but she remained in the chair.

But what Ted said had softened Lolly's anger toward Edwin, and she reached over and squeezed Edwin's soft, fleshy hand, then held it. He studied their hands intertwined like that. Maybe, Edwin let himself think, everything could start over from this day. If there was hope for Ted, why couldn't Edwin's life get better, too? Everyone was touching and smiling, and there was a vibe that Edwin could feel, a sense of new possibilities. And for the first time all day he thought about Robert Kennedy — not his funeral train, but Kennedy himself, his selflessness, his compassion for others. So much hope had died with him, it seemed. Who would stand up for so many who needed championing?

He didn't want to get bogged down in that thinking now, though. Something was happening here in their backyard, and he wanted to try to hang on to it as best he could. Ted did deserve to see his kid. They were all deserving. And if Georgia got to play with Ling-lee the way she wanted, then that was just more happiness to go around.

But could Lolly ever be satisfied if it just remained the two of them? He had his doubts. He looked at Lolly's face, and more than anything he wanted to take her into their bed and make love to her, with the sunlight streaming through the window, like the old days. He gently tugged on Lolly's hand, and she understood that he wanted her to sit with him. Lolly let her head fall back, closing her eyes, and a kind of serenity spread across her face in a way that thrilled Edwin. Then she stood up and positioned herself over him. She kissed him for the first time that day, and in the eagerness with which he kissed her back she let the last remnants of her anger drain away. Both couples were kissing now, and the girls next door pressed their faces and their Barbies' faces against the chain-link fence and watched.

Delores had always preferred Ethel to
Jackie. Jackie's beauty made her seem
unreal, somehow, as if she belonged under
glass or behind a velvet rope in a museum,
whereas Ethel looked like she could have
been a fun roommate or the head of fund-
raising for the PTA. Bobby and Ethel,
Delores had read, liked to throw parties that
could turn raucous. Once, Ethel had jumped
into their backyard pool with her clothes on
— to the astonishment of her guests. Soon,
Bobby was in the water with his clothes on
as well. It was said that Bobby and Ethel's
kids could be a little rough around the
edges, and Jackie eventually forbade Caro-
line and John John to play with them.
Delores didn't remember seeing Ethel in a
little pillbox hat even once.

Delores had once believed she would be
the wife of a politician herself. During her
freshman and sophomore years at Penn

State, she dated a boy named Darden Clayton, who had attended Delores's rival high school. Darden's dream was to become mayor of their hometown by the time he was thirty-five. He planned to run the town council by thirty, and before that he was counting on being the youngest alderman in the town's long history. He liked to tell Delores what, as wife of the mayor, she would be expected to do: be involved in children's charity work, perhaps, to organize the mayor's Christmas party for the town's most prominent citizens, to attend with him the openings of a new hospital wing, a retirement home, a new Little League field. Their sophomore year Darden was elected class president, but it proved to hold little training for Delores, as there were few responsibilities to which she, as his girlfriend, was obliged.

Delores took comfort in knowing so clearly what was ahead for her; the idea of having so visible a role in a small town made her sit through classes with a kind of dreamy distance. She enjoyed her psychology and behavioral studies and Introduction to Classical Music classes, but she could no longer invest herself in the course work the way she had in her first semester there. If Darden was going to be mayor by thirty-five, he said, he'd want to have children old enough so that they could sit still and listen intently during his swearing-in ceremony and pose properly when asked by a newspaper photographer. If all went according to plan, by the end of their first year of marriage Delores would be pregnant.

Darden Clayton didn't yet understand that in politics, so little goes according to plan, but he understood that in times of crisis, a politician must be decisive and steer away from anything that can be damaging. In the spring semester of their sophomore year, Delores believed that she had missed her period. She waited a week before she mentioned this to Darden, though she knew that the more sensible step was to see a doctor first. They were walking in the campus quad, holding hands, and all around them young Alpha Delta Pi pledges in matching blue T-shirts were linked arm in arm and singing "Alley Oop" as a couple of senior sisters led them with the grand, sweeping arm movements of a conductor. Delores felt so keenly happy at that moment, and the possibility of a baby seemed to her, suddenly, like one more reason to be grateful for the direction her life was going. Without breaking their stride she told Darden about the late period. If it did turn out that she was pregnant, she said, they could simply get married early. As she spoke, she was sure he would be impressed with the way she had thought it all through. "I've been so distracted by it the last couple of days — but not in a bad way," she said. "I sit in class and I don't hear a word the professor says."

Darden's face tightened, but already he liked to practice a mayoral sense of calm, and he squeezed Delores's hand before saying, "Well, we'll find a way to deal with it, if you are. It's a whole lot easier to get this kind of thing fixed these days. I know a couple of guys whose girlfriends have done it. It's not true that your only choice is to drive down to Mexico."

Delores nodded, and as Darden looked on at the singing pledges, she squinted to push back the hot rush of tears. "You know, it's just, you don't start your career in politics by getting your girlfriend knocked up in college," he said. "You do that, you can look forward to working as a middle manager at the local water plant. Politics is just that tough. But everything will be fine. If you are   if your period doesn't come — I'll help you through everything. I'll be there for you. We just have to think like a team."

Five days later, Delores's period came, but

her weepiness over the course of that week had been inexplicable to him, and he became uncertain about Delores as a mayor's wife. She was too unstable for him, he decided, a possible liability.

Two years after graduation, a girlfriend convinced her to come along on a blind double date. Arch King was just back from Korea and starting up in the tire business. He was large and unapologetically loud, and when he laughed he slapped his wide palm across the table. At the end of their first date Delores was surprised by how easily she let him kiss her — wet, with Arch moaning slightly — and the toothy grin he flashed when they said good night made her feel alive and beautiful.

"I think you're going to be seeing a lot of me, Delores Banks," he told her on the front steps of her apartment building, called Langley Arms. When he was walking — backward — to the car, where his buddy sat waiting behind the steering wheel, Arch noticed the sign and flexed his muscles like an old-time circus performer. "You belong in *Arch's* Arms." His laughter exploded into the night air, and when Delores got upstairs and found her roommate still awake, she said, "I am *floating!*"

By the time they had picked out a chapel

for the wedding and arranged the accommodations for a five-day honeymoon at Lake Erie, she had long convinced herself that being the wife of a politician would have given her a rather empty life — an endless parade of gestures and poses that served everyone but herself; with Arch, everything was what it appeared to be. He had no secrets, no deeper aspirations but to work for himself and provide comfortably for his family. He liked to prop his size thirteen feet up wherever he was, and anyone who showed too many table manners was a bore and possibly a snob. And like Darden Clayton, he knew exactly what he wanted and didn't want for himself. Fighting in Korea, which he generally talked very little about, made you know exactly who you wanted on your side, he said. He and Delores had been married for two months when he told her that — they were tucked into their little backyard table, eating steaks he had cooked to well done. In a year he would get the loans to open up his Tire King shop, and six months after that they would have a baby boy. Dwight D. Eisenhower was still president. He had gotten Arch's vote both times.

Roy took a few pictures of Jamie pulling the bowstring back to his ear. "There's never a reason you should miss," Jamie said. "Once you work out the physical mechanics, which aren't that hard, the only thing that can screw you up is your mind." Jamie had just hit eleven bull's-eyes in a row, but now he seemed tired. He put the bow down and closed his eyes.

"The old job at the garage is still there if I want it," he said. "Standing offer from Jurrel. Same crew's still there. Lonnie and Dave. Fat Phil. Mr. Jurrel said take my time, let him know by July if I want to come back. Basically, if you're leaning over an engine or underneath the car, one leg's as good as two. It might be charity, but he knows I know what the hell I'm doing."

Jamie traced one of the arrows with his fingers. "Maybe Sutton and I will get an apartment together."

Roy wrote in his notebook. "You said 'charity,' a second ago, talking about how some people respond to the war and wounded soldiers. What's it been like for your family — your coming back under these circumstances? How would you say they've responded?"

"Look, what am I really going to say to you, a reporter? Huh? They're completely flipped out, in case you haven't already picked up on that. They're trying to do the best they can, you know, but my mother and Miriam, it's like I'm some sickly little kid, all the touching and hugs and . . . They don't know what to do, but, you know, that's not for your story. My dad's different. He's been cool, but for this little article here, let's say this. Here you go: they've been great. Really supportive, just treating me like nothing's different. They're glad to have me back home, of course. But they don't treat me like a cripple, and I don't think that's how they see me in their eyes. There, that's the stuff you're looking for, right?"

"I'm just looking for anything you want to tell me," Roy said. "Whatever the truth is, or whatever version of the truth I can get."

Jamie opened his eyes. "Well, that's the version you're getting."

■ ■ ■ ■

When Roy interviewed Ellie, they were sitting in the same spot in the backyard where he and Jamie had.

"Oooh, I'm so nervous," Ellie said. "I know that's silly, but I just want to say the right things."

"Oh, there's nothing to be nervous about," Roy said. "Just think of it as a conversation. And that's what it is, really. I just want to get your perspective on a few things, your thoughts about Jamie."

He asked her about her initial reaction to Jamie's being drafted, and she said, "Joe served in World War Two — he was stationed in the Philippines — so we believe — and Joe in particular — in serving your country. So that's a real pride in this family. Now, that said, Vietnam is —" She stopped herself, because she and Joe had had some disagreements about Vietnam, and she didn't want to say anything that he — or others in the community — could take issue with. "— is a different kind of war." And she thought she should leave it at that.

He asked her how they had stayed in touch with Jamie before his injury and how they found out about his leg. He asked her how she thought Jamie was coping. And in every answer she spoke carefully, like a child reciting from memory. Everything she told him was what he mostly expected her to say, but he pursed his lips in a show of admiration as he wrote down some notes while his tape recorder turned its slow cogs. When he finally told her that was everything he could think to ask her, she began to cry.

Roy's mother had cried frequently when he was a child — for reasons he rarely understood. Sometimes he found her dabbing her cheeks with a tissue when he walked into the living room or the kitchen, and sometimes she began to tear up when she dropped him off at school. "Don't mind your crazy mother," she would say, but he wouldn't step out until she recovered herself. When she pulled away, he could see her waving good-bye until she was all the way down the street.

"I know it must be tough," Roy said, at last, to Ellie. "I guess all my nosy questions don't help any."

"What Jamie has been through is traumatic — and we can't pretend like everything is the same," she said. "Because it isn't."

PENNSYLVANIA

Delores knew she should check in with her mother-in-law. She pulled into an Esso station and put a coin in the pay phone, all the while watching Rebecca wrap her red crepe paper around her finger.

"Hey, Mama, it's me. I thought I'd stop to see how everyone's doing. It is so *hot.*"

"Are you on your way now?" the old woman said. Delores thought she could hear the television in the background.

"I'm not able to just yet," Delores said. "But soon. I have one last thing that should finish up in just a little. I just wanted to make sure the boys were doing okay. Are they behaving themselves?"

"Oh, dear. I didn't know it'd be the entire day."

"You don't have to entertain them, Mama. They can entertain themselves."

"And they can't ride with you in what you're doing?" the woman said. "Did Arch know about this being the whole day?"

"I'll be by just as soon as I'm able," Delores said. "It really is so helpful, your taking them like this. Rebecca and I went by the church earlier for delivering meals."

"Well, we'll be waiting, I guess. Do I need to feed them supper, too? I don't know that I have anything that would suit them. They don't like to eat what I eat."

"I'm going to get them for supper, Mama. Don't worry about that. Don't worry about anything."

When Delores got back in the car, Rebecca puffed. "I want to see the *train*," she said.

"So do I," Delores said, cutting back on the air conditioner. "Right now that's *all* I want."

Sutton arrived in his Dodge Charger, whose engine he and Jamie had rebuilt before Jamie was drafted. They liked to open up the hood and contemplate what else they might try to modify. Since Jamie had gotten home, Sutton was eager for them to work on it together, but they hadn't gotten past talk.

"So what are you writing about Jamie?" Sutton asked Roy, when Jamie and his mother had gone to the yard's edge to ask their neighbor Emma Wilkinson about her husband, who was leading a platoon in Suoi Da.

"I don't know exactly," Roy said. "I'll sit down and see what all the interviews add up to. Do you want to tell me something about Jamie, something I might not know yet?"

"I don't want to be quoted or anything like that — you know, official. That would be weird, since we're buddies and every-thing." Sutton swiped at something. "I was just curious."

"You're sure? Could be good for the story. That's what I'm doing — talking to the people who know him best."

"Yeah, I know," Sutton said. "I mean, but I don't know what it's like to fight in a war or kill anyone. He tells me things, you know, so I sort of get what he went through, or how he's doing now. I don't know. I wanted to go over there myself, but my damn leg."

"Jamie told me about that," Roy said. "He said you tried to go through the physical anyway."

"Well, they didn't let me get very far. Fuckers." Sutton let out a laugh. "What about you — you have a deferment, I guess."

Roy nodded.

"Shit," Sutton said. "I wanted to go. Fight for my country."

"Why?" Roy said. "Would you tell me on the record? That doesn't have anything to do with Jamie, but it's kind of an interesting point for the article, maybe. Jamie's lost his leg and he's home from the war. You have an injury to your leg and can't go, but you've tried anyway. Just tell me why you wanted to go to Vietnam. I'd only print what you tell me. You don't have anything to worry about."

"It's funny that it's you writing about Jamie," Sutton said.

"How so?" Roy asked.

"Well, Jamie dated Claire, but then you and she spent a lot of time together, it seemed like. I could never quite figure out that whole situation. You know: Were you in love with Claire? Were you guys really just friends? Why was it that you seemed to spend more time with her than Jamie did? It was just kind of funny. I bet Jamie was shocked to find out you were the reporter."

"What are you saying, that Jamie hated my guts in high school?" Roy laughed to show that he was making a joke, but to Sutton it seemed a reasonable question.

"I don't know that he *hated* you," he said, and then he combed further through his memories of those days. "I mean, he was just kind of jealous, I guess. He wasn't going to kick your ass, though." Sutton watched Jamie adjust his crutches as he talked to Emma. Then Roy watched an idea flicker across Sutton's face. "So what was the whole story there, anyway?"

"What do you mean?"

"You and Claire were just friends that whole time?" Sutton asked.

Roy watched a bee land on one of the daffodils that bordered the yard. He was surprised by how tempted he was to confide in Sutton. He was so fully back in that place now, that longing. He was aware, too, that he could say something to turn the delicate situation with Jamie into something more volatile, and that would jeopardize his story. If Jamie became upset, he could withdraw all his quotes from use. Roy needed the internship, and he couldn't afford to create any problems for himself.

What he couldn't tell Sutton was that when he and Claire played Monopoly at her house, Claire liked to put on her grandfather's old top hat, and that they made each other laugh with their crude Chinese accents every time they passed Oriental Avenue. He couldn't tell Sutton that his and Claire's favorite place to talk had been on top of a large fiberglass whale in Rowan Park, which went mostly forgotten because of the newer parks in town, and that one afternoon, while lying back on top of its head, they imagined a summer working together in Washington as guides at the Museum of Natural History, and lunching together on the lawn of the Mall and spending their evenings poking around in the bookstores of Georgetown and Dupont Circle. And he couldn't tell him that on the afternoon of the senior prom, which Claire attended with Jamie, she was trying on three different dresses as Roy sat back on her bed, and after slipping into the first gown, she stopped turning her back to him, but let him watch her dress and undress — unhurried and without any self-consciousness. By that time, he knew, she had stopped pretending that his devotion to her was strictly out of friendship, and she was going to let him look at her the way he wanted to. He understood that he was not to move, that this was not Claire's invitation to seduce her, but a consolation prize, of sorts. What she didn't realize was how pathetic he would feel around her from that day on.

Instead, Roy looked at Sutton and said, "That was all. Just friends."

Sutton nodded, but in that gesture he was acknowledging the truth that Roy couldn't confess. They understood each other. Sutton, Roy realized, was like him in some essential way. He was the confidant, the supporting role wherever he went. Sutton's injury had all but cemented that, and even Jamie's loss of a leg wouldn't change the dynamic between them. Jamie's swagger would be mostly gone, and his fortune with women didn't hold much promise, but Sutton would still be the sidekick. Their friendship centered around everything from Jamie's past — his football heroics, Claire the beauty queen, and now his Vietnam stories — and whatever future they had as friends would hold to that pattern. The leg was an irrevocable setback for Jamie — his first — but he wasn't going to let someone like Sutton move ahead of him.

"The air conditioner's broken. Sorry," Ted said. "The old van's kind of falling apart on me." Over his shoulder he could see Lolly trying to figure out what to do with a pair of speakers in the backseat, their wires protruding like whiskers. "Just put those anywhere, Lol. They're busted up pretty good."

"That means he's going to keep them in his apartment," Georgia said. "Ted can't throw out a broken speaker. He has to use them as stools or shelves."

"Hey, a speaker is a beautiful thing," Ted said.

"Oh, so romantic," Georgia said and laughed. She reached over and fingered a thick curl falling over his headrest.

"Okay, so here we go," Ted said. "Hey, babe, hand me that Cream tape, will you? Some 'Disraeli Gears' would be good about now."

"Ted, do you mind if we don't play music right now?" Lolly asked. "I wouldn't mind just a little quiet on the way. Just to, you know . . ."

"Lolly's right," Georgia said. "I know it doesn't feel like it, but it is kind of like we're going to a funeral, in a way."

"Sure, sure," Ted said. "That's cool."

"Thank you," Lolly said. Her hand was resting on Edwin's knee as Ted pulled out into the street.

"You know," Ted said to Georgia, "Lolly worked for John Kennedy's presidential campaign."

"You did?" Georgia said. "Wow. What was it like?"

"I was just a volunteer," Lolly said. She described the cramped state office she reported to, how she called registered voters and sometimes walked door-to-door, handing out fliers that emphasized the distinctions between Kennedy's policies and Richard Nixon's. As she talked, the wind from Ted's window picked up and blew Edwin's hair back. He looked out at his neighbors as the van rumbled past. There was Major Drew, mowing his yard with the same stony expression he wore whether his children were playing in the sprinkler or he was washing his red Corvette; and there was

261

the woman whose son got attacked by a dog last summer and had to get all the stitches; she was planting bulbs in front of the house. There was that teenager who had tried to sell Edwin some grass that time by the park, but all Edwin had on him was change. And here was Mrs. Lamaza, or Lavaza. One of the neighbors had told Lolly that ten years before she had won the title of Miss Venezuela. Now she was talking to the postal carrier, Hal, in a yellow halter top and swatting at the heat, as if a perfectly timed strike would correct the temperature.

They all lived on his block, and as Edwin thought about it, they were, when it came right down to it, probably all pretty decent people. Word would eventually get out about the Galaxy. Neighbors might start hinting around for an invitation on hot Saturdays like this one. And that was understandable. He couldn't fit them all in, of course, but maybe there were other ways to look at it. He could possibly have a party in shifts, or invite a few houses each weekend. It wasn't unthinkable. And he'd get the chemicals balanced out, no problem. He just needed to make the right adjustments.

PENNSYLVANIA

At first Delores thought she had hit a squirrel and that somehow the squirrel's body had become wrapped around the tire. When that stopped making sense, she wondered if something had become loose or broken off in the trunk. When it finally occurred to her that the sound was a flat tire, she imagined how disappointed Arch would be that she didn't have more appreciation for that sensation.

She pulled into the parking lot of Winn-Dixie and traced her fingers around the hot edges of the rear right hubcap, searching for the hole as a way to redeem herself. But she could find nothing. She then went to the passenger's side; Rebecca was drowsy, her eyes flickering little recognition that the car had even stopped at all.

"We have a flat tire, pumpkin," Delores said. Rebecca scanned her mother's face for something more. "This is just not our day, is it? Not at all."

"Daddy can fix it," Rebecca said. Her voice was so small and quavering that it took Delores a moment to realize she had even spoken.

"He fixes all kinds of flat tires, that's true," Delores said. But the flat tire was one more incident that required some puzzling through. She and Rebecca were supposed to meet the others in a half-hour. Arch would drop whatever he was doing and drive over to fix the tire himself, but she wasn't ready for him to see Rebecca like this. Too, there would be the question of where they were headed now. And why wasn't she on her way to pick up the boys and relieve his mother? Next to the line of grocery carts and a slew of yellow and green plastic wading pools, Delores spotted a phone booth. There was, she supposed, the slimmest of chances that Arch would send someone else over — Rudy Barre, the assistant manager, who had been Arch's number two since he opened the business and idolized Arch like a younger, less capable brother; Danny Adalpho, who was in his early twenties and knew more about cars than anyone in the shop, but whose constant sullenness meant they had to keep him away from customers; and Carlos Furero, an older man who had immigrated from Cuba and infused the shop with a gentle wisdom when it came to cars and people. He had been kind to Delores and had taken an interest in little Rebecca in particular, and Delores had the feeling that he alone was the one she could turn to for help.

Delores called the shop, ready to hang up if Arch picked up, but it was Rudy's voice that came on the line. Delores lowered her voice. "Yes, may I speak to Carlos," she said. Rudy paused for a moment, and Delores imagined him craning his head toward the garage. "Hang on," he said, and called out Carlos's name. In the background the high scream of a drill whirled.

"Hello?" By the uncertain tone of Carlos's voice, she could tell that it was unusual for someone to call him at work.

Delores kept the same low rumble in her voice. "Carlos, this is Mrs. King, but I don't want Arch to know I'm calling, so don't say my name out loud. Do you understand?" The telephone was in the small office, which held little more than the counter, the cash register, and a tall vinyl chair badly torn and duct-taped across the center.

"Yes."

"Carlos, I have a flat tire, and Mr. King just put new tires on the car a month ago.

He tells me I'm always driving straight over potholes, and he's going to be so upset when he hears I've driven over something again. And what I'm wondering is, could you possibly drive over and put a new Firestone on, and I'll pay you in cash, and he'll never have to know. It will be our little secret. Is there any way you could do that, Carlos?"

She could hear Arch talking to a customer, most likely, and Carlos said, "I bring tire to you," taking measure of just how he might explain that. "Yes, I understand."

"Oh, that is such a relief. And you can get away? You can tell Mr. King someone you know called and needs a new tire? I'm not far. I'm just in front of the Winn-Dixie, on the boulevard."

"Yes, I tell him that," Carlos said. "Is no problem. The truck is here. I help you."

"Oh, thank you, Carlos," she said. "I knew if I could get you on the phone, everything would be all right. We'll be waiting for you, then. I have Rebecca with me."

"I see you soon," he said.

Walking back to the car, the glut of lies she had told in a single day made her feel like she had drunk something spoiled. Arch had put new tires on her car because he always liked to give her new tires every twelve months, but she never drove over potholes, and the subject of her getting flat tires had never come up, since she almost never did. If Arch were to find out that she had called Carlos instead, she could probably convince him that she was simply embarrassed. But she knew Arch would fire Carlos for lying to him. He valued Carlos's experience, but he had his complaints about him: Carlos worked too slowly; Carlos talked too much while he worked — about his beloved Havana and the beautiful women there and the music of Arsenio Rodriguez and how Cuba produced the greatest baseball pitchers in the world; his hatred of Fidel Castro. Carlos could be prickly when told what to do. He liked to do things his own way, Arch said. The old man had run his own garage for fifteen years in Havana, and he had never fully gotten used to having to answer to someone else.

"One of Daddy's trucks is going to come and fix our tire," Delores told Rebecca, who nodded and said that she was fixing her doll, that her doll had had a bad fall, but that she was all better now.

"She's lucky she has you," Delores said.

As they waited, Delores wondered how Ethel was holding up. The day had surely exhausted her. And what about all the poor children! There was still so much ahead for all of them: the arrival in Washington, the burial at Arlington National Cemetery. Where were Ethel and the children going to spend the night? she wondered. Was President Johnson putting them all up in the White House? How many rooms did Ethel need for a family that big? How, Delores wondered, could she face going back into their house, their swimming pool, their bedroom, without Bobby?

"You knew what tires you had," Carlos said in approval. "You are wife of tire man. You know." He was rolling the new tire from the truck to Delores's car.

"Well, if he saw something besides a Firestone on this car, he'd have a heart attack," Delores said. "Or shoot it."

Carlos smiled. "He shouldn't notice difference," he said. "This one is new, but your others look good. Not much different. Maybe this one a little shinier. Best thing you can do is drive through big mud puddle, let them all get dirty." His smooth, bald head was beaming in the sunlight, and he let out a full, proud laugh. Then he set out his tools to remove the flat, but his hands froze when he spotted Rebecca, who had just crept out of the car and hidden herself behind Delores's leg.

"Oh my gracious," Carlos said. "Little Rebecca. Beautiful Rebecca." He looked up at Delores, incredulous. "She was in accident?"

"She fell from the monkey bars this morning," Delores said. She did not want to say more, but neither did she want to sound unconcerned, so she added, "And she's been so brave. Just a lot of bad boo-boos and bruises, but nothing more."

Carlos took a step to have a closer look, but Rebecca retreated farther behind Delores's leg. Angela and Faye and Betty Jean would be looking for them shortly. Delores did not want to give in to impatience, but now Arch's complaint about how easily Carlos stopped working as he talked was already making her anxious.

"Poor, poor girl," he said. He forced himself to smile, showing his one gold tooth, and said, "Rebecca, I am sorry for you. But that does not change that you are still beautiful girl. Does it hurt to smile, if you go like this?" He stretched his mouth wide with his oil-tipped fingers, revealing the rest of his teeth. Rebecca hid completely from view, then peered around to see if his smile was still waiting for her. It was.

"I don't smile like that," she said.

"Oh, that's a shame," Carlos said. "You

269

should smile big and wide, even with bruise." He stretched his lips even farther, and Rebecca giggled this time before she could catch herself.

"No," she said.

Carlos looked at Delores, and he could tell by the way the corners of her mouth strained that she had had a difficult day. He began to position the jack under her car, his eyes closed in what looked like a mockery of rapt attention before he had it in position. "She will be smiling again soon, and feel much better."

"I know," Delores said quickly.

When he had the back of the car elevated, he removed the bolts from the tire. Then he methodically spun the tire, searching. "I no see — ah, here is our little friend. Is nail." He reached in and held up the nail with some admiration for the damage it had managed to do.

"It was bad luck," Delores said, "but we'll be back on the road in no time."

Rebecca stepped closer to Carlos and stared at the nail, which he put in his shirt pocket.

"Bad nail," he told her. "Bad, bad nail. Tell me, Rebecca, were you on the way to come see your friend Carlos at shop?"

Rebecca said no. Then she added: "We're

going to see a train."

"Oh, train," he said, and Delores watched his face for any recognition. "The train for Robert Kennedy?"

Delores nodded.

"Now he was great man," Carlos said. "Always talking about the poor. He say many important things. Things that need to be said, but only he say them. Now that, that is tragedy." He fastened the new tire and began to tighten the bolts, first with his fingers. "My wife and children go see train. In fact" — he looked at his watch — "they go there now. To wait."

When he picked up the lug wrench, he said, "I wanted to see train, too, to pay respect. But of course, Mr. King, he no like the Kennedys. As you know." He smiled at this, as if to say to Delores, *But that's okay.* "I ask, but is Saturday. And as I say, with him, Kennedys . . ." He began to spin the wrench around. "Okay, soon will be fixed and ready to go."

"Well, we weren't going to tell him, to tell you the truth," Delores said. "You're right, he gets very worked up about his politics. But I think Bobby would have made a great president, myself. I want to be there just as much for Ethel, though, too, with all that she must be going through."

"Yes, he would be great president. Bobby Kennedy care about the poor, the disadvantaged. The Negroes, Mexican people. All people. And he and his brother were very tough with Fidel. Fidel feared them. They would have killed Fidel if they could have. And that would have been a joyous day for all of Cuba, if you ask me. Bring back freedom for Cuba."

He had stopped tightening the bolts. "Same tire. He will not notice."

"I'm sorry he won't let you go," Delores said. "It would be for such a short time, too. The train is just going to whiz by, really." Delores looked at her watch. "I hope it's on schedule. I think everyone ought to be able to pay their respects."

Carlos looked down at the ground, unsure what to say for once, and then he noticed that Rebecca had climbed into the driver's seat. "My wife will be there. Maybe you will see her. You've not met."

"No, we haven't," Delores said.

"We were married in Cuba, and then we come here because with Fidel, is too hard for the businessman. You cannot be success, or you have too much power, and power is problem for Fidel. Only I come here first. For almost a year I am here and not see her. Then finally she come. The hardest time of my life, not to be with my wife. We were still young. And she had our baby in Cuba. When she come here, she have big boy in her arms and say, 'Carlos, this is our son.' Now that was the happiest day of my life. I cry and I cry, right there in airport, and she say, 'Oh my gosh, now I have two babies.' "

"Well, maybe I will see her. I'd like to say hello. But if you think we're about done here, we'll get on over there."

"Yes, yes," Carlos said. "Mr. King will be looking for me. He always says, 'What take so long?' He likes very quick, very fast."

"He certainly counts on you," Delores said, reaching into her purse. "Now I need to pay you for it."

"Let me tighten once more, to be sure."

After counting out the money, Delores reached out to stroke Rebecca's hair, and was startled not to feel her. She spun around, and her panic caused Carlos to stop what he was doing. "Rebecca?" she said, but as she spoke she spotted Rebecca's legs sticking out from the car. Rebecca was lying down on her back, her body underneath the large steering wheel. Her eyes were closed, and her lips were slightly parted. "Rebecca, let's wake up, honey. Time to go see the train."

Delores cupped her hands around Rebecca's face and watched her breathe out little darts of air.

"Rebecca, let's wait and sleep after. I'm not going to be able to carry you the whole time like that." She put one hand underneath Rebecca's head and sat her up, but Rebecca slumped against the seat, unresponsive.

"Rebecca, wake up, honey!" Delores cried out. Carlos, who had come to stand behind Delores, now leaned inside.

"She is all right?"

"She's not waking up," Delores said in a loud, trembly voice. "She's so limp. Rebecca! Rebecca, wake up! Right now."

"Here," Carlos said, and ran around to the other side of the car. "We're going to help her. Maybe because of accident? Little Rebecca, wake up for your mommy. You give Mommy big scare." He tried to scoop her into his lap, but Delores still had her by the shoulders and did not want to let go. Rebecca felt like a large puppet, all limbs and heavy head. Her skin was cool and dry.

"Is not good," Carlos said, and tried to look into Delores's eyes. "We should take her to hospital. Is not good we can't wake her up. She hit her head?"

Delores's body began to quake. "Rebecca, wake up, Rebecca!"

"We drive her in my truck. Tire is not yet tight enough. Here, I lift her. She's going to be okay. Do you have water, at all? Any cold water? We splash her face. It might wake her." Carlos held Rebecca against his chest, her head flopped over his shoulder. A few shoppers had stopped on the way to their cars, trying to make out the commotion.

"I think is accident," Carlos said. "Her head."

Inside the cab of the truck, Delores held Rebecca's face. "Please, Rebecca. Wake up, baby girl."

"At hospital she will be fine," Carlos said. "The doctors will know what to do. I take her to Mercy," he said, referring to the hospital that loomed over downtown. Delores had never been to Mercy. Of the two hospitals in town, Mercy was the one, she knew, filled with patients who had no insurance, patients who were stabbed by a family member, patients dropped off at the emergency room by cars that stopped for only a few seconds, then kept going. But it was the closest, and maybe once there, Rebecca's doctor would come.

The black truck screeched out of the congested lot as Carlos gripped the wheel tightly, stealing a glimpse at Rebecca every few seconds. "I will call Mr. King when we get there, tell him to come. You tell doctor what is wrong. She will be all right. They just need to wake her. They will know how. Little Rebecca, do not worry. I will get us there. Is going to be all right."

Carlos was speeding but well in control, cutting around a Volkswagen, a station wagon with lumber sticking out of the back window, a van with a crudely painted, menacing-looking Viking holding an over-sized sword. They got on the boulevard and soon reached the Kmart, where, stuck behind cars at a red light, both Carlos and Delores watched a stream of mourners cross in front of them on their way to the train tracks. One woman held a sign that read: "RFK: Never Forget."

Delores repositioned Rebecca so that she could kiss her forehead, and when the light turned and they could move again, Carlos accelerated in such a way that pushed Rebecca hard against her mouth.

"I go fast as I can," he said, as a way of apology. "It won't be long now. Is going to be okay. Everything will."

One of the porters who had delivered ice to Lionel's snack car had reported that Rosey Grier was in one of the cars "bawling like a baby," though he had said it without judgment. Big Rosey was a hero to most of the porters, and they had all taken comfort in learning that he was one of the ones who had caught the gunman.

Inside Lionel and Big Brass's car, the mood continued to be subdued, though both men observed, now that the trip was clearly going to take so much longer than planned, the male passengers loosening their ties slightly and trying to move their mouths away from set frowns. The men with the press tags around their necks wrote in their notepads, and sometimes they stopped and talked to each other or pointed out the window to a sign or someone hanging off a bridge for a better glimpse. Lionel took Big Brass's cues on everything, including Big

Brass's own hushed demeanor.

"Understand, this ain't like no other day," he whispered to Lionel. "You see me being solemn, and that's what's right for this day. Trip to Savannah or Philly, that's another story. If you're a passenger, I'm going to be your friend. If even for two minutes, while you're waiting for your drink. You'll see. You've got to make them feel like they're your only customer in the world — if you want the tip, that is. And you want the tip. But this day, this is something else. All we can do is get everybody through it."

The long crowds of mourners from state to state felt like they'd been plucked from a dream to Lionel — he'd heard so much about the train that would carry the senator's body, but no one had said much about all the people who would turn out to see it. When no one was ordering anything from the bar, he and Big Brass stole glances out the window behind them. There were flag patrols and Boy Scouts, nuns and bikers, crowds huddled under express ramps and in long green fields where families held hands, the women sometimes weeping as they waved. There were girls in two-piece bathing suits and men who had worked themselves into their old military uniforms stored in the closet and held a crisp salute as the train went past. There was a family of seven that had lined up according to height.

A week earlier, Lionel's father had read a newspaper article about a recent Kennedy rally and collapsed the paper noisily against his lap. That meant that whoever was in the room was supposed to stop what he or she was doing and listen.

"This is going to be the first chance you get to vote for the president," he said to Lionel, who was sitting on the couch and had put down his sketch pad with some irritation. "And I don't know if I've lived through a more important election than this one."

Lionel admitted that was true.

"You cast your vote for Bobby Kennedy, and you're casting your vote for the whole Negro race," he said. "Bobby Kennedy is all we've *got* right now."

Lionel turned away from the window and shook his head at Big Brass in marvel. He hadn't followed Kennedy's campaign the way he wished he had; after Dr. King was shot down, he had mostly tuned out the news and retreated into his drawings and notebooks when he wasn't preparing for the semester's final exams. But since Kennedy's assassination, his parents had watched the nightly news accounts for hours at a time and read aloud the stories in the newspapers, and they kept talking to Lionel about what all this likely meant for the country — and how profoundly the country might have changed if Kennedy had gone on to be elected president.

"This right here is Robert Kennedy's America," Big Brass whispered. "These are *working* folks. And he got shot because some people were afraid what he might do. What he *would* do. Same with his brother, same as Reverend King. And seems like that's how it is now in this country — take down the man who wants to help the people who need it the most." Big Brass poured himself a soft drink and held it in his mouth before swallowing. "Makes you wonder how we supposed to go forward. Someone answer me that. How we supposed to keep electing leaders to lead this country if they're just going to get killed every time? Can anyone answer me that?"

A reporter who had paid his respects to Mrs. Kennedy mentioned to Big Brass that she was doing very well, considering. While everyone else around her was falling apart, the reporter said, Mrs. Kennedy was trying to cheer people up. She told a joke to one of her girlfriends that the reporter didn't quite follow, but the point was, she was telling a joke. But Big Brass didn't believe that. That just couldn't be.

Lionel's lower back had turned stiff, and he couldn't remember when he had kept a hat on so long. The work was already monotonous.

Here and there he had time to think about Adanya. He wondered if she looked different somehow, though it had been just three weeks since he had seen her. But women talked about the glow, and if he saw her now, he wondered if he would recognize it. Could anyone else?

They had met the first week of that freshman year. A half-dozen students from his dorm were meeting up with some girls they had met at the first football game, and Lionel's roommate dragged him along to make the numbers work out. They met at a restaurant called Tubby's, Adanya seated in front of him. When Lionel introduced himself, she smiled and pointed to her throat, then shook her head. Lionel didn't understand until the girl next to Adanya put her arm around her and said, "We've been in rush, so we've been singing and shouting all week, the way they make you do. And Adanya lost her voice *completely.* They haven't made their selections yet, and she's worried no one is going to pick her because she can't say anything. But I told her they wouldn't turn such a cute face down." The girl then reached over and squeezed Adanya's cheeks before Adanya playfully slapped her away.

"Well, at least you know you won't end up saying the wrong thing," Lionel said. Adanya smiled, and as Lionel talked for the rest of the dinner, she kept on smiling. He asked her questions she could answer by shaking her head, and then for fun he asked her questions she couldn't answer that way. When he asked her what she planned to major in, she pantomimed playing the piano — she was a music major. When he asked her where she was from, she pointed to the floor. It took him a while to understand that she was from right there in Winston-Salem.

Within a few weeks they were spending all their time together, and he had already been fed twice at her parents' dinner table. In the evenings she would play piano in one of the music hall practice rooms, and he would bring his books or his art pad and sit in the corner of the cramped room and draw his characters. Lionel was planning to introduce what would be the first black superheroes in comics. His favorite creation was Reginald Warman, aka Black Justice, who had no superhuman powers to speak of but had trained as a detective and won international weight-lifting competitions; he was kicked out of the force by a corrupt white police chief who was caught by Warman taking payoffs from the city's most notorious gangsters. The police chief planted drugs in Warman's locker as a way to get him locked up, but this costly mistake gave birth to Black Justice, and Black Justice had been a thorn in the chief's side ever since, always apprehending the criminals before the chief's inept police force could. Black Justice's calling card, which he had pinned onto a suit jacket of one of the criminals he left piled in a heap for the police to arrest, was a black X made of iron.

Lionel had reams of characters with intricate biographies and stacks of notebooks that charted their current visual incarnation. Adanya liked hearing Lionel chronicle their stories — some written down, many still forming in his mind, though she had no particular interest in comics. She admired him for wanting to do something no one else had been able to do, for his conviction that there was a place in such a white-dominated business for him and his characters. That spring semester, they became pinned, and sometimes they laughed at how

283

ludicrously secure they felt in their relationship, in each other. The plan was that they would wait to get married until after graduation, and the idea of children hovered out there on the horizon, real but plenty far away. She wanted to come to New York and, like her mentor, Alice Coltrane, start playing with New York jazz musicians on the scene. And with the two major comics publishers, Marvel Comics and DC Comics, based there, New York was the natural place for him as well.

But now there was a baby. Adanya could have the baby, he figured, and eventually return to classes while her mother watched over the child. But they would have to be married for her parents to support them in any way, and in any case, they would have to live with Adanya's family until graduation. He liked both her parents well enough, though they were much more traditional and conservative than his own, and their house was small; it was impossible to envision all five of them living there and his not feeling miserable. Or, Lionel wondered, would Adanya possibly consider putting the baby up for adoption? Maybe they could talk about all the options in some reasonable way.

On his break Lionel read her letter once

more, the whiff of perfume still faintly on the page, despite how many times he had opened and closed it. He studied the little heart she made at the bottom, plump and radiating. Since they'd been dating, her hearts had improved measurably.

Lionel rejoined Big Brass, who was due his own break now.

"You think you're ready to handle the bar for a little bit, rook?" Big Brass asked him. "I was going to take five." As the trip had extended, more passengers were coming into the snack car, and a few had asked Big Brass for drinks Lionel had never heard of. There was a list of drinks and their ingredients under the bar, but it looked at least twenty years old, with the type badly faded, the paper worn so thin that it wouldn't survive another folding.

"Yes, sir, take your time," Lionel said, too confident to be convincing, but Big Brass moved behind him and clapped him on the shoulder. They were approaching a packed station platform, and the conductor slowed the train to a speed so halting, it felt like it was being pushed by crew members. From his window Lionel caught a glimpse of the crowd: most were so slick with perspiration that they looked as if they had just stepped out of a rain shower, but they were suddenly

285

revived by the train's arrival. As the train went past, the crowd surged all at once as several police officers shouted their gruff warnings about getting too close.

The snack car was filled with smoke, which had begun to irritate Lionel's eyes, but maybe he would get used to this, too. The men with the press tags around their necks talked casually to men Big Brass had told him were senators and congressmen, but it was clear these were not conversations that would make their way into the next day's paper. The reporters ordered the most drinks. The air conditioner had remained broken, and with each state the train passed through, the reporters' ties became more open at the throat.

A man in a dark suit, with a face not much wider than the knot of his tie, entered the car and moved purposefully to the bar. "Mrs. Kennedy would like a Coke," the man said brusquely. The request hit Lionel like an electric jolt. How much ice did she like? Should he send along what was left in the can? Lionel tried to steady himself and poured slowly. When he handed the man the drink, the man stuffed two dollar bills into the tip jar.

Lionel wondered if it was possible for him to go to the last car, before the coffin was unloaded at Union Station, and steal a glimpse — at least for his father. This was too risky, he knew, and he wasn't going to ask, but until Big Brass was back from his break, it was nice to try to imagine how he could do it.

WASHINGTON

Inside Union Station they were all stretched along the platform of track 17. The man behind Maeve had his arm pressed against the middle of her back, and the woman next to her was pushed squarely against her shoulders. That woman was getting the occasional report from the man next to her and told Maeve that the train was even further off schedule. It was only puttering through Delaware now.

Sometimes there was a sudden, violent surge of movement, pushing Maeve and those around her almost off their feet. The air was as heavy as wet laundry, but if Maeve pushed her way through, back up to the main hall to quench her thirst, she knew she would never get her place back. As it was, her position in the crowd didn't seem half bad. She was fifteen feet from the platform's edge, toward the end.

"It's so hard on the legs, and I'm *used* to

288

being on my feet the whole day," the woman next to Maeve said. Around her dull blond hair, she wore a kerchief which mostly matched the scarlet shade of her lipstick.

Maeve nodded vaguely. For the last couple of hours she had mostly avoided attempts at conversation, but it was occurring to her that this was probably only making the time go by that much more slowly.

"Are you here by yourself?" the woman asked.

Maeve said she was.

"My sister was supposed to come, but she decided to drive up to Maryland because she thought she would have a better view. She was smart."

Maeve smiled.

"They're just lining the tracks the whole way, the reports say," the woman said. "Sometimes it's miles at a time. It's amazing. It's a real tribute."

" 'Tis," Maeve said.

"Where are you from, if I may ask?" said the woman.

"I live in Boston," Maeve said. "But I'm originally from Ireland."

The woman's face brightened. "You drove all this way from Massachusetts? My, I'm impressed." She tugged on her kerchief, trying to straighten it but only making it more lopsided.

"Actually, I was already here — on vacation, really."

"I see. My husband and I honeymooned in Boston," the woman said.

Maeve smiled once more.

"He was home on leave — this was during World War Two," the woman went on, grateful for the occasion to talk. "He had two weeks, and we didn't know each other very well at all. We had gone on a few dates the prior year, in 1942. And he was called up. We exchanged some letters, nothing — the way I saw it — too serious. I did send him a picture because he had asked for one, but it wasn't anything glamorous. My mother had a picture of me out in the yard washing our dog. I sent it to him without thinking anything of it. He always said that picture was what sealed it. When he came home on leave — we lived in Rhode Island then — he had arranged to have dinner, and it was all candle lights and a nice booth. And wine. And before the check could come, he had gotten down on his knee and proposed. And that was that. He wanted to be married right away, before he went back, and that's what we did. We eloped and drove the two hours to Boston for nearly a week — stayed at a little inn in Beacon Hill. And then he shipped off, just like that. Just like I knew he had to."

Maeve looked into the woman's eyes, then said, "That must have been hard, having to be apart so quickly like that."

"Oh, I never saw him again," the woman said. "No, he was killed in Normandy. About three months later."

"My goodness!" Maeve said. "Oh. So tragic."

"That it was," the woman said, and she showed a smile that made clear there were no more tears for him. "But it was happening to so many young men. It was a long time ago. And yet." The woman stopped and brought her husband back into her mind once more. His hair was dark, with a little cowlick in the front that she played with constantly that one week together. One of his teeth had been chipped in a fight when he was a teenager, and she followed along the uneven bottom of it with her finger, the sharp edge like a broken shell. One of his eyes was blue, the other green, and when they married she wondered if she ever would get used to that. It was as if he were two men in the same body. She remembered the way he looked leaning down for his duffel bag at the airport on their last day together. He sucked in his lip, like a child determined not to cry.

"Yes, a long time ago," she said. "I've been in Washington for twenty years." Ordinarily, she might have stopped there, but going back to being silent was too much for the woman to consider. "I work as a tour guide at the Capitol. Taking visitors through the House chamber and the Senate chamber, the interior galleries, through the rotunda. Narrating the history. I've been there for sixteen years now."

The Capitol was a world away from holding babies and changing diapers and singing little nonsense songs to lull them into their naps, and suddenly Maeve felt a little foolish. "Did you ever get to meet Senator Kennedy, then?" she asked.

"I did get to meet him once, yes," the woman said. "Just about a year ago. Before he entered the race. He was standing by himself, just outside the Senate chamber. There was about to be a vote, and he was standing almost like a nervous schoolboy, almost like he had to work up the nerve to go inside. I was between tours, and I just walked over to him. I explained that I worked there, and he wanted to know all about what I did, how long I had been here, and he told me his favorite painting in the Capitol, which he said was *Westward the*

Course of Empire Takes Its Way, by Emanuel Leutze. Said he liked the sense of 'manifest destiny' of it — I'll always remember that. He was exceptionally charming. Talking to me like I was the only person in the world."

"That's wonderful," Maeve said. Her legs felt rubbery, her shoulders pulled to the ground. She tried to bend her knees, and that was the last thing she remembered before everything went dark.

MARYLAND

Despite his deadline, Roy had stayed for the train because he was sure the scene in their backyard would give him some powerful image, some metaphor to work with: Jamie's war injury seen against the body of the man who was likely to have been the next president, who might have ended the war. Jamie surrounded by family, the Kennedy family possibly gathered around the casket. Roy was trying to write the lead paragraph in his mind when the rumble of the train's locomotive engine announced its arrival. Everyone on the Wests' back lawn jumped to their feet and rushed to the edge of the tracks, except Ellie, who waited for Jamie to get his crutches under his arms. As he moved to join the others, she ran her hand over his back and said, "Well, here we go." Next door, the two Wilkinson boys had mostly fallen apart waiting for the train, and their mother was inside putting them down to bed. But now she came running out, as if the train were returning her husband from Vietnam.

Miriam stood next to Roy and wrapped her arms around herself. "Oh God, oh God," she whispered, and her eyes swelled with tears, though to Roy she seemed to be willing herself to cry. Mr. West took off his Baltimore Orioles cap and placed it over his heart. As the train crossed in front of them, Roy noticed that Sutton held his hand in a crisp and well-practiced salute. Next to him, Jamie put all his weight on one crutch and held the other one aloft — still, as if he were holding a flag. His chin jutted out, the way it did in his senior portrait in the Burton yearbook.

As the first cars rushed by them, Miriam suddenly dropped to her knees. Roy quickly bent down and put his arm around her shoulder, and he was surprised at how quickly she moved into him. He said, "It's all right," though she couldn't hear him. He could feel Mrs. West turning her gaze toward them, but he could not take his eyes off the train. When the car bearing Robert Kennedy's body sailed past them, Roy was surprised to feel a fierce desire to pull Miriam even closer against him, to kiss her damp cheeks. But he knew it was really just Claire he was thinking of.

WASHINGTON

"There you are," said a voice.

Maeve was lying down on a low-slung cot, next to a few others similarly spilling over the small frames. She felt dizzy and couldn't be sure she wasn't dreaming. The man's voice wasn't Irish, but it reminded her of her father, the surprise in it, the tenderness. "Where am I?" she asked. "What happened?"

"Well, first of all, you're just fine," said the man. He wore a white coat, and his hair was a nearly perfect match in color. "Fine now, that is. You're in the station's first aid room. You fainted. But lucky for you, you fell right into the arms of the woman next to you, so no head bump. But don't feel bad. You're hardly the only one to have fainted out there. The heat, the hours of standing, especially with the long delay. I wonder if you've eaten anything."

"Just breakfast," Maeve said, and she sat

up, which made her even woozier.

"Easy now," he said. "I'm Dr. Rayburn, by the way. I'm on loan, so to speak. I work over at Georgetown Hospital. How about we give you a little orange juice, just to get some sugar into you."

Maeve nodded and took a paper cup from the nurse, whose starched white cap looked like it might topple off. "Thank you," Maeve said, and took two long sips. "I've never fainted before."

"It's nothing to worry about," the doctor said. "It's your body's way of just shutting down if it's too weak or your brain isn't getting enough oxygen. There can be a few factors, but I suspect it's the heat and the lack of food. You're not hypoglycemic, are you?"

Maeve didn't know what that meant, but she shook her head no.

"It takes a little time to get your full energy back. And I want to see you standing up first and trying a little walking before I let you go." He then attended to a man who had possibly broken his ankle.

"Did someone bring me over?" Maeve asked the nurse. "Is the woman I fell into still here?"

"You were brought through on a stretcher," the woman said with the cheer of someone describing a shooting star.

"My goodness," Maeve said.

"Your purse is right there," the nurse pointed out.

Maeve put her feet on the ground and lifted them a couple of times to test her strength.

"How does that feel?" asked the nurse, who was as plump as a pumpkin.

"Fine enough, I guess," Maeve said. "So has the train already come, then?"

"Still on its way," the nurse said. "It won't get here until dark at this point. Some people were killed in New Jersey along the way, and they've just really slowed it down."

Maeve's mind felt too cloudy to ask what she meant, or maybe she hadn't heard correctly. But she shook her head in an appropriate recognition of such news. She then took a few steps away from the cot and circled around.

"You're looking better — in the face," the nurse said. "You've got some blood back in your cheeks."

"Oh."

"Well?" the doctor asked.

"Okay," Maeve said. "A little weak."

"You should eat something. There are places in the station, and the sooner the better. Take another few minutes, make sure you're strong enough. And no fighting your way back into that crowd. Do you have someplace where you can go and rest? Are you anywhere close by?"

"The Churchill Hotel," Maeve said.

The doctor shook his head to indicate that he didn't know it, but the nurse let out a coo of satisfaction. "Would you believe my husband was the concierge there for a long time? Until about two years ago. It's such a lovely hotel."

"Your husband was the concierge?" Maeve asked.

The nurse put her hand to Maeve's forehead. "Your skin is dry now, too. You were very clammy before. Yes, for nearly fifteen years. He loved it there. They have a colored man who took over for him. They say he's very nice, but I haven't been back in since Ralph died."

"I'm sorry," Maeve said.

"Thank you," the nurse said. "Well, I'm sure they'll take good care of you over there. Now do you have cab fare? You really shouldn't be walking or even taking a bus. What you want to do is just climb into one of their comfortable beds and take it easy."

Maeve agreed. She put her purse around her shoulder and turned to thank the doctor, who was still kneeling over the man's ankle. "Take it slowly," he called out to her.

"Yes. I will."

The nurse walked alongside Maeve to the exit, her thick fingers on the small of Maeve's back. "Yes, the Churchill was a big part of our lives. That's so interesting that you're staying there, of all the places in Washington."

"The concierge there now is very good," Maeve said. "I think your husband would have been pleased with how well he does."

"Oh, that's nice to hear," the nurse said, and she could see her husband again putting on his blue blazer in front of their bedroom mirror, the Churchill insignia over his breast, the fringes of his hair still damp.

The nurse gave Maeve's back a little pat. "I'm sure he would have," she said.

Maryland

Ellie walked Roy out to his car. She had been quiet since the train had passed, and he wondered if she had disapproved of his attempt to comfort Miriam. Now, as he fished for his car keys, the sound of loose change in his pocket was startlingly loud.

"It's been a real pleasure, Mrs. West," he said. "I know it's been a sobering day with the funeral train, and I want to thank you for letting me spend so much time with your family, and for being so generous."

"Jamie has good days," she said, "and sometimes he has days where I know he's struggling. On days like that — like today — I really see his hurt so clearly. And as his mother, I will never be able to make that hurt go away. That's what is so painful for me."

"Yes, ma'am." They stood there for a time, both swatting at gnats. Finally, Roy said, "I may well call you tonight, if that's all right.

If there's anything I'm not sure that I have exactly right, I'll call to verify it with you."

"You know, Claire cast a spell on all of us. When they broke up, we all really missed her. Deeply. I suppose I really had come to think of her as my own daughter in some way, even though they were both so young, and I never really imagined they would stay together always. But when she was gone, I grieved for her in a way that I would have never let Jamie know about. Even Joe never really understood, I don't think, what she had brought to us, our home. And your being here today has brought all of that back. How things used to be, how much simpler and innocent."

Roy smiled, or tried to. "Well, thank you again," he said, and he stuck out his hand. But Ellie leaned in to hug him instead. She put her hand around his neck and put her chin over his shoulder and held him like that.

"We'll look forward to reading the article," she said in a choked voice, and then, willing herself to believe, she added, "and on this day we'll try to remember those whose struggles are greater than our own."

During her father's wake, Maeve's uncle, Colum, did his best to entertain. In the next room, Larney was stretched out on the dining room table, his hands folded over a rosary and resting on top of his good blue suit. While Colum told stories about the troubles he and Larney got into when they were boys, Maeve sat a few feet from her father, shaking her head at how unskilled Colum was as a storyteller. He would get ahead of himself, then, when trying to backtrack, he would ask, "Wait — did I already explain how we got there?" If someone laughed, he would turn and insist, "But that's not the best part." But generally there were no best parts to his stories.

The drunker Colum got, the harder he tried to keep the mood festive, until Maeve's mother finally put her arm around his shoulder and said, "Let's leave it at that, then, Colum." Then she said to anyone who was listening, "My husband is dead, and I will be, too, if I have to hear any more of that."

Her father's mouth looked particularly slack, Maeve thought, and it saddened her that he would be buried with such a frown. She wondered if she pushed his lips upward whether they would droop back down, and she started to move toward him when her mother came in and sat next to her.

"He always looked good in that suit," she said. Maeve nodded that that was true.

"If I turned my back on your father for a second, he was always off somewhere. If I was setting the table, then he remembered he was supposed to meet the boys at the pub. If I said I needed firewood, he would forget the bundle we had out back and head into the woods with his ax. Be gone for two hours, he would. And now he's done it again. And how am I supposed to manage this time, Larney? Hmmm? I'm asking you that much. How will we get by this time?"

She put her face in her hands and rocked back and forth. Maeve put her hand on her mother's shoulder and she was surprised when her mother leaned into her. Her mother smelled of baking soda, and there were coarse, wiry strands of gray shooting out from her unraveling bun at the center of her scalp. Maeve pulled her closer in and took over the rhythm of their rocking, slower now, not back so far against the chair. "There we are," Maeve said after a moment, and she felt like she was cradling a gigantic baby. She put her lips to her mother's forehead, the way she often did with her sisters when they were upset or had hurt themselves. "I know," she whispered in her mother's ear.

That was the last time they had touched like that, Maeve was remembering on the cab ride back to the hotel. She had been trying to decide if she would even tell her mother about trying to see the senator's casket. There wasn't much point, she figured, since it had ended in failure.

Maeve thought she should feel more foolish for fainting than she did, but in some ways, the fainting had brought a kind of relief. Seeing Robert Kennedy's casket might have just compounded the misery of it all. Part of that misery — the part that was selfish — was an increasing certainty that there wouldn't be any more contact from the Kennedy family. If she had ended up working for the Kennedy family, Maeve would have been so busy with so many children around that no one would have even thought to consider her life outside work.

"So how do you like Washington?" the cabdriver asked. He had been looking in the rearview mirror a few too many times for Maeve's taste, and he had taken half the drive to work up his nerve to start a conversation. He wasn't much older than she, if at all, and his voice was so full that it sounded like he was speaking through a cabinet speaker.

"It's beautiful," she said without enthusiasm.

"Sure. Of course, it's a lot less beautiful right now. The city really got torn apart back in April. That was madness."

He looked back at her in his mirror, hoping he could go on. "I was working the night of the riots. I had parked on the street and was getting a little dinner, and while I was eating, my cab got blown up. Got hit with a Molotov cocktail. Boom! Everyone inside had to run out the back, and we just kept on running. Running for our lives. Just crazy."

Maeve looked out at the tranquil downtown streets — the young men whose faces beamed slightly from razor burn and who were anticipating an evening of buying drinks for women in miniskirts; the tourists who hadn't expected their children to be so depleted from a day of walking and who now carried them collapsed over their shoulders. "You were quite fortunate, then," she said at last.

The driver thought about that. "I mean, I'm sure I'll get drafted — it's kind of a miracle I haven't so far. But here I am ducking bombs and I'm still in *Washington?*" He realized that he had veered into a rant and tried to recover. "That was a real crowd back at Union Station. You're not just arriving, though? I noticed you didn't have any luggage."

"Maybe you're noticing too much, then." She flashed a hint of a smile before she could suppress it.

"Maybe," the driver said, but he saw some promise in her expression in his mirror. In the shadows of the backseat he could see the fine angle of her jaw as she turned away. "Maybe. So are you here visiting someone?"

They drove another block in silence, and he could barely look at the traffic in front of them as he waited for whatever else she might say.

"If you must know," Maeve said, and she found just the right note of resigned anticipation, "I'm meeting my husband."

New Jersey

Michael and his mother were sitting on their porch swing. He had been quiet since he got home — quieter than any other day since his return, but she had refrained from asking too many questions. Besides, sitting out on the porch was his idea, and that tempered her concern. For dinner she had fixed flank steak and the frozen French fries he liked, and now they were working on two orange Popsicles from the icebox, their slurping sounds helping to drown out a low chorus of crickets hidden in the grass that needed mowing.

The sun had dipped almost out of view and had left the sky resembling a scoop of rainbow sherbet, Michael thought, but he was content to think it without saying so to his mother.

"We'll have to go to the movies sometime soon," she said.

Michael nodded. "Yep."

She absently let her hand touch his hair. He often moved closer when she did this — for his whole life he had believed there was no better sensation than feeling his mother's nails draw little circles across his scalp — but she could feel a rigidness to his body now.

"Yeah, that will be good," she said. "I've missed my movie partner."

Michael nodded and closed his eyes.

"I was so worried about you," she said, and she was embarrassed that her voice had cracked. There was no mistaking it. Michael kept his eyes closed, but he didn't mind about the crack. It was all right if she needed to cry. This was their swing, their porch, their house. No one was going to tell them what they could or couldn't do.

"Here we are, Maggie-McDunnough-just-one-drink-I-don't-believe-in-wearing-a-ring." The cabdriver brought two glasses of Irish whiskey — an order he had first thought to be clever but now lamented as unoriginal — to their corner table. He had hoped that the bar, which he frequented several times a week, would be quieter, since she didn't seem like someone who would be willing to raise her voice to be heard, but it was a Saturday night, and he had little reason to be surprised by the raucous crowd. And he was pleased for the people he knew here — already he had spotted a lot of the regulars — to catch sight of him with a woman so striking. They would, he was sure, ask him about the dark-haired beauty later that week.

Maeve took the glass and swirled the liquor around while looking past his shoulder, as was her habit with men who showed any interest in her. He studied the long, elegant slope of her nose and considered how close he could lean forward. "So you say you like Washington so far, then," he said. She had barely said anything to him since getting into his cab, and he knew enough that if he said anything much duller, she was going to insist he take her on to the hotel.

"I do," she said, and took her first sip, which burned her throat more than she had imagined. Maeve generally took a dim view of alcohol — mostly because she had rarely been around people whose company didn't greatly deteriorate with drinking.

"Well, like I said, I probably won't be here much longer," said the driver, whose name was Steve, though recently he liked to introduce himself as Vincent. He was finishing an adult education art class and had developed some affinity for Vincent van Gogh. "I'm sure I'm going to get called over. And who knows? If I survive, maybe it'll give me some rich experiences to draw on. I'm an artist, so I might get my horizons expanded being in a foreign country like that."

"And what sort of artist would you be?" Maeve asked. He watched her drink more of her whiskey and could feel the time expiring with every sip. Even if she really was married, which he didn't believe, she *had* given in to having a drink, and that let him hope for at least a slim chance with her.

"I like oils," he said, a rare answer of brevity that he thought made him sound self-assured. But when her face didn't reveal the barest hint of being impressed, he added, "Yeah, I like painting street scenes, portraits — I do a lot of portraits. That's probably my forte. I haven't sold a lot yet, but I haven't really put a lot of time into the whole commercial racket of it — selling for money. Working with dealers. I like just really focusing on the purest aspects of it — trying to capture a person's soul, their whole being, just letting that come through on the canvas." He had only completed four paintings: a picture, from memory, of a collie he had as a boy; a portrait of a girl he dated for two weeks; a portrait of a girl he dated for one week; and a self-portrait in his yellow taxi.

"So you're the starving-artist type — is that it, then?" Maeve said. "Drive around a taxi while you nurse your talents?"

He couldn't tell if she was mocking him. "Pretty much," he said. "Painting, making a little bread how I can, studying the greats, just trying to grow as an artist."

He nodded at someone he recognized in an exaggerated tipping back of the head. "So do you like any particular artists or styles? Modern? Expressionism?"

Maeve took another sip — two more, he noticed, and her glass would be empty. "I'm not very well versed," she said. "I wouldn't know how to talk about what I like, really."

"Do you like van Gogh?" he asked — too eagerly.

"Maybe," Maeve said. "What's a famous work of his?"

"A lot of his self-portraits are really well-known," he said. "He painted a lot of fields of flowers. You'd recognize them, I'll bet. I can't think of the names. But I don't really paint flowers too much. I like painting people."

"Yes, you said *capturing* people. Let me ask you a silly question. Why would anyone want to do that? What do you do with that, capturing a soul? You have to be really interested in people to do that sort of thing, I would imagine. Maybe that's why I'm not much of a connoisseur. I don't much like art with people in it."

She seemed engaged for the first time, he thought, and he wanted to offer an intellectual response. He looked up at the light fixture to give the impression of sorting through any number of complex theories on the matter; he was trying to remember something from the two chapters he had read from a biography on van Gogh that he had checked out from the library, but the early pages had dealt mostly with the painter's childhood.

"Why don't you like people in paintings?" he said. "I've never heard anyone say that before. Is that because you're only into abstracts? Like Jackson Pollock?"

Maeve shook her head. "I guess I find portraits a bit intrusive," she said. "A bit *too* intimate, or personal."

"But that's the whole point," he said, smiling like a schoolchild who finally knew an answer. "You *want* the intimacy. You want it to be personal. That's what I was saying earlier. You want the whole person to come through. Yeah, intimate."

Maeve shrugged. "Oh, well. That's why I don't much fancy it."

His mouth began to droop. "Huh." He tried to think of a different point of view to offer when he saw that she had finished her glass.

"Well, my husband will wonder what's keeping me," she said. The lies she had told him were easy, but she couldn't help feeling a little exhilarated by the old pleasure of them. Part of her wanted to sit there for the rest of the night and build more intricate stories, layer upon layer, but she was still feeling a little light-headed and fragile.

"Okay," he said in a mournful bass note. "I guess we can't keep him waiting." He felt for the car keys in his pocket. "What does your husband do, anyway? Is he some kind of Irish diplomat or something?"

"He's a writer," Maeve said. "And thank you for the drink."

They worked their way up from the table, and as they walked out the door he saw that the bartender's eyes were fixed on Maeve. That should have lifted Steve's spirits, and he could still have offered the bartender a sly smile that suggested he'd have plenty to fill him in on next time, but he felt too defeated for that.

Once back in the cab, he glanced in the rearview mirror and said, "So I don't guess you've ever let anyone paint your portrait before?"

"No, no. Not at all," she said. She almost laughed at the idea, it was so absurd. After a couple of turns she saw that he was back to watching her in the mirror.

"Yeah, I figured," he said. "I was just curious." The car turned a corner, and Maeve could see the outline of her hotel.

316

"So what does your husband write, exactly?"

"As a matter of fact," she said, "all of his books are about people. The things they do, the things they say. They're" — she waited for the right word to fall — "intimate. They're all very intimate."

PENNSYLVANIA

Delores and Arch were on either side of Rebecca's hospital bed. She was surrounded by so much equipment that she looked tiny, like one of her dolls. Occasionally one of the monitors, connected to her body by thick, gray cords, beeped or chirped, and they would turn their gaze in alarm to the bank of equipment, not knowing which of the pieces had sounded, or why.

The doctor had explained that there was swelling on Rebecca's brain, but he was less concerned about that than the fluid buildup in her lungs. What he said about her unconsciousness was less clear to them, but as he spoke Delores kept looking down at Rebecca. Her face was exceptionally pale, and the tube down her throat had left her thin lips white and dry. Every time the doctor finished a thought, Delores looked down at Rebecca and smiled, as if to reassure her that these were all good things they were hearing.

They were uncertain how much longer they could remain in the room. Visiting hours were over in a few minutes — at nine o'clock — as one of the nurses had said earlier, but were parents considered visitors? They hadn't thought to ask. Delores couldn't imagine stepping away for anything besides getting a Coke from the machine around the corner, and the waiting room down the hall might as well have been the next town over. She didn't know when the doctor would be back to check on Rebecca, or whether he would do so again until the morning, unless her condition changed. She should have asked him about that, she thought now. Her mind felt emptied out, as if someone had turned her upside down, like a purse. All she and Arch had been able to manage was to nod and say thank you whenever the doctor or nurse came in. She hoped that Arch better understood everything they had been told.

Arch hadn't asked much about the accident itself, and it was clear now that Delores's version of the day would get no further scrutiny. She had explained that she called Carlos about the tire only because she knew how busy Arch was on Saturday, and hearing this he had simply shaken his head in agreement.

"You hungry?" Arch asked. "I don't know what they have in the cafeteria. Cafeteria food. But I can go get you something, if you want."

"No, you go. I can't eat."

Arch didn't move. "You know, the last time we were in the hospital, she was seven pounds, eleven ounces. Seven-eleven. That was always easy to remember."

"She came right out, didn't she? About an hour of pushing, and *whoosh.*" Delores's mouth began to quiver, and Arch reached over and held her hand. With her other hand Delores gripped her face.

"Hey, hey, she's going to make it through this, Delores," Arch said. He squeezed until Delores could look at him. "She's going to wake up. They think she's going to."

"If I had brought her to the doctor right away, she wouldn't be like this. We wouldn't be here." Delores had kept circling back to this point, and each time Arch tried a variation to the same response. There was something almost soothing about the repetition of it, like the way the nurse kept coming in to check Rebecca's vitals, or the constant paging of another doctor over the floor intercom.

"It's nobody's fault, D," Arch said. "Children fall. Children have accidents." Then he added: "And sometimes parents have to bring them to the hospital."

For a time they listened to the low drone of the machinery in the room, and then Delores thought to ask, "What do the boys know?"

"I told Mama to just tell them that they want to keep her overnight, just to watch her, and that I'd bring them over if she's still here after the morning. So that's what I'll do."

Across the hall, they could hear two nurses complaining about a doctor's handwriting.

"Her doll is still in our car," Delores said. "I wish she had it with her."

"We'll get it," Arch said.

"She pretended that the doll had gotten hurt, and she was taking care of her."

"I'll pick it up."

Delores gripped Rebecca's hand and got to her feet, hovering just a few inches from Rebecca's face. One of the nurses across the hall was telling someone that visiting hours were almost over.

"We're right here, Rebecca," Delores said, and then she heard the nurse knock on the door in the next room over.

"His color looks so much better than it did this morning," they could hear the nurse saying. "I think the doctor is going to be surprised that you've been on your feet like that. You're already ready to leave us, aren't you, Mr. Miller?" Mr. Miller, in a fatigued hum, said that he was.

Arch stood up and reached over to put his hand against Rebecca's cheek. He began to speak but stopped himself; his face caved in all at once.

The nurse had shuffled over in her sensible shoes. She knocked lightly on the door. "Visiting hours are just about over, I'm afraid." Arch's body stilled immediately, as if he'd been caught at something.

Arch and Delores looked at each other, each searching for some response they could offer. "But we're her parents," Arch said at last.

"I know it's hard," said the nurse, who had found in her sixteen years as a nurse that there was no reply more effective. "And we're going to take good care of her."

The bell of the elevator down the hall rang through. It was the only pleasant sound produced in the entire building.

The three of them stood there, not moving, until the nurse stepped out; she'd be back in a few minutes to lead them out.

Arch reached across the bed and put his hand on Delores's shoulder, patting, squeezing some more. Delores nodded, as if he had said something neither of them had thought of, something wise and reassuring.

In the hallway, one of the nurses said to another, "I still have to get trained in that," which reminded Delores of Ethel and the train for the first time in hours. That morning, Delores had asked, "How in the world is she supposed to get through this?" Angela had replied, "She's a Kennedy," and in that she was communicating some truth that only women could understand.

Despite everything Arch had said and done from the minute he had arrived, she had never felt so alone. The thought of stepping into the house with Arch and the boys, without Rebecca, made her feel nauseated, and she leaned back into the chair. That was when she caught sight of the wheels on the bed. She couldn't block out the image of Rebecca being pushed quickly from hallway to hallway, a sheet pulled over her face, and the multitudes of nurses and visitors stepping out of the way, their backs pushed against the white walls, their eyes cast downward at the speckled tile floor as a tribute to the dead in the only way they could offer.

"You okay?" Arch asked, but Delores couldn't answer. She knew without looking that the nurse was standing in the doorway, but not yet ready to speak. She was waiting. They were all waiting.

NEW YORK

When the train pulled into Union Station, it was separated into two. The tangled mass of restless mourners watched this with some puzzlement; a deep-boned fatigue had settled in by now, and despite the arrival of the train, they couldn't yet set aside their crankiness that the train's journey had taken twice the estimated time.

The passengers, who during the long ride had seemed to recover from their early shock and begun to find themselves again, now braced for the equally difficult experience of the burial. As the train came to a stop, the men straightened their ties, and the women checked their compacts only to find that the heat inside the cars had drained away all traces of makeup. The food and drinks had long ago run out, but before the passengers shuffled onto the platform, they still stuffed single bills into the tip jar, and Big Brass had to empty it out again and again in the time it took for the car to empty. They thanked the two porters and shook their hands. Big Brass kept saying "God bless you" to them, and Lionel found he could think of no other line to offer and said nothing. Then the train became unbearably still and quiet, and an exhale from the engine trembled through the cars.

The pallbearers had moved to the last car, with the senator's casket, and at some silent signal they gripped the brass handles and lifted until they had it off the chairs. They had to navigate it with great delicacy out of a window that was removed once the train came to a stop, and more than one shuddered at the idea of hitting a corner and jostling the body of their close friend inside. A slow dirge from the navy band finished its last notes as they stepped onto the platform.

At the sight of the coffin and the morose faces of the men carrying it, the noisy station was reduced to the hush of a museum. The mourners had gotten themselves through the day with conversations about the riots and Nixon and Ethel and the war, and also the shameful job manager Jim Lemon was doing with the Washington Senators and the countdown to the week at Ocean City or Virginia Beach and the challenges of finding a reliable babysitter and Burt Lancaster's performance in *The Swimmer* and the musings of what the Beatles would come up with next. Now they were all jolted back to their gloom, and only the sound of low sobs competed with the still-hissing engine of the train.

President Johnson and Vice President Humphrey were there to meet the train, along with their wives, and were swarmed by a team of Secret Service agents locked together at the shoulder. Police officers helped the crowd slowly open up a path for the pallbearers, a few feet at a time, and though everyone close enough to touch the casket would have remembered doing so all their lives, they knew to refrain. Lenny Carol, forty-seven, an electrician from Arlington, studied the fabric of the flag draped across and wondered if Kennedy could have truly ended the war in Vietnam and whether his son, Lenny Jr., would also arrive in Washington in a coffin covered with the American flag. Ike Benson, twenty-nine, who drove a tow truck in Southeast, thought back to watching his cousin's black-and-white Zenith as Robert Kennedy announced the death of Martin Luther King in Indianapolis, then went on to say, "But the vast majority of white people and the vast majority of black people in this country want to live together . . ." And Ike Benson was still wondering just how true that really was. Evelyn D'Amato, whom Robert McNamara brushed against as he moved past, was a sixty-eight-year-old retired schoolteacher from Adrian, West Virginia. She liked to picture Heaven as a place of picturesque, serene landscapes and imagined Robert Kennedy and his brother John together again, walking along an ocean shore — maybe on their beloved Cape Cod — both men shaking their heads not in sorrow or self-pity, but in concern for what would happen next to their America.

The pallbearers moved off the platform and onto the waiting hearse, parked in the station concourse. Some in the crowd roped off across the street gasped at the sight of the car as it pulled onto the street, then lamented that they had made any sound at all. The hearse motored past the Senate Office Building, where on Robert Kennedy's door a typewritten note read: "Due to the death of our Senator, our offices are today closed to the public. Thank you." The people of Washington lined the route, some of them dotting the tops of buildings, some with candles, and while other parts of the city carried on as they did any other Saturday night, the streets that led to Arlington were as silent as outer space.

Out of all the hundreds of thousands of mourners who had turned out that day, the ones in Washington had most fully imagined some version of this, understanding more than anyone the true cost of politics. Senator Kennedy, it was now clear, had simply asked too much of his country.

There were some who took the smallest comfort in the fact that this time the assassin had not come from within, that he was not someone who looked like their mechanic or their son's football coach or the chatty neighbor down the hall. But for most, none of this mattered. Dead was dead.

The car drove down Constitution Avenue, past the Justice Department, where Kennedy had once worked, then took a brief pause by the Lincoln Memorial, where tourists and residents alike had turned up all day and night, studying Lincoln's troubled gaze for any guidance about how to endure such violence. The hearse continued across Memorial Bridge, and there some young black mourners raised their fists in salute. Seeing this, some young white mourners affected the same gesture, unaware of their mistake.

There had never been a nighttime funeral

at the cemetery, and floodlights had been set up. By the front gate were thousands who had waited for hours to see what they might. After the long procession of cars arrived and the vast crowd had taken its place, Ethel and her children filed delicately toward the gravesite, which was just south of President Kennedy's grave. The Archbishop of Washington spoke quietly into the night air, and then the flag was removed from the coffin and folded into a triangle. First it was given to Ted Kennedy, who then handed it to Joe Kennedy, the eldest son, whose resemblance to his father was, on this day, too much for some to bear. Joe then gave it to his mother. The Harvard University band, whose members had flown in from all over the country to be here, held their instruments as steadily as they could and played "America the Beautiful," which no one thought to question.

Lionel could hear Buster Hayes's loud voice from several cars away.

"All right, all right," he was saying, almost singing to himself. When he reached their car, he said, "Well, the young buck has survived his first day. Put 'er there, young buck," and stuck out his thick hand. "Mr. Trent, how did he get along?"

"Very good, very good," Big Brass said. "Did fine." He began to close up the bar, his arms and hands swirling across the surfaces as if he were motorized. Lionel looked on, unsure how to assist, but Big Brass said, "I'm going to take care of this, son. We'll teach you about cleanup on the ride back. I think what we all want to do is finish up the job right and move on. A train carrying a dead man's body starts to wear on you after a while, and one wants to step out into the night air and still know that he is *alive*. Am I telling the truth, Mr. Hayes?"

"Yes, sir," Hayes said. "A train carrying the dead and causing more to die on the way — it's going to take a while to shake that off. Young buck, you probably don't even know where we're bunked up when we're in Washington. So we'll take you into town and maybe even buy you a drink, if we can find a bartender that will serve that baby face of yours. They caught the man that killed Martin today, and that's worth raising a glass to."

Lionel couldn't imagine getting through the night without talking to Adanya — and Adanya's parents wouldn't like it if he called late. And he knew that no matter how his conversation went with her, it would be difficult to be around a group of strangers, listening to their stories into the night.

"I appreciate that, Mr. Hayes," Lionel said, "but if you just give me the street address, I'll be along before too long. I feel like I need to get out and just do some walking."

He watched Hayes exchange glances with Big Brass. He didn't want them to think that he was above socializing with them.

"Look here," Buster Hayes said. "You don't know Washington, and right now a young Negro can have a very hard time of it here. Do you understand what I'm saying? Parts of this city look like they been *bombed.* And I know what I'm talking about, because I fought in World War Two, and some streets look *worse* than what I saw in France. You got buildings reduced to piles of rubble, buildings burned down to *nothing.* And it's black boys that did all that. So a Negro has got to be careful. All right, look: stay well clear away from Seventh Street Northwest — it's all been torn up to hell. And Fourteenth Street? You don't have no business there right now. And maybe *never.* Other bad parts you're not going anywhere near, unless you were looking for them. Just be smart, and be aware. Do you hear what I'm saying?"

"I'll be careful," Lionel said. Hayes wrote

down the address for the sleeping quarters, and then Lionel picked up his bag and, after a couple of wrong turns inside the station, found his way out onto the street.

Though the sun had gone down an hour ago, the sidewalk still carried some of the day's heat, and as he took a few tentative steps Lionel wondered when he would ever get some relief. Packs of sailors, laughing and slapping one another on the back, stumbled through the street like circus clowns, and one of them bumped straight into a man trying to light his pipe. "Hey, watch it!" the man called out, which made the sailors howl like jackals.

The first order of business was to find a pay phone and hear Adanya's voice. Her parents would likely be home, so there wouldn't be much she could say to him without them hearing, but just as they had on the first night they met, she could answer yes-or-no questions. Was she feeling okay? Did her parents know? Could they talk soon without the worry of them listening to her? Adanya was spending the summer giving piano lessons, and he would need to ask her about that as well. But it would be difficult to pretend anything else was half as important.

Compared with the skyscrapers of New

York, the buildings in Washington looked like they had been cut down at the root. Taxicabs spun around him, but they were quieter than the ones he knew and seemed to have no use for their horns. Eventually he spotted a phone booth, and after a man in a rumpled gray suit finished up his call and stumbled out, Lionel stepped in and fished out Adanya's number. The mouthpiece reeked of beer. Lionel took out a pocketful of coins and pressed them in, and after each one fell, his heartbeat thundered. By the time the phone rang, he could barely breathe.

He let it ring for the length of time it took an elderly man to shuffle across the street and disappear around a corner, then set the phone back on the cradle. It was nearly nine thirty, and perhaps they had gone out, the three of them, to the movies, or maybe there was a potluck dinner at the church. Though his company-issued shoes were cutting into his feet, he decided to walk with no particular destination. He understood that the sleeping barracks were in the southeast part of town and that he would have to catch a taxi at some point, but he was hungry and set out to get a sandwich. He had already developed a strict summer budget for himself, and he would have been content to find a hot dog stand, but the vendors had already closed up and gone home for the night. He walked along Massachusetts Avenue for half a mile before he came across a black police officer on foot, and he asked the man to steer him in the right direction. The officer studied Lionel's uniform for a moment in admiration and encouraged him to walk another two blocks until he came across a Nathan's. The officer understood that Lionel didn't know the city, and he added, "You shouldn't have any problems there."

Lionel walked on, and once he found it, he took notice of two pretty young women waiting outside whose caramel-colored faces shone with makeup. "Ask him," he heard one of the girls say.

"Excuse me, baby," the one in the blue jeans said. "Do you have the time?"

Lionel told them that it was close to ten o'clock.

"They're not coming," the other girl said, letting her shoulders drop. The air around them was heavy with an overly sweet fragrance, and the streetlight bounced off the glossy finish of their lipstick. "There's no way. And I'm not waiting anymore."

Lionel reached for the door when the girl in blue jeans said, "You look like you just getting off work."

"That's right," Lionel said, his hand still on the door.

"You work in a hotel or something?" the girl asked.

Lionel laughed. "No. I work on a train."

"Oh, a train. That's nice. Where you coming from?"

"New York," Lionel said.

"Okay," the girl said. "We've been to New York. We *love* New York. They know how to treat girls right up there. Here they're a bunch of *dogs.*"

The other girl moaned in agreement.

"We were supposed to meet our dates here half an hour ago, but they stood us up. Or something. Had us standing out here as if we don't have anything better to do."

"I'm sorry," Lionel said. The other girl, who was wearing a red halter over a miniskirt and vinyl boots, eased over next to him. She studied Lionel's uniform, smiling as a piece of chewing gum swam across her teeth.

"Saturday night, too," she said. "That ain't right."

"That's too bad," Lionel said.

"Well, we're out now," the girl in blue jeans said. "And it's early. Forget them sorry fools."

"What's your name?" the other girl asked.

"Lionel."

"My *brother's* name is Lionel," she said.

"He don't look like *him,*" the girl in blue jeans said, then laughed. The girl in red was unsure if she could also laugh, then decided she could.

"*You* should take us out instead," the girl in blue jeans said. "We like you better than those two bums anyway."

"But you need a change of clothes," the other one said. "You got a change of clothes in that bag, baby? You don't want to go in looking like you're going to be serving drinks." She let out a throaty laugh.

The bottoms of his feet burned, and his back felt like he had had a tire iron strapped to it. His head was spinning from all that he wanted to talk over with Adanya and also from the endless miles of grief he had seen: the sobbing mothers clutching flowers in one hand and their toddlers' hands in the other; the softball team whose coach had just ordered her players to take off their hats; men on crutches who still hadn't fully comprehended what had happened back in Than Khe and Quang Ngai and Chu Lai.

Just then he saw two men approaching — clad in jeans and bright, silky shirts halfway buttoned, one with a purple comb in the side of his Afro. The other man flicked his

337

friend's shoulder at the sight of the two women and smiled. "I told you, man," he said.

Lionel took this as a good sign.

MARYLAND

Only the weekend editor was still in the office; Roy's story was the last to be typeset, and now Roy was waiting to know what he thought. The weekend editor's nickname, Roy had learned, was Mr. Sigh, because every time anyone gave him copy, the first thing he did, after reading the article and sitting down with the reporter, was to let out a long, deep sigh.

Roy tugged at the knot in his tie and thought about putting his feet up on his desk before deciding against it. He had never spent so many hours reporting a story, and he had never written one so long. He filed it at seventy newspaper inches, although Mr. Sigh had no intention of running it that long. Roy had spent the drive over organizing the piece in his mind, and when he sat down to his Selectric typewriter, he spent the next thirty minutes on the first two paragraphs.

Claire would have appreciated the irony of the whole situation, he thought. Too much time — and too much disappointment — had passed for them to have a sincere laugh over anything, and the fact that it had all happened because Jamie had lost a leg cast a pall over the whole episode, even if he could have told her. She wouldn't have approved of the way Jamie had tried to belittle Roy, but there were always two sides of Claire. That was how she could date Jamie and be just as close to Roy, as different as they were. That was the essence of Claire. It was like Mrs. West had said — she charmed everyone, and you never quite got over her.

But who was Claire's confidante now? Roy wondered. There was probably a slew of sorority sisters with whom she shared her most intimate thoughts and love-life details, and no doubt her fiancé would have been every bit as intolerant of Roy had he and Claire stayed close.

Mr. Sigh came out of his office, his face already set in a show of professional suffering. Roy straightened himself in his chair and waited as the man stood over him, ready to exhale his verdict, ready to teach the young man all the things about crafting a story he still did not know.

The women's voices grew raised and angry.

"Well, we don't wait that long for anyone," the one in blue jeans said, "and now we *have* our date, thank you very much." She looked over to Lionel as if she had known him for a lifetime and took his arm.

"Who is this brother? The motherfucking Good Humor man?" one of the men said. His eyes were wide-set, his purple blouse rippling in the breeze. The other man stepped over and tugged lightly on Lionel's jacket sleeve, then dropped it and cackled.

The other man was bigger than his friend, his neck as thick as a bucket. "This ain't a date. This is the boy that's going to *drive* you *home* after your date."

Lionel knew he had played a part — a minuscule part — in something honorable and historic, and now, just as quickly, here was more of the kind of mindlessness that was making a simple walk in the city these days its own dodgy venture. "This uniform says I've been working on a train, the train carrying Robert Kennedy's dead body from New York," Lionel said, his voice rising with each word. "You fellas know anything about that? Senator running for president, brother of President Kennedy. Was trying to help the black man more than anyone in this country right now."

The two men let their grins dissolve.

The woman in red stepped to the other side of Lionel. "You didn't tell us *that*," she said. "Damn."

"You fools should show some respect," her friend said. "He's got an important job, and what you got?" She began to pull Lionel away when the bigger man took hold of her arm.

"Hold up, hold up there," he said, and tried to soften his expression. "Hold up just a minute there now. We just had a little business that ran late, and that's done, and we made plans with you ladies, and that's why we come out all this way. And here we all are. So let's just put aside this *anger* and get on with the evening. Can we do that? Nate, tip the conductor here for holding our place, and then let's go and have a good time."

At that moment Lionel knew the night

was on a course that he would regret for a long time, that he might remember all his days. It wasn't too late to drop the girls' arms right then and walk in the other direction, but he wasn't raised like that. And as someone who spent his days dreaming up endless ways superheroes dealt with all vestiges of the criminal element, there was a small part of him that wanted to experience how the volatile situation might play out. Plus, there was some question of the ladies' safety. Even if they did relent and go along with these two, would the evening end peacefully for them?

Lionel looked to the women for any cues, but all four seemed to be waiting for what Lionel would say or do next.

"Fellas, look, I'm not even *trying* to take these ladies out, all right?" Lionel began. "What I really want to do is call my *own* girl and then head over to Southeast for the night. So no one is trying to take your dates. But it's pretty clear they don't want to go with you. So let's all leave it at that, and then let's all go our own ways here. Let's just keep it dignified." Lionel exhaled.

"Damn, I thought Dr. King got shot and died in *Memphis* a couple months back, but nah, here he is, preaching good as ever," the thinner man said. "Nate, we brothers rioted

343

for nothing, 'cause Martin Luther right *here.*"

Lionel watched the bigger man, since he figured he would be the first one to act. Did he have a switchblade in his pants pocket? If so, maybe Lionel could use his suitcase to block it, and he could land a punch before striking out at the smaller man.

"This is a waste of our damn time," the woman in blue jeans said to the two men. "Arnelle and I are walking this way, away from all y'all. You want to fight? That don't make a bit of difference to me. Just don't take up my Saturday night!"

She began walking, pausing for a second for Arnelle to catch up. Arnelle made a kissy face to Lionel before ambling off. Lionel was as shocked as he was relieved. Wasn't it obvious that he was trying to defend them? The girls were halfway down the block now, the slap of their heels against the pavement too faint to hear. Lionel picked up his suitcase and shrugged his shoulders, which he meant as a way to say to the two men, simply, "Women!" But he hadn't been able to turn around before the smaller man said, "Brother man, we're not finished here. Where the hell you think you're going like that? What you got — a shoe-shine kit in that bag? You ain't done with work yet."

The larger man nodded thoughtfully, as if his colleague had made an inarguable point. They had already forgotten all about the girls. "He ain't even offered to fluff up our pillows or nothing," he said, and he thought that would draw a bigger response from his friend than it did. But his friend liked to believe that he was the more clever of the two.

Lionel took in everything around them. There was not a steady stream of cars passing by, but whatever was going to happen would take longer than thirty seconds, and enough drivers would surely see the commotion. Whether any drivers would stop and try to do something about it was another matter.

"Reach in that bag of yours and get your kit out, boy," the smaller man said. "We don't have all night."

Lionel nodded once, and he gave off a contemplative expression meant to suggest he was considering which tools would be best suited for the job. It was clear that he would have to hit first — and quickly — if he had any chance of getting away. He bent down, his finger on the zipper of his bag, and glanced up. The men exchanged satisfied glances, though they were also a little amazed that a shoe shine was exactly what

345

they were about to get. Lionel was closer to the big man, and he decided that he'd attack him in the midsection first, since the man was so exposed for the moment. If he could cause him to double over, he'd have a few seconds to try to put the smaller man on his back, and then all he could do was run — in his slick-soled shoes, on his tender and rubbed-raw feet.

Just as he was about to spring upward, the smaller man pulled his left boot back and kicked at Lionel's head, but Lionel was able to throw his body back, and instead of the toe of the boot landing straight across Lionel's face, the boot tip glanced off Lionel's neck. The bigger man leaned in as Lionel staggered to his feet and caught him by the collar and threw an uppercut to his gut. As Lionel crumpled forward, he could see that the few people walking past had stopped to look on — not in repulsion, exactly, since they had clearly seen worse, but more out of a sense of obligation. The smaller man took a couple of steps toward Lionel and tried again to kick his head, but Lionel stifled the blow by catching his boot. Then he twisted it, causing the man to tumble sideways. Lionel caught too late in his peripheral the dark blur that was the bigger man's fist, and when it landed just under his eye, Lionel was determined not to let it knock him to the ground. The force of the punch put so loud a high-pitched ringing in Lionel's ears that it was hard to believe he was the only one who could hear it. Lionel wavered but managed to steady himself and put his fists up, more for show than anything. The smaller man had gotten up and was coming for him, and his friend all but stepped aside to oblige him. Lionel drew back his fist as if he were going to charge the man, and then he turned and knocked the bigger man square in the mouth. The smaller man registered surprise that Lionel could land a punch, and in his pause, Lionel then took the bigger man by the shirt collar and let fly his left elbow across the man's head. Watching this, the smaller man seemed to remember that he had something in his back pocket that would be useful. But Lionel wasn't going to give him the chance and dove into him, grabbing him around the waist and knocking him down so that Lionel landed directly on top of him.

It was then that Lionel thought of his Black Justice character and how he would have handled the two thugs. Black Justice would have approved of his having attacked the bigger man first, and Black Justice would have admired the quick way Lionel responded to the man reaching for something in his back pocket. No one was used to more dirty tricks or uneven fights than Black Justice, and that required hyper-speed decision-making and reflexes. That was part of what Black Justice was known for. But just as Black Justice could never count on help from others, so this was true for Lionel. There were maybe ten people who stood watching the fight now, only one of them female, and as a spectacle the fight had more or less earned its credentials, but it had done nothing to encourage the breaking up of a lopsided match.

Lionel was on the smaller man. He thought a solid punch to the head might retire him, but the bigger man, who had shaken off the shock of Lionel's two blows, was another matter entirely. Lionel's punch had been, miraculously, swift and efficient, and he could thank the two years during high school when he worked out regularly at Bald Eagle Gym, a few blocks from his house, after failing to make the football team, for that. Yet the larger man, with blood pooling out of his nose, was still in a state of disbelief that a man thirty pounds lighter than he — in a starched gray *uniform,* no less — had caused such injury. His eyes were blinking in wonder, like a little boy whose punishment far exceeded what he had imagined.

If the police arrived now, Lionel's suit, ripped and bloodstained in two places, might win him a more compassionate assessment, but the police were also just as likely to take them all in and let a judge sort it out in the days ahead. That would be the end of Lionel's job, for starters, and what came after that was too much to let register as even a flicker in his mind. Lionel jumped off the man and ran left of the bigger man, who lunged for him but without full vigor. Lionel snatched his bag and began sprinting back in the direction he had come. The drumming of his shoes against the sidewalk drowned out the ringing in his ears, and he tried not to meet the stares of those who stopped in their tracks to watch him.

When he had charged hard for two blocks, he looked back to see if anyone was following him — police officers, either of the two men, a bystander who hadn't approved of the outcome. There was no one, but if a police car crossed in front of him now, they'd stop him based on his appearance alone. He then darted into an alleyway, wrestling off his jacket. Though he knew it was a pointless gesture, considering the ruined condition of it, he took care to fold the jacket once before pushing it into the bag.

The most important thing was to lie low, to let an hour or more pass before he stepped out again. He pulled a wooden crate out from a stack of them and found a way to sit down on it, letting his head rest against the brick wall. He eased off his shoes and examined his hands in the dim light. His right hand was badly cut across the knuckles, but nothing more. It was his first night in Washington, and he had wanted so little from it: to talk with Adanya for even a minute or two, to stroll around the city after a cheap dinner. Lionel hadn't been in a real fight since he was in tenth grade, but as an artist he had spent countless hours plotting fights and drawing them. Every once in a while one of his heroes lost a fight, and when he did he would slink away into some place of hiding and nurse himself back to health. Dark Matter, who as a custodian in a nuclear power plant had been exposed to nuclear radiation and could turn his skin into an unbreakable alloy, was once beaten so badly by the Sledgehammer that he had retreated into hiding for a solid month until he could recuperate. But such setbacks were rare in Lionel's world of heroes. Mostly they never had to explain a pulpy face after a beating, and if they had to limp around for a day or two, there was no one around them who questioned what was wrong. All his heroes were loners. Their choice was always to fight. But how did they live with that month after month, year after year? Lionel wondered now. It was a question he had never asked himself before.

WASHINGTON

When she stepped into the lobby, Maeve was eager to tell Mr. Hinton about the nurse's husband, though now she remembered that in her daze she hadn't thought to ask his name. But instead of Mr. Hinton, Maeve found that one of the bellboys was in his place. He couldn't have been much older than she, with a touch of acne on his chin, and the fact that he had kept on his little red cap — a monkey's hat, she decided — made her even angrier that he was standing there.

Seeing the young girl's pretty face, the bellboy stiffened his posture and cocked his head slightly at an angle he thought served him best. "Hello, miss," he said. "Can I help you?"

"I was looking for Mr. Hinton," she said. "Is he not here?"

"Mr. Hinton finished up a while ago. But is there something I can do for you?" He smiled a little too eagerly, and this put Maeve in no better a mood.

"No, that's all right," she said, and turned away. She would see Mr. Hinton in the morning, before checkout. But then, she couldn't be sure that he worked on Sundays. Standing, Maeve felt a little wobbly and decided she should lie down before she collapsed again. But if that unpleasant elevator man was still on his shift, she would take the steps to the sixth floor, no matter the risk.

Instead, the elevator opened to its empty walls. She had eaten only a little soup at a restaurant in Union Station that wasn't very good, but now she wondered if she should have forced herself to eat more. When the elevator came to a stop, the jolt made her stomach drop. Inside her room the air conditioner sounded even worse, but now she was grateful for the cacophony of its well-worn parts. She turned on the television set and sat on the edge of her bed, kicking off her shoes. She hoped to find some news report of the funeral train, but there was a baseball game on one channel, and a western on the other, and she was too tired to do any more searching. She pulled herself back onto the bed a bit more, and she thought again of the doctor from the station and how in that first moment his voice had reminded her so much of her father. Right before she drifted off, she remembered a story her father used to tell. Maeve had been sick with fever, and she had slept the better part of two days when she awoke to find him by her bed, holding a wet cloth to her forehead.

"Well, hello there," he said.

She smiled weakly, not ready to speak. But he could see that she was in the mood to listen. When was she not? This particular story always started like this: "Did I ever tell you about the time Frankie Farland caught the nuns sleepwalking in the cemetery?"

NEW YORK

Lionel stepped back onto the street, keeping his head down, but also constantly glancing over his shoulder, staying alert. Black Justice never let anyone take him by surprise, and since Lionel had created all the character's sharp instincts, it was critical that he apply them himself this night.

Lionel had a street address, but it was on the other side of town. He knew enough that in the nation's capital it could be hard for a black man to get a cab, and for over twenty minutes, cab after cab passed him, many with empty backseats. More than once Lionel caught the expression of a white driver looking him over as he drove — the on-duty sign lit above — and wincing, or shaking his head in dismay at the very idea of stopping for him. Lionel kept walking. When a breeze picked up, the city still smelled faintly like a bonfire.

Eventually, a cab driven by a black man

caught sight of Lionel's outreached hand and turned around to pick him up. He could only see Lionel's left side, which was unhurt, and Lionel kept his face turned so that his right side was out of view. He thanked the driver for stopping and gave him the address. Almost immediately Lionel saw another pay phone, and it pained him all over again to not hear Adanya's voice.

When the cabdriver eventually came to a stop, they were in front of a single-story building that had been in need of repainting twenty years ago. Lionel paid the driver, and when he got out he was confronted all over again with his injuries. He stood for a while, appreciating the silence. Once inside, the laughter coming from the far end shot out like a car backfiring, which made him all the more mournful. He rounded the corner of a cinder-block wall, and there, among a dozen bunk beds, were the men from his crew, hovering over a game of cards. The air was heavy with sour smoke. He could see Buster Hayes dealing out a hand, and Big Brass was to his side, hoisting a bottle of beer for the last swallow. It was Big Brass who saw him first.

"What in *the* hell?" he said.

Buster Hayes finished delivering the cards, and his mouth twisted downward.

The rest of the men turned around, and they gazed at Lionel as if he were wearing some costume they couldn't discern.

"I got into a little trouble," Lionel said, and tossed his bag on what appeared to be an available bed.

Buster Hayes pushed back his chair and walked over. He was in his T-shirt and work pants, his suspenders down by his knees, and as he walked he made a clicking sound in his jaw.

"You got into a hell of a lot more than a *little* trouble," he said. He took hold of Lionel's head as if it were a piece of produce, turning it from side to side. "Just wanted to stroll around," he called back to the other men. "Young buck said on his first time in the city he just wanted to walk around and maybe see the sights. Now look at this shit. Did you get mugged?"

"Not exactly," Lionel said.

"Did a white man do it?"

Lionel shook his head.

"Uh-huh. Just fighting, then." He released him and began to walk back to the game, but stopped and approached him once more. "I know your father raised you better than that. Your father the only reason you have the damn job, and you want to be out *brawlin'?*"

The men moaned in unison.

"This is one damn mess," Buster Hayes said.

Lionel was trembling slightly — out of pain, out of nervousness, fatigue. "I'm sorry, Mr. Hayes," he said in too weak a voice to please Buster Hayes. "All I wanted to do was get a little bite to eat, call my girl, and get some sleep. That was all I wanted to do. But I got caught up in something, and it got physical."

Now Big Brass came over for an inspection of his own. He was puffing on a cigar, and made sure Lionel could hear the sound of him chomping on the bit.

" 'It got physical.' That's a damn shame," Big Brass said. "Let me ask you this: How you think you going to show up for work tomorrow and work like that? Passengers don't want to be served by someone look like he been sparring with Joe Frazier. With a face like raw meat. Good God Almighty. Mr. Chalmers, can you make any sense out of this?"

Mr. Chalmers put his cards down and blew out cigar smoke in a big gust. He looked at Lionel carefully, stroking his chin for effect. "All the young man had to do was come back here and surrender some of that first day's pay in a friendly round of cards. I don't rightly see how we can bring him aboard tomorrow, lessen the Lord plan to work a miracle on that face between now and six A.M. And maybe He will. But I wouldn't bet my hand on it."

Buster Hayes scanned his face once more, in case he had missed something earlier. "Nothing to do but go to sleep, young buck. In the morning I'll talk to the office and see what they want to do. We'll tell them some damn shit. Say you got hit by a policeman's stick, but of course, if I tell them that, they're going to think you were trying to burn some *other* building down, so I can't do that. Let me think on it. We'll figure something out. I don't know what."

"Thank you," Lionel whispered, and turned to consider the rows of bunk beds.

"Take the last one, there," Buster Hayes said. "Up top. Mr. Chalmers is below you, and Mr. Chalmers don't sleep on top of nobody."

"Except Mrs. Chalmers," another porter from the cards table called out to gut-busting laughter.

Lionel unzipped his bag with the intention of washing up, and when he turned to look for the bathroom, the men went back to studying their unpromising hands of cards. He stepped into the small bathroom, where a single bulb cast a dull light over the scratched-up tile floor and two shower stalls and two toilets. The bulb might as well have been a power plant for as loudly as it hummed.

Lionel glanced in the mirror and quickly turned away, not yet ready to confront just how rough his face was. If he couldn't work the return leg of the trip, would someone in the main office let him heal up and give him a second chance? There was no guarantee of that. Even so, his parents would be ashamed that he hadn't shown the good sense to walk away from those two thugs. He could hear his father's voice now: *That's my name you carrying around with you, and you fixed it so that you couldn't even work your second day on the job? Because you had to fight some hoodlums over a girl you didn't even know? When you got a steady girl? Boy, you showing us we've done nothing but fail with you.*

The men around the table were still complaining about or chuckling at the problem rookie who had just joined their ranks. Lionel wanted nothing more than to have Adanya cradle him right now, to hear her say "Hush" in a voice as soothing as a soft blanket. Maybe he was going to have to go down there and marry her, come back to

campus that fall as husband and wife. He
would do that; he would do anything for
her. Having a baby didn't mean he couldn't
still study or work on his comic books.
Adanya wouldn't let him stop, anyway. But
everything felt so unfamiliar and unsteady
right then, surreal. It was like a comic he'd
been working on he called the Night
Avenger, about a night watchman in Har-
lem who fell asleep during every shift, and
when he woke up he was someone else —
and always in peril: an escaped prisoner being chased by guards; a messenger fighting
off a gang of kung fu assailants. And just at
the moment he was about to be killed, he
would wake up again in the dark and quiet
bank. Only, when he returned home each
morning, he would bear the scars from each
violent outing. In his fog, that was all Lionel
could hope for now — to wake up and find
himself having drifted off while on break on
the train.

Lionel's wants in life were relatively few,
but leaning over the sink, trying to clear his
head, they felt remarkable and unrealistic:
He wanted to be back in Winston-Salem
with Adanya. He wanted to make it through
college and make his parents proud. He
wanted to stay as far away from Vietnam as
possible, and he wanted to go his whole life

and never again be called *nigger,* to never have any man — white or black — put his hands on him. And he wanted to bring out his own drawings and characters to an audience of readers who had never seen black superheroes before, never even imagined that in a white world they could exist. But with so much evil in the world, why couldn't Black Justice and Dark Matter and The Boulder help with the fight? Didn't the world, now more than ever, need all the help it could get?

Mr. Hinton reached into his pants pocket, his fingers running over a row of jagged metal edges, and picked out his house key. When he stepped in, he flipped on the porch light and was dismayed to see so many new dead bugs inside the light fixture over the door, the bodies like smudged fingerprints.

He lived in Anacostia, where he was born and raised. At eighty-seven, his mother still lived on her own in the house that he grew up in, five blocks away. He often stopped by to see her on his way home from work, but tonight he had dropped by Hank's Bar for a couple of beers. He and Hank had been friends for half his life or more, and on Saturday night, Hank was always glad to see his old friend.

"My man," Hank shouted out at the sight of Mr. Hinton. "Now I *know* it's Saturday night." The bar was only half full, and almost no one there was under forty, and most of them men. But you didn't go to Hank's to pick up a woman. And Mr. Hinton hadn't done that in more years than he cared to count.

He let Hank pour him exactly two beers, and when he declined a third, Mr. Hinton said, "Not that my gut agrees with me on that." At Hank's you could count on hearing Ray Charles and the Cadillacs and Ruth Brown and Louis Jordan, but nothing on his jukebox had been recorded after 1960. This was nothing any customer had ever thought to complain about.

Now that he was home, it wasn't too late to call his mother, since she didn't go to bed until well after the evening news. She had no doubt watched the funeral that morning on television, and she would be eager to know if there were other tidbits he had learned about the service or the funeral train while at work.

"Hello, Robinson," he said to his fifteen-year-old cat, who waited until the man sat in his recliner to greet him. He stroked the cat around the ears for several minutes until his fingers tired, and this helped the cat forgive him for being gone for so many hours at a time. Robinson leaped up into his lap, sputtering like an old generator. "Uh-huh, I know you've missed me," he said to the cat. "I know that much."

Six years into his job at the Churchill, in 1937, Mr. Hinton was listening to one of the bellmen describe the strange guest in room 445 when a radio report announced that the Hindenburg had become completely engulfed in flames while landing at an air station in New Jersey. Four years later he was fixing a leaky staff toilet when word reached the lobby that Pearl Harbor had been attacked. He had just finished pushing a cart of ten bags on a Sunday morning twenty-two years later when a fellow bellhop told him a church in Alabama had been bombed, and that four little girls were dead. That same year, Mr. Hinton was standing just outside the kitchen on his fifteen-minute break, chatting with one of the dishwashers, Miguel, when over the radio it was announced that President Kennedy had been shot in Dallas. In his first week on the job as concierge, he watched through the front windows of the hotel as a long parade of protesters marched through the streets, their arms stiff and raised to the heavens, demanding that President Johnson pull American troops out of Vietnam. A middle-aged father and his two sons from Chicago watched from the next window over, and finally the man said, "All those hippies want is to be free, but you think they'd be willing to fight for that freedom?" The sons assured him that they wouldn't.

And it was just two months earlier when Mr. Hinton had stepped out into the night air and fell into a harsh coughing spell as the dark smoke of a city being burned poured above. As he tried to make sense of what was happening, a group of young black men ran past him, one of them holding his arm as pools of blood trailed behind. June, from the front desk, quickly pulled Mr. Hinton back in and convinced him it was too dangerous to get into his car. That night he slept at the hotel for the very first time.

There was almost nothing in his life that he hadn't experienced through the filter of the Churchill, and he sometimes wondered what he would do if something of national consequence happened while he was sitting in his home.

He needed to feed the hungry Robinson, but getting back up anytime soon seemed unimaginable, so sore were his hips, his knees, his ankles and feet. He could have fallen asleep in a matter of seconds, but he needed to check in on his mother. Otherwise, on Sunday morning, after he drove over to pick her up for church, the first thing she would say would be, "Well, hello, stranger." She would not say it unkindly, but neither could she pass up the opportunity to let him know that a day without hearing from him was unsettling. What if she had needed a prescription refilled? What if she had fallen? Or needed orange juice? She would even manage a half-smile when she said it. But her son knew about the difficulties of living alone all too well. What if *he* had fallen? How would she know? How long before anyone would find him? They needed to stay in constant communication; they were all each other had.

His mother believed that his never getting married was a fate worse than disease. How she had ached for grandchildren. He was an only child, and she had held out hope that he would still marry even at fifty, but fifty came, and then sixty came, and there was her boy, Earl, still on his own, no companions he ever spoke of, no dinner dates that she ever heard about. He was married to his job, he sometimes said to end her prying.

"Well, don't bring it over to dinner," she said. "It's too big to sit at the table." She could be clever like that, even now.

Finally he reached over for the telephone, much to Robinson's frustration, since he was dislodged in the process, and stuck his finger into the holes and dialed. Her phone would ring once, maybe twice, but never more than that before she picked up.

"Hey, Ma," he said.

"Hello yourself," she said. Her voice was sharp for this time of night. "You just got in?"

"Just now," he said, his voice so low and tired that he repeated himself to be sure he was heard.

"Uh-huh," she said. "Well, I know you work hard." Then there was a pause. There was always a pause before her first question, which was always the same. "So," she said. "How was the day?"

BACK FROM VIETNAM, HOMETOWN HERO FINDING HIS STEP AGAIN

By Roy Murphy
Special to the Gazette

Jamie West is back home after a tour of Vietnam that lasted two years. But coming home has required more than the usual adjustments for a soldier. Four months ago, just east of the village of Than Khe, Private West had finished cleaning his gun, which he was known to use with more precision than any other soldier in his company. But he never had a chance to train it on the enemy on the morning of February 5, when Vietcong artillery fire filled the sky where Alpha Company awaited further instructions from command in Saigon.

West's best friend was just a few feet away when a missile struck, setting him ablaze. West immediately ran to tackle him and smother the flames when another missile struck the foxhole West had just jumped out of. He could not save his friend, despite his valiant effort. Nor could he avoid being struck by the shrapnel that shredded his lower leg. It was amputated at an Army aid hospital a few miles from Than Khe, and after receiving many weeks of physical therapy at the 8th Field Hospital in Nha

Trang, he was discharged and on his way home.

"He lost his leg trying to save someone else," says his mother, Ellie West. "If that's not a hero, I don't know what is."

Private West is more modest about his wartime efforts and maintains that any soldier in his company would have attempted the same rescue of Private Allan Landreaux. He was just the closest to him at that moment, West says. But he doesn't deny that the loss of a leg is requiring an adjustment.

"There's no choice but to get used to it," he says. "But there are still some times in the day when, for a split second, my mind forgets, or my body [forgets]."

Before being drafted, West worked as a mechanic at Jurrel's Garage after helping lead the E. E. Burton Panthers to first place in their division as wide receiver on the football team. West says he still thinks about his days playing football, of what it was to run like a gazelle across the field and into the end zone. But neither does he fall into pity when he talks about his injury. His parents avoid that thinking, too, he says.

"They don't treat me like a cripple, and I don't think that's how they see me in their eyes," West says.

Currently he is entertaining a standing offer from Mack Jurrel to rejoin the crew at the garage. But right now, the young man is still learning how to get around and to maneuver in new ways. As an expert marksman, West was eager to get back to his passion for archery. Now he sits down when he's ready to shoot his arrows, but he seems to have lost nothing of his skills. For this reporter, he demonstrated his steely technique by hitting bull's-eye after bull's-eye from 30 yards. It's a hobby that his mother says gives him a sense of comfort, and it's a reminder that though he has lost a leg, he is still capable of a great many things.

West knows that he's not the only soldier to have suffered such extensive injuries in Vietnam, a war that shows no signs of ending anytime soon and which is increasingly seeing more wide-scale protests in Washington. One man who wanted to end that war, Senator Robert Kennedy, was shot and killed Wednesday night in a California hotel after winning the state's Democratic primary. As it turned out, the Wests' backyard sits right in front of the train tracks that carried Kennedy's body en route to Arlington National Cemetery on Saturday. Despite the four-hour delay caused by the tragedies in New Jersey (see "Funeral Train Causes

371

Deaths in New Jersey" on 2A), the Wests were pleased to have the chance to observe the train passing by. When the 21-car train sailed past, emotions were running high in the West family, and Miriam West, 17, who will be a senior at E. E. Burton High School, was given to many tears as the family caught a glimpse of the senator's casket. Private West gave a salute of a different kind. He raised his crutch in midair. When asked why, the reserved private shrugged. Not everything, he said, could be explained.

A NOTE FROM THE AUTHOR

The Train of Small Mercies is a work of fiction based on actual events. The details that relate to Robert Kennedy's funeral, the funeral train, and the burial are true. My primary sources included accounts from *The Washington Post, The New York Times,* and *Time* magazine. I also interviewed reporter David Broder, who was on the train for the *Post.* Thurston Clarke's *The Last Campaign: Robert F. Kennedy and 82 Days That Inspired America* (Henry Holt and Company, 2008) was very helpful to me for understanding the spirit of Kennedy's brief presidential bid — and also the effect it had on Americans of all persuasions.

The novel was inspired by the extraordinary photographs in Paul Fusco's *RFK Funeral Train* (Umbrage Editions, 2000). Fusco worked for *Look* magazine at the time of Kennedy's assassination, and he was assigned to shoot the senator's burial at Arlington National Cemetery. After the train left New York's Penn Station, Fusco was moved by the lines of mourners — sometimes unbroken for miles — gathered along the tracks, and he kept his camera trained on them until the arrival at Union Station in Washington. He had shot well over a thousand pictures before stepping out onto the platform.

Leaving Penn Station a few minutes after one p.m. on Saturday, June 8 — and already late by then — a doleful journey turned even more tragic. In Elizabeth, New Jersey, a man and a woman who was holding her granddaughter were killed by another train named the Admiral, headed to New York from Chicago, as it plowed through an overflow of mourners waiting for the Kennedy train. The granddaughter was thrown into the air and not seriously injured. Soon after, a man in Trenton, New Jersey, was critically wounded while standing on top of a boxcar for a better view and touching an 11,000-volt wire. Later that day, a Kennedy press officer announced that the man was dead, but in fact he survived and gave an interview to *The New York Times* in 2009, in which he revealed the Kennedy family had helped him with his extensive medical bills.

After these grisly incidents, the Kennedy family threatened to stop the train if other trains couldn't be halted. For the duration, the Penn Central traveled at a significantly reduced speed, and the 226-mile trek ended up taking twice as long as was originally scheduled.

The coffin was placed in the last of the twenty-one cars and propped up on chairs so that it could be seen; at times, it had to be braced from falling.

By day's end, it was estimated that there were anywhere from 500,000 to 2 million people who had turned out by the railroad tracks to catch a glimpse of the train's historic journey and to pay their respects. Many of those mourners lived in small, rural towns that were bisected by the rail lines. Old and young turned out in the simmering heat, black and white, the poor and middle class, the distraught and merely curious. There were choirs singing "The Battle Hymn of the Republic" and Honor Guards and mothers in curlers with babies on their hips and older women who had thought to bring flowers but who realized, as the train roared past, they were unsure what they should do with them. Some mourners, including many African-Americans, having come to expect this tragedy, dropped to their knees in anguish as the train passed — not only for the loss of an essential voice in the fight for civil rights, just two months after Martin Luther King Jr. was killed, but for the violent state of lawlessness their country had become.

Hubert Humphrey went on to win the Democratic presidential nomination and lost to Richard Nixon in the national election. America didn't officially end direct involvement in the Vietnam War, which Robert Kennedy had come to bitterly oppose, until early 1973. The U.S. casualties numbered near sixty thousand.

As it turned out, *Look* magazine didn't publish Fusco's pictures taken from the funeral train, and they remained largely unseen until their first publication thirty years later. An expanded edition of that work, *RFK* (Aperture, 2008), included an additional seventy pictures never seen before. That book, to my mind, offers some of the most searing portraits of American grief ever captured. It's a country that has come to know too well the cost of seeking justice for all its people, and while a sense of hope has not been completely extinguished, never has it seemed so far out of reach. For a single day, at least, politics were put aside for something more fundamental, more humane: a man who had dared to challenge, sometimes to condemn, the country he loved was dead, and here was a chance to say thank you for the work he did and had intended to do. The people who gathered along the tracks that day were too late to save Robert Kennedy, but they could honor his vision by going about their lives with renewed moral courage and conviction.

"Few will have the greatness to bend history itself," he told a group of young people in South Africa on their Day of Affirmation in 1966, "but each of us can work to change a small portion of events, and in the total of all those acts will be written the history of this generation."

ACKNOWLEDGMENTS

Bill Routhier, Beth Castrodale, and Audrey Schulman were extraordinarily generous and insightful writing group companions for many years.

Melissa Bank offered me invaluable comments on this novel — and true and timely encouragement throughout. Wells Tower weighed in at an essential time, and Marianne Gingher provided a spark that I very much needed. Ron Carlson imparted a guiding and instrumental lesson early on.

At *The Washington Post,* Len Downie and Patricia O'Shea selected me for a fellowship at Duke University, where some of this novel was written. Debra Leithauser offered me the gift of time.

At Putnam, Diana Lulek provided always cheerful and expedient assistance. At the Friedrich Agency, Lucy Carson gave me a steady and reassuring line of counsel on all matters throughout. I thank my agent,

Molly Friedrich, for her fierce belief in this novel and my editor, Marysue Rucci, for her remarkable care with it. To them I'm profoundly grateful.

I thank Max Steele (1922–2005) for putting me on the path in the first place.

I'm indebted to Jack and Martha Fleer for their ongoing support; my brother, John, for his enthusiasm; my mother, Ann Rowell, for her unwavering faith; and my sons, Griffin and Anderson, for their patience. And to my wife, Katherine, for all the days and nights.

My father, Glenn Rowell, kept a house full of books but didn't get to include this one. Still, he loved everything the author ever produced.

ABOUT THE AUTHOR

David Rowell is an editor at *The Washington Post Magazine* and has taught literary journalism at American University. He lives in Silver Spring, Maryland, with his wife and their two sons. This is his first novel.

The employees of Thorndike Press hope you have enjoyed this Large Print book. All our Thorndike, Wheeler, and Kennebec Large Print titles are designed for easy reading, and all our books are made to last. Other Thorndike Press Large Print books are available at your library, through selected bookstores, or directly from us.

For information about titles, please call:
(800) 223-1244

or visit our Web site at:
http://gale.cengage.com/thorndike

To share your comments, please write:
Publisher
Thorndike Press
10 Water St., Suite 310
Waterville, ME 04901